The 40-year-old Rookie

A Major League Story of
Perseverance and Faith

Reese Barton

Published by Cross of Grace 2025

FIRST EDITION

ISBN: 979-8-9888766-3-2

Cross of Grace Publishing

www.reesebarton.com

For my grandson, Lincoln. His innocence and passion for life are a godsend.

You need to persevere so that when you have done the will of God, you will receive what he has promised.

— Hebrews 10:36

Prologue
Navin Field, Detroit, MI - Monday, 10/7/1935

Ty Tyson, the voice of Detroit baseball, refused to sit as he watched the crowd of over 48,000 stand and cheer for their Tigers. The atmosphere was electric, and the city was hungry for a championship. The depression had taken a toll on Detroit, but none of that mattered right now. It was Game Six of the World Series, and their team was up three games to two. It was the bottom of the ninth inning with the score tied at two. Tyson didn't have to remind listeners it was almost a year ago to the day that the Tigers lost to the Cardinals 11-0 in game seven of last year's series after being up three games to two. That loss came right here at Navin Field. Right here and right now was the story, and the 40-year-old rookie that fans embraced as their own was coming to the plate. The moment was here, and Tyson was ready to call the action.

"It looks like the meeting on the mound is over, and French is ready to pitch. Graham closes his eyes and looks up into the heavens. He smiles and then steps into the box."

CHAPTER 1
Monday—July 7, 1980

Arthur Graham sat on the newly donated bench that faced the church's courtyard. It was already eighty degrees at 8:30 a.m., and it was looking like a beautiful summer day was taking shape. Arthur smiled as he tossed some breadcrumbs onto the ground. He watched as the birds landed and ate the crumbs. He smiled and grabbed another handful.

"Don't fight, my friends, there's plenty for all of you," he stated as he smiled and tossed more onto the ground.

"Whatcha doing, mister?" A voice asked.

He froze as he was reaching into the bag.

"You guys can talk?"

He heard laughter to his left.

"Birds can't talk."

He turned to see a young boy standing next to the bench, smiling in his direction. Arthur laughed and motioned for him to take a seat.

"I didn't know anyone else was here. Please, young man, have a seat."

He scooted further to his right to make some room. The young man took a seat next to him.

"My name's Lincoln Fisher. What's yours?"

Arthur smiled and held out his hand. "My name is Arthur Graham, Lincoln. Pleased to meet you."

Lincoln took his hand, and they shook.

"Pleased to meet you, Mr. Graham." He looked down at the bag full of breadcrumbs. "Do you mind if I feed them some?"

"Not at all. Reach in there and grab a handful."

Lincoln grabbed a handful of crumbs and threw them out onto the ground. More birds landed and ate. He smiled and looked over at Arthur.

"Why are you here so early, Mr. Graham?"

1

"Well, son, you'll find as you get older you don't need as much sleep. I usually get up around 6:30 a.m. most days. Sometimes it's earlier."

"On your own? Nobody makes you get up that early?"

Arthur laughed. "If I'm lucky, some days I sleep in until 7:30 a.m. Why? What time do you get up?"

"During the summer, I usually sleep until 10:00 a.m. Some days later."

"My goodness, that's a long time to sleep in." Arthur looked at his watch. "What has you up so early on this fine summer day?"

Lincoln sighed, "My dad. He has a job to do here at the church, and since my mom is gone for the next few weeks, I have to come with him. Well, maybe just for a week because I might stay at my friend Billy's house next week."

"Oh." Arthur laughed. "Is he the one building the addition to the worship center?"

"Yep. Well, him and his company."

"Well, that'll be nice."

"Yeah, he does good work."

"You can come sit with me this week and feed the birds."

"I guess I might as well. Are you here every day?"

"Most days."

"Don't you have anything else to do?"

Arthur smiled and looked at Lincoln. "Well, since I retired, it has become one of my favorite things to do."

"Retired?"

"I used to be the pastor of this church for forty years."

"Forty years? Wow! How old are you, Mr. Graham?"

"I just turned 85."

"What day is your birthday?"

"June 27th."

"Cool. Mine is June 25th. But I just turned 12."

"So, I'm just a few days older than you," Arthur smiled.

Lincoln laughed out loud and watched as the birds continued to peck away at the ground.

2

"So why did you retire?"

"I felt it was time to turn the job over to my son, Dillard. Then, Mrs. Graham and I could travel a little and feed the birds."

Lincoln looked around.

"Where is Mrs. Graham?"

"Feeding the birds really isn't her thing. So, I come here in the morning and feed them and read my Bible. You know what a Bible is, Lincoln?"

"Of course I do. We go to church on Sundays."

"Where to?"

"We go to Grace, over on Lahser."

"Oh, that's a nice church. I know the pastor there well."

"Yeah, Pastor Steven is a nice guy. He gives us suckers sometimes."

"Well, that's nice."

"Yeah. I like Sunday school. Right now, we're learning about Jonah."

"Ah, the fella that got swallowed by the big fish."

"Yep, that's the one."

Lincoln put his hand into his jacket pocket and pulled out a baseball. Arthur's eyes lit up as he watched the young man toss the ball into the air and catch it.

2

Chris Fisher watched from a distance as his son sat on a bench and talked to an elderly gentleman. His thoughts drifted momentarily when the pastor's firm voice interrupted him.

"Mr. Fisher, are you okay?"

Chris looked at him and answered, "Yeah…yep, I mean yes, pastor, I'm fine."

Dillard followed Chris's gaze until he noticed his father talking to a young boy sitting on the bench that faced the church courtyard.

"Is that your son?" Dillard asked.

"Yes, sir, it is. His mother's gone, and he'll be coming to work with me. Don't worry, he won't distract me from getting the job done." Dillard laughed. "I'm not worried about that, Mr. Fisher. Your company's reputation is solid. I was just going to tell you not to worry about the old man sitting next to him. That's my father, Arthur. He was pastor of this church for a little over forty years before I took over almost five years ago."

"Oh. Okay. I just didn't know. I didn't mean to offend you."

"Offend me? For being an attentive father. Never."

"I just hope my boy doesn't drive him crazy talking his ear off. All he wants to do is play, talk, eat, and sleep baseball right now. If your dad knows nothing about baseball, he will when Lincoln's done." Dillard smiled. "Dad knows a little about baseball, so they should get along just fine."

3

"Do you know anything about baseball, Mr. Graham?" Lincoln asked.

"I do," he answered with a smile.

"Probably not more than me."

"Probably not, but I have a really good story that might interest you."

Lincoln caught the ball and then focused his attention on Arthur. "Is it a story about baseball?"

"As a matter of fact, it is. Since we're going to be bench buddies for the next week, or possibly longer, would you like to hear it?"

"Only for a week. Remember, next week I might be at my friend Billy's."

"But what if I'm not done with my story at the end of the week?"

"Like my dad says, 'Let's play it by ear.'"

Arthur chuckled, "That's fair." He tapped his chin. "Where to begin. Maybe from birth."

"When were you born?"

"June 27, 1895."

"Wow!"

Arthur laughed so hard that it started a coughing fit. Lincoln did what his mother always did when he coughed and started patting Arthur on the back. When he finally gained his composure, he looked over at Lincoln.

"Thank you, young man. It's been a while since I've laughed that hard."

"Sorry, I just didn't expect to hear 18 in front of the year."

"That's alright. I'm old, and I know it." He smiled. "So, do you play baseball, or do you just go around throwing a ball into the air?"

"I play. I'm in a league right now."

"Is that so? Why aren't you playing right now?"

"We don't play on Mondays. We practice on Tuesdays, Thursdays and Fridays from 6:00 p.m. until 7:00 p.m. And we have games on Wednesdays at 6:30 p.m., and Saturdays at 10:00 a.m."

"That's a big commitment."

"I know. I give up sleeping in on the weekend."

"Not from you. From your parents. They must really love you to make that kind of commitment. I hope you appreciate that."

"Yes, sir, I do."

"Good. It's a tough job being a parent. Do you have brothers and sisters?"

"My sister Lucy is 10 and my brother Jack is 8."

"That's a full house. Do they play sports as well?"

"Naw. My sister is what my mom calls 'a girly girl,' and my dad says that Jack has the 'attention span of a gnat.' It's true," he finished.

Arthur chuckled. "So, you're the serious one in the family?"

"With baseball, I am."

"What position do you play?"

"Third base."

"Say…that's a hot corner. You can't take your eye off the ball for a second."

5

"Boy, you said it. Two weeks ago, we were playing in a game and a kid got hit right in the junk…I mean…um…the."

Arthur stepped in to help him. "The beans."

Lincoln laughed. "Yeah. The beans. My mom doesn't like me telling that story, but it's kind of funny."

"Unless you're the guy getting hit in the beans."

They took a moment to laugh out loud together.

Arthur continued, "So, are you any good?"

"I made the all-star team last year, and the coach says I'll probably make it again this year."

"Really! Well, that's impressive."

"Thanks. I really love playing. When I'm not playing, I watch the Tigers as much as I can, and every once in a while, my dad gets tickets for me and him."

"That's nice. Who's your favorite player?"

"Lance Parrish."

"What? He's a catcher, not a third baseman."

"I know, but he's a lot of fun to watch. He hits the ball hard."

"Yes, he does. He reminds me of a young Hank Greenberg."

"Who does he play for?"

Arthur turned to look at him.

"I thought you said you knew baseball?"

"I know a lot, but I don't know everything. Who is he?"

Arthur smiled.

"He's one of the greatest baseball players that ever played the game, and a part of the story I'm about to tell you."

"Who did he play for?"

Arthur leaned in and whispered, "The Detroit Tigers."

"Awesome!" Lincoln paused and then asked, "Is this a true story or one that you made up?"

"It's true. Should I start?"

"Wait one second." Lincoln reached his hand into the bag and pulled out some more crumbs. He threw them onto the ground and watched as the birds flocked to them once again. He smiled and then looked up at Arthur. "Okay, I'm ready."

"One more thing." Arthur reached his hand into a different bag and pulled out a shiny red apple. "I brought two just in case I met someone. You want one?"

"Sure, Mr. Graham, thanks. My dad likes the green ones, but I like the red ones."

"Me too. The green ones are a little too sour for me."

"Yeah. They make my insides flinch."

Arthur chuckled as he handed him the apple.

"So, you're a big Tiger fan?"

"The biggest."

"Do you know when Tigers Stadium was built, or any of its history?"

He scratched his head and thought for a moment. "Not really. I guess I mostly just know about the players."

"Then you'll learn something right out of the gate."

Lincoln focused all of his attention on Arthur. "Okay."

"Since we're starting our story in 1912, you should know that on April 20th of that year, Tiger Stadium, or Navin Field as it was called then, was built. Also, as a side note, Boston's Fenway Park opened the exact same day."

"Cool."

Arthur paused to see if Lincoln was going to add to that profound statement. He didn't.

"Okay. Well then, let's get started."

4

Fort Worth, TX, July 1912

The Fort Worth Panthers seventeen-year-old second baseman Arthur Graham stood just outside of the batter's box and stared down the opposing team's pitcher, Ricky Klein. There were runners on first and second base, with one out in the seventh inning, and the score tied at two. Arthur's mind was racing as he tried to figure out what pitch he was about to see. He was 0 for 2 on the day, with two strikeouts. Both ended with a swing and a miss on a well-placed curveball. The count was currently 2-2, both strikes again on the curveball. "It's gotta be a curve," he whispered under his breath. He stared over at the umpire, who was standing there with his hands on his hips.

"Play ball," he screamed.

Arthur stepped back into the box and readied himself. He took a deep breath in through his nose and then exhaled through his mouth and stared back out at Klein. He was one for twelve against Klein this season. The one being a tactically placed bunt down the third base line in the two teams' first meeting of the year. Klein checked both runners and then set his sights on home plate. Arthur gripped the bat tight and prepared for the curve as Klein delivered the pitch. Fast ball. His timing was extremely late, but he managed to catch a small piece of the ball and foul it into the catcher's mitt. He looked back to see the catcher scramble to hold on to the ball, but it popped out of his mitt and onto the ground.

"Foul ball," the umpire screamed.

Arthur breathed a sigh of relief as he stepped back out of the box and closed his eyes. He reminded himself that baseball was a game of inches. The home run was exciting, but a base hit here would produce a run and the lead. "Be a team player," he whispered as he stepped back into the box and got ready. Klein received the sign from his catcher and went into his windup. Arthur choked up on the bat and prepared for whatever was coming. Klein followed through and delivered another fastball that was headed for the lower outside corner of the plate when Arthur swung and connected. The ball jumped off his bat, sending a sharply hit line drive down the first base line just past the diving first baseman.

"Fair ball!" the umpire screamed as it went by them.

The Panthers' dugout erupted with cheers as everyone stood and watched as the three men started running around the bases. The right fielder chased the ball down and was scooping it into his glove as Arthur was rounding first base. In one beautifully crafted motion, he scooped it, popped up, and threw a bullet into second base. Arthur slid just as the ball was coming into the bag, and he felt his foot hit the base just before the infielder's glove tagged him.

"Safe!" the umpire screamed as he threw both hands out to his sides to drive home the point.

The home fans cheered as Arthur popped up from his slide with a smile on his face. He looked over to see the runner on third pumping his fist. He then shifted his stare toward the dugout, where his teammates were celebrating the runner who had just crossed home plate, giving his team a 3-2 lead. The next batter would go down on strikes, swinging at that lethal Klein curveball for the third out of the inning, but the score would hold up and the Panthers notched a 3-2 win on the heels of Arthur's two-out double.

After the game, he was collecting his gear when one of his teammates, Bob Schilling, came up and gave him a pat on the back.

"Way to hang in there, Artie. I thought for sure you were getting the curveball."

Arthur laughed, "You and me both. I scraped that thought process after he threw the heater on the pitch before and almost got me."

"Well, it was the right call." He winked at him. "See you at practice tomorrow."

Behind Schilling, there was an exaggerated throat clearing. Arthur watched as Schilling rolled his eyes and then took a step to his right. Standing behind him was a young lady wearing a white dress. Her hair was golden, and her eyes were bright blue. She smiled and walked toward him.

"I'm Esther. Pleased to meet you, Arthur." She extended her hand, and her smile grew wider.

She had the face and movements of an angel.

"The pleasure is all mine, Esther," he stated as he took her hand in his and held it.

They took a moment to stand in silence and stare at each other.

9

Schilling cleared his throat and put his hand on her shoulder.
"We've got to get going, Esther. Great game, Arthur."
He gave them one more second before he physically pulled her hand from Arthur's and turned her around.
"Yeah, great game, Bob," Arthur finally got out as he continued to stare at her.
"Goodbye, it was nice meeting you," she stated as Schilling walked behind her and escorted her up the steps and out of the dugout.
"Nice meeting you, Esther."
He continued to stare in her direction until she was out of sight.

5

"Whoa! You played minor league baseball, Mr. Graham?" Lincoln asked, with a surprised look on his face.
Arthur laughed.
"I told you that you were going to like this story. How the heck did you know the Panthers were a minor league baseball team?"
Lincoln smiled. "I told you I knew a lot about baseball."
"Yeah, you did." Arthur smiled. "How old did you say you were?"
"Twelve."
"How did you learn about the minor leagues?"
"Me and my dad like to go to the library. He reads about history, and I read about the history of baseball."
"That's nice. So how much do you know about the Detroit Tigers?"
"I know a lot from 1953 on. That's when Al Kaline started playing for them. He's my dad's favorite player. I also know that they won the World Series the year I was born, in 1968."
"That's right. Do you know anything about all the great players that have played in Detroit?"
He thought for a moment before he answered.
"I read about Ty Cobb, Al Kaline, Mickey Lolich, Bill Freehan, and know all the Tigers on the team now."

"That's a lot of talented players who wore the Old English D."

Arthur smiled. "You know I met Cobb and Kaline?"

"No fooling?" He asked in a high-pitched voice.

Arthur laughed. "No fooling."

"What was Al Kaline like?"

"He was an outstanding baseball player, and a gentleman to boot." He smiled. "And Ty Cobb might be one of the very best all-around players to ever play the game."

"Cool. Did you ever play with any of them?"

"Let's not jump ahead in the story. We'll get to that eventually."

"Okay."

"I brought a ham and cheese sandwich. You want half?"

"Sure. Thanks Mr. Graham."

He reached into the bag and pulled it out.

"You can thank Esther. She made it."

As Lincoln took the sandwich from him, he paused and looked up at him.

"The same Esther from the story?"

"The one and only."

"Cool." He took a bite. "How old was she when you met her?"

"She was sixteen and beautiful."

"Wow! You guys have been together for a long time."

"Married for sixty-five wonderful years."

"Whoa!"

"Whoa is right."

"You guys must really love each other."

"We must. You got any girls in school or around the neighborhood you like?"

Lincoln's face told him what he needed to know, but he added emphatically, "Gross! No way. Girls are the worst."

Arthur laughed. "In time, you'll feel differently."

Lincoln took another big bite of his sandwich, but let his face continue to do the talking. "If you say so."

"Alright, where was I?"

11

6

Fort Worth, TX, October 1912

The Panthers finished the season at 59-81. In his first full season playing minor league baseball, Arthur was tested out at just about every position. The only positions he didn't play were catcher and third base. In 307 at-bats, he had 87 hits, which resulted in a respectable .284 batting average. Included in those hits, he had 2 home runs, 14 doubles, and 4 triples. He had 42 RBIs and stole 11 bases out of 13 attempts. He pitched in 14 games and held a record of 1-3 with 2 saves. His ERA was 4.2. The young man from Texas had caught the eye of a few scouts from the majors, but not enough to get a tryout. When the season ended, he did what most minor league ballplayers did back in 1912. He went back to his regular job.

Arthur started at Dillard's Hardware Store in July 1911. In June of that year, he had turned 16, and his father told him he needed to get a job. A job builds character. It gives one a sense of purpose, and it prepares them for independence. He stressed to Arthur that he needed to figure out what he wanted to do with his life. That he was no longer a boy and needed to think like a man. Arthur conveyed his love of baseball to his father. That he wanted to be a professional baseball player, and that he could make a decent living doing so. Both of his parents were always supportive of his dreams, so his father made him a deal. He asked that Arthur find a job for the summer, just to see what it was like to work a regular job and bring home a steady paycheck. If he still wanted to pursue his dream of playing baseball, then the following summer they would support that dream and help him out the best they could. That summer, he worked four to five days a week and thoroughly enjoyed his time at Dillard's. The owner, Jack Dillard, was like a second father to him. Between stocking shelves and cleaning the store, he and Mr. Dillard would throw the ball around whenever they got the chance. They talked baseball extensively, and whenever the time permitted, Jack and Arthur would take in a Texas League game together. Sometimes Arthur's father, Jim, would join them. Jim and Jack were deacons together at the local church, so his parents didn't mind Arthur spending so much time around Jack. At one of those games, Arthur spoke to the coach of the Fort Worth Panthers, who invited him to try out for the team in the spring. When school started back up in the fall, three days a week, he would go home, do his schoolwork, whatever chores he had to do, grab a quick bite to eat, and then head to Dillard's to work for a couple of hours.

When the spring of 1912 rolled around, Arthur got his tryout. Over a three-week period, he really impressed the coaches with his blend of speed, arm accuracy, and at-bats. They had lost three players from the year before, so they were looking to replace them with youth and talent. Given his great tryout, his age, and his already six-foot frame, they took a chance on him. The only problem is that they didn't know which position fit him best, so that summer they made him a utility player that they plugged in as needed. They gave him a fair wage, one that would allow him to focus just on playing ball, and they concentrated on finding a position that would be the perfect fit. They were very pleased with the season he had and invited him to play with the team the following year.

7

"So, did you go back and play?" Lincoln asked.

Arthur looked over at him with a grimace on his face.

"Why so impatient? The purpose of the story is to enjoy the adventure. It's a long story, but a good one. I thought you might like the journey, but if you want me to just summarize it quickly and tell you the ending, I can."

"No, I'm sorry, Mr. Graham. I just got excited because I didn't know you played professional baseball and rubbed elbows with some big names."

He gave him a pat on his knee.

"That's okay, son. I guess I understand that. It was only Texas League baseball, not quite professional. More of a Class B league. So, where was I?"

Before he could continue, the voice of Chris Fisher interrupted him. "Lincoln, son, it's time to go." They both turned around to see him standing behind them. He made his way around them and to the front of the bench. He extended his hand to Arthur. "I'm Lincoln's father, Chris. It's nice to meet you, Pastor Graham."

Arthur stood and shook his hand.

"It's very nice to meet you, Chris, but please call me Arthur."

"Okay, Arthur it is. I hope my boy didn't talk your ear off."

Arthur laughed. "Actually, I think I did most of the talking."

He looked over at Lincoln and smiled.

"Well, that would be a first."

"Mr. Graham was just telling me about his baseball days." Lincoln responded.

"Now that's something that will grab his attention," Chris remarked.

"He met Al Kaline, dad."

"Really. What was he like?"

"He is a true gentleman. Are you a student of the game like our young Mr. Lincoln here?"

Chris laughed.

"No, sir. These days I watch it when I have time and try to throw the ball around with Lincoln as often as I can, but I'm no student. There was a time I watched it regularly, but a wife and three kids later keep me busy these days."

Arthur smiled. "I can understand that. Well, Lincoln here has a fine grasp of the game if you have questions."

Chris chuckled, "Yeah, he fills me in on it most days." He looked over at Lincoln and smiled. "Well, you ready to go, sport? Jessica's supposed to call us in about an hour."

Lincoln looked at Arthur. "That's my mom."

Arthur laughed, "I figured. We'll pick this story up tomorrow when you get here."

"Okay, Mr. Graham. See you tomorrow."

Arthur shook Chris's hand again and bid them both a good night. He sat back down and threw the birds some more bread.

CHAPTER 2
Tuesday—July 8, 1980

When Lincoln arrived at the church, Arthur was already sitting on the bench reading a book. Lincoln walked over and sat down.

"Good morning, Mr. Graham."

Arthur held his place with his thumb and sat the book on his lap and looked over at him.

"Good morning, Lincoln. How did you sleep?"

"I didn't get as much as I wanted, but I slept well." He rubbed his eyes.

Arthur laughed. "Why didn't you go to bed earlier?"

"It's summer vacation. You're supposed to stay up late and stuff."

"Says who?"

Lincoln scratched his head and thought for a moment.

"I don't know. I guess I just stayed up because I could. Dad went to bed early, but I wanted to eat junk and watch TV."

"What did you watch?"

"Kung Fu movies where the voice doesn't line up with the guy that's speaking."

"And you like these movies?"

"Of course. It's kind of our thing. We usually watch them together, but he said he needed to get to bed early to be rested for his work today."

"I'm sure he would rather have stayed up with you, but he's got a big job ahead of him."

"Yeah, I know. Did you watch any TV last night?"

Arthur paused before he responded.

"Well, let's see. When I got home, Esther and I worked a puzzle together. We worked on that for about an hour. Have you ever done a puzzle?"

"Yeah, mostly when I was a kid. It's been a couple of years, though."

Arthur scratched the base of his nose as he covered his smile.

"Well, this one has 1000 pieces, so it's challenging."

"Whoa! I never worked on one that big."

"It challenges the mind, and it's something we enjoy doing together. Anyway, after that we had some dinner, sat on the front porch for a bit sipping on some iced tea and reading, and then we went back inside and watched the Wheel of Fortune, and then the news before we turned in."

"What time did you get up this morning?"

"Around 6:30 a.m."

"6:30 a.m.! Why so early?"

"When you get older, you go to bed earlier, so you get up earlier, and when you get up earlier, you go to bed earlier."

They both laughed.

"What do you do when you get up that early?"

"I like to start the day reading the Bible."

"Reading the Bible? Weren't you a pastor for like 40 years? What don't you know?"

Arthur laughed out loud.

"I'll have to share that one with Esther. I read it over and over for a couple of different reasons. To constantly remind myself of God's love and direction for my life, to remind myself how I should treat others, and I really enjoy the stories."

"Like Jonah and the big fish?"

"Yes, like Jonah and the big fish."

Lincoln reached into the bag that he had brought with him and pulled out two peaches.

"My dad said that it was nice of you to share your lunch with me yesterday, and he felt terrible about forgetting to pack me one, so today we packed two peaches and two sandwiches so that I could share with you."

"Well, that's very nice. Do you know I walked right out of the house and forgot my lunch on the counter today?"

"No fooling?"

"No fooling." Arthur smiled. "Did your dad not eat yesterday,

17

either?"

"My mom says that while he's working, he focuses so hard on the 'task at hand' that he forgets to eat. She packs him a lunch, but he said that he usually eats it on the way home, so she won't get mad."

"Ah…so she's the lunch packer in the family? That explains why he forgot to pack your lunch yesterday."

"Yeah. He remembered on the way home because his stomach growled. He gave me the responsibility of packing lunches while my mom is gone."

"Did you pack him a lunch today?"

"Yep. Same as ours. A peach for a snack and a peanut butter and jelly sandwich."

"What kind of jelly?"

"Grape."

"Good boy. That's my favorite."

"Mine too. I mean nothing against the other flavors. Grape is just better."

"I couldn't agree more, Lincoln. So, where was I yesterday?"

"You finished your first minor league season with the Panthers in 1912, met Esther, and got a job working at Dillard's."

"Oh yeah. Nice recap. You were paying attention. Okay, let's see." He tapped his fingers on his chin while he thought. "Well, let's continue."

2

Fort Worth, TX, June 1913

The coaches were all in agreement that Arthur was an offensive asset. He could hit for average, and he could deliver a clutch hit or walk when asked. He displayed above average power, but with a little work and some weight training, he would get better. Offense wasn't the problem. Defense was a different story. He had good speed and a cannon for an arm, but his judgment was lacking. In

1912, they tried him in multiple positions, hoping to find the perfect fit. The experiment didn't go very well. So, they started from scratch. In the outfield, he had the speed to run down balls, but when the ball was in flight, he had a hard time tracking it. This resulted in too many missed or dropped balls. They tried him at the infield, but he had a hard time scooping the ball cleanly. He knocked it down most of the time but was always just late on the throw to first base. They felt that because he had such a powerful arm, pitching might be his calling. Two and a half months into the season, he was 1-6 with an ERA over six. He had a good fastball, but that's all he had. Most teams figured this out early in the game, and when he couldn't produce any variety in his pitches, they usually put on a hitting display. Management was perplexed about what to do with him. The errors had cost them a couple of games, and the players were getting frustrated with his play. Arthur was very much in tune with what was happening because when he was in the field, his stomach did somersaults. He willed the ball to be hit to anyone but him. Then, on June 13, 1913, fate stepped in. It was during the second game of a doubleheader against the Dallas Giants that he got the call. The Panthers backup catcher, Steve Hornick, didn't show up that day, which meant their starting catcher, Chet Michaels, would have to play both games. The Panthers squeaked out a win in the first game, 3-2, but in the bottom of the ninth on the last play of the game, Michaels injured his shoulder diving for a pop-up. He made the catch to secure the win, but separated his shoulder. The team learned about the injury between games. Arthur didn't play the first game but was sitting in the dugout when he heard the manager, Walt Morris, and the third base coach, Bill Nance, talking about game two.

"What are we going to do, Walt? Hornick really screwed us this time. That boy is about as unreliable as they come."

Morris just scratched his head and stared out at the field.

"I don't know, Bill. We need to find a more reliable backup. And it looks like Chet might be out for a bit, so we have to find another starter for a few weeks."

19

Nance looked over at him.

"Tomorrow I'll start looking, and by the end of the day I should have a..."

He was interrupted.

"Can I get someone to warm me up?" Darnell yelled from the mound.

Nance turned around to see that Arthur was the only player sitting in the dugout.

"Hey kid. Throw on some catching gear and go warm up, Darnell."

"Yes, sir," Arthur replied and hurried down to the end of the bench to put on the gear.

Morris and Nance continued their conversation while Arthur suited up and headed for the plate. After a while, they stopped talking and contemplated the issue in silence. They took turns spitting chew over the rails as they stared out at the mound. They both noticed that Darnell was throwing a lot of balls in the dirt, wide of the plate, and high enough that the catcher had to leave his crouch to spring up and snag it before it made its way to the backstop. They turned at the same time and looked at each other.

"Hey Bill, are you seeing this?"

"I sure am. That kid has snagged every ball. Not one has gotten by him."

"After Darnell is done, let's have him throw some balls to second to see if his arm is accurate."

"Good thinking. At the very least, we can throw him in to start this game and then evaluate him moving forward."

They watched Darnell warm up for another ten minutes, then Morris shouted to the second baseman, Buck Sheehan. "Hey Buck! Go to second and take some throws from Graham."

"Sure thing, Skip," Buck responded.

While he jogged over to second, Morris shouted out to Arthur.

"Hey kid, take the pitch and then pop up and throw the ball to second. Treat it like you're trying to throw the runner out who's stealing."

20

"On it," Arthur responded.

They watched intently as Darnell went into the windup and then delivered a fastball right down the center of the plate. Arthur caught it, and then in one smooth motion he popped up, and gunned the ball to second base. It cleared a ducking Darnell by a few inches and made Sheehan's glove pop as he snagged the ball six inches above the bag and slapped it down. Sheehan stood up and stared at Arthur. "Nice throw, Graham," he yelled.

Morris and Nance were so stunned that they just stood there in silence. Sheehan threw the ball back to Darnell.

"Again," Morris finally stated.

The next fifteen pitches were a variety of fastballs, curves, and change-ups. They were caught cleanly or scooped up by Arthur and thrown down to second base. Every throw was a laser that was between six and twelve inches above the front of the bag. Nance looked over into the dugout to see their right fielder, Mike Patty, sitting on the bench tying his shoe. Patty had good speed and had stolen twenty bases last season.

"Mike. Go to first and see if you can steal a bag," Nance ordered.

"Sure thing, coach," Patty replied.

Nance focused his attention on Arthur.

"All right, kid. Let's see what you can do against a runner."

Arthur nodded to him as he watched Patty jog over to first. He now knew that this was more than just helping Darnell warm up. This was an audition. He crouched down behind the plate and readied himself for the pitch. Patty had a modest lead at first. Darnell went into the windup and then delivered a fastball right down the middle of the plate. Arthur's glove popped, and within a split second, he was already on his feet, throwing the ball to second. Sheehan caught it and slapped his glove down at the front of the base. Patty slid perfectly into the tag.

"Yer out!" Sheehan yelled.

Sheehan threw the ball back to Darnell. Nance looked over at Morris. There was a smile on his face.

"We might have stumbled onto something here, Bill," Morris stated with an eyebrow raised.

"You might be right." Nance scratched his chin. "Let's see exactly what we've got."

They grabbed a player to be a hitter and another to play first base. The instructions were simple. Treat it like it's an actual game. The hitter would stand in the box, and Patty was instructed to steal when he felt comfortable. Darnell took the mound and pitched out of the stretch. The batter took his position in the box, and Arthur was in his crouch, flashing signals to Darnell. Patty took his lead, and the first baseman straddled the bag to hold him close. Arthur flashed Darnell the number one, and he nodded in agreement. From the stretch, he came up into the resting position and held it. He peeked over his shoulder at first to see Patty with a substantial lead. He quickly spun and fired the ball over to the first baseman. Patty dove back into the bag and barely got his hand in before the tag. Nance was now at first base, playing the role of the umpire.

"Safe." He shouted.

Darnell got the ball back and went back into his stretch. He came to rest once again and looked over to see Patty with more of a normal lead. He delivered a fastball high and inside. Patty stayed put. Arthur tossed the ball back, and the play resumed. This time he nodded yes to the curveball. Patty maintained a normal lead and watched as Darnell went into his windup. He took off toward second base.

"Runner," came the shout from the first baseman.

 The pitch started inside on the hitter but curved and dropped into the lower outside corner of the plate. Arthur snagged it and came up throwing. The throw was high, but Sheehan made the catch and slapped Patty's foot a half second too late.

"Safe," Nance yelled.

Arthur's heart was racing. He had never felt this type of adrenaline at any other position. Patty returned to first as Darnell got another ball. The hitter stepped back into the box, and Arthur took his position behind the plate. He taped the inside of his right thigh, and Darnell gave him the nod for the pitchout. He went into his stretch and checked on the runner. Patty was smiling as he danced back and forth for a moment and then took his lead. He threw the pitch toward the plate, and Arthur leaped up from his crouch. He fielded the pitchout high and outside and went into a throwing motion before he stopped and checked the runner at first base. Patty eased back toward the bag with a big smile on his face as Arthur held the ball. "You've gotta be sharper than that, kiddo," Patty stated as he wagged his index finger at Arthur.

Arthur smiled and tossed the ball back to Darnell. Morris was thrilled with what he was seeing at the moment. The kid can scoop and block balls behind the plate, throw to second with accuracy and heat, and now he is showing signs of having situational instincts. He looked over at Nance standing at first base, and they nodded to each other.

"I think that's enough," Nance shouted.

"Everyone, do some stretching. Arthur, come see me," Morris yelled as he looked over at first and motioned Nance to join him.

Arthur jogged over and joined the two coaches as they sat in the dugout pointing at the lineup card.

"You wanted to see me skip," Arthur asked.

Without looking up, he responded, "You're playing catcher in the second game. Do you think you can handle that?"

"Yes, sir, and thank you," he stated as he smiled.

He had no sooner got the words out of his mouth when Hornick came jogging up.

"I'm here for the second game, Skip," he stated as he looked at Arthur. "Hey, what's he doing with the equipment on?"

Morris finally looked up.

"HE is wearing the equipment because HE is playing the second game behind the plate. YOU are sitting in the dugout."

"He's never caught a game in his life. Why would you want to put him behind the plate?"

Nance intervened. "Because, unlike you, he shows commitment to

23

this team by showing up when he's supposed to be here."

"Whatever. This should be fun to watch." He looked over at Arthur and managed to get out a sarcastic, "Good luck, kid. Try not to let too many make it to the backstop. Darnell has a wild arm."

3

"The guy seemed like a sore loser," Lincoln stated.

"Steve was an alright guy. He was a good catcher when he wanted to be, but he had no discipline in his life."

"Coach says that you have to have discipline, or you won't amount to a hill of beans," he smiled as he said it.

Arthur laughed.

"He's not wrong. Discipline is key in a lot of areas in your life, not just in baseball. Earlier, when you asked me about reading the Bible, that's an example of discipline."

"I guess I understand that. Can I ask you another question?"

"Sure. You can ask me anything, son. I'm an open book."

"Why didn't they just make you the designated hitter if you were such a good hitter?"

"That's an excellent question, Lincoln. The designated hitter rule wasn't implemented until 1973."

"But pitchers still go to bat in the National League."

"That's the difference between the two leagues. The American League feels it produces more offense if you substitute an everyday hitter instead of letting the pitcher bat, while the National League feels the pitcher should hit because that's the way it's always been. They're more traditionalist."

"Trad-ition-a-list?" He enunciated.

"Yeah. It just means that's the way it's always been, so that's the way it'll always be."

Lincoln scratched his head and thought for a moment.

"Okay. Which way do you like best?"

"I like the DH. I think it's better for baseball, and great for the aging baseball player who can still hit, but maybe doesn't play the field so well anymore. It makes the game more exciting. You?"

"I like to hit, so I guess I like it too."

Arthur pulled a clean handkerchief from his pocket and handed it to him.

"Here you go, kid. Wipe your mouth. You got peach all over it."

"Thanks. I get kind of messy with fruit sometimes."

He laughed, "So I noticed." He tapped his chin. "Where was I? Oh yeah."

4
Fort Worth, TX—June 1913

In the top of the first inning alone, Arthur snagged four of Darnell's wild pitches before they made it to the backstop. By the time they finally got the Giants out, Darnell had thrown five wild pitches, hit two batters, but only given up a single run to make the score 1-0. As they walked into the dugout to sit down, Darnell threw his glove against the wall and walked to the end of the bench. Nobody looked his way or said a word to him. Morris looked over at Nance, and they both just shook their heads at one another as Nance climbed the steps to make his way to coach third base.

"Arthur, get your gear off. You're batting third!" Morris shouted at him.

Arthur made his way to the end of the bench and sat down next to Darnell. He started taking off his equipment when Darnell spoke.

"I don't know what's wrong with me out there."

Arthur stopped and looked at him. "You're in too big of a hurry."

Darnell turned toward him. "Too big of a hurry?"

"Yeah. You're pitching as if there's a clock on you. Slow down and take a deep breath before you pitch. When you go too fast, I've noticed that you release the ball late. Then you try to compensate on the next pitch by releasing the ball too early. Just take a deep breath and relax. When you slow it down, theirs nobody out here who pitches better."

Darnell scratched his chin and thought about what Arthur had said. "If you think I'm going too fast, then slow me down. Give me some sort of sign before I throw the next pitch. We'll see if you're onto something."

Arthur smiled and patted him on the knee. "Will do."

Darnell watched as Arthur finished getting his equipment off and picked up a bat. He walked into the on-deck circle to take some practice swings. Hornick walked over and sat next to Darnell. "What was that all about?" he asked.

"A pep talk from a kid who's been playing catcher for all of ten minutes." Darnell responded.

Hornick laughed. "Putz. Some people just think they know everything. Don't worry, I'll be in there before long."

What he didn't realize was that Arthur impressed Darnell. Starts were the norm like this for him. It usually took him a couple of innings to settle down before he got his stuff under control, but by the time that happened, it could already be four or five to nothing. Generally, they just let him fester at the end of the bench without coming and saying a word to him. Not even the coaches. In the bottom of the first, with a runner on second, Arthur made solid contact with a fastball that was on the lower outside corner and sent it flying over the left field wall. The Panthers led 2-1 when they took the field for the top of the second. Darnell had taken Arthur's advice to heart between innings and pitched a flawless second by striking out the side. As the game progressed, the offense continued to fire on all cylinders. At the end of the fifth inning, the Panthers were enjoying a comfortable 7-2 lead. Between innings, Arthur continued to walk down and sit next to his pitcher, and Morris noticed that the two of them talked non-stop, using hand gestures like they were building something. During the game, he didn't ask questions because Darnell had pitched five good innings of baseball, giving up two runs on only four hits, striking out seven, and had no wild pitches since the first inning. Arthur was also having a day. He was two for two with a home run, three RBIs, a walk, and had thrown out a base runner attempting to steal second to end a rally in the last inning. Nance walked over and stood next to Morris as they watched Darnell throw his warmup pitches in the top of the sixth.

"Good day so far, wouldn't you say?" He asked.

"I would." He answered.

Nance paused and then added. "What did we stumble upon here, Walt? We tried this kid at every position except for catcher. We knew he had a good arm. How come we never put two and two together? What does that say about us as coaches?"

"We already had two decent catchers, and were looking for a player that would help us out in the field. We just couldn't see the forest for the trees, I guess."

"You ever give much thought to the saying, 'The Lord works in mysterious ways?'"

He looked at Nance and laughed.

"Not really, but it makes perfect sense in this case, doesn't it? He must like us because he could see that we were both too blind to see that we had the makings of a good catcher right in front of our faces."

"Let's not jump the gun just yet. His catching career has only been five innings."

"We both know talent when we see it, Bill. That's where he belongs. Behind the plate."

They both stared down the bench at Hornick to see him sitting there staring at his feet.

"He knows it too," Nance observed.

"Yep. That's a man who knows he just lost his job."

They turned their attention back to the field to continue watching the game. Darnell allowed the first two batters of the inning to reach on base hits. When the third batter came to the plate, Arthur could see

27

visibly that his pitcher was upset. The first pitch was a ball in the dirt that Arthur had to scoop. The second pitch sailed high, and he had to leap out of his stance to catch it and keep it from going over everyone's heads. He threw the ball back to Darnell, who caught it in disgust and turned to face centerfield. He massaged the ball and stared out into the stands for an extended period until he heard the umpire yell, "Play ball!" He turned and took his place on the mound. When he looked up to get the sign from Arthur, he didn't see him crouching behind the plate. Arthur was standing on home plate, staring back at him. Arthur simply looked at him and mouthed the words, "Slow it down," as he took both of his hands and made a pushing motion toward the ground. Darnell gave him a nod, and he took his position behind the plate. They agreed on an inside fastball as Darnell came up out of the stretch and set himself. He tried Arthur's breathing exercise to slow things down. He delivered a picture-perfect fastball that painted the inside corner of the plate. "Strike one," the umpire yelled.

Arthur threw the ball back to him and gave him a fist pump. Darnell smiled as he caught it. He repeated the routine. A deep inhale through the nose followed by an extended exhale through the mouth. The changeup delivered caught the bottom of the strike zone. The batter had been expecting another fastball and swung late. He made contact with the ball but produced a ground ball to Sheehan at second. It was a tailor-made 4-6-3 double play. Darnell got the ball back and could now breathe a sigh of relief. The next batter attempted a bunt down the third-base line. Arthur was all over it. He popped up from his crouch, ran the ball down, and fired a perfect throw to first that just beat the runner. Bad inning avoided. The Panthers finished the day with a doubleheader sweep. Darnell pitched a complete game, allowing three runs on seven hits, while striking out eleven. Arthur finished the day three for four with a home run, four RBIs, and a successful day behind the plate. The Panthers won the second game by a score of 9-3.

"So, you were a catcher after that?" Lincoln asked.

"I was. When I crouched down behind that plate, it just seemed right. My coaches were convinced. I was a catcher."

"In the majors?" He asked with excitement in his voice.

Arthur missed that youthful energy. Where the simplest possibility could seem like the greatest thing in the world. He smiled. "They knew I was good enough for the Texas League, but I'm not sure they were convinced I was a player with major league potential."

"So, did you ever make it to the majors?"

"You'll have to wait and see. My story isn't finished yet. Remember how we talked about the journey?"

Lincoln smiled, "Yeah." He tossed some crumbs onto the ground before asking, "So, did you start the rest of the season?"

"When Michaels came back from injury three weeks later, we rotated in and out of the lineup."

"But I thought you did a great job?"

"I did. The coaches were very pleased with the way I played and with the way I could manage a game behind the plate, but Michaels was a very good catcher too."

"What happened to the other guy?"

"The next day, they cut him from the team and found someone else. He backed me up for three weeks until Michaels returned, then they cut him."

"Tough business."

Arthur laughed, "You're telling me. Just wait until you hear the rest of my story."

"Did he ever play again?"

"No." Arthur's mind drifted for a moment. He didn't feel the need to share with the kid that Hornick just couldn't overcome his addiction to alcohol. That's the reason he was always late or just didn't show up. Finally, he looked at him and stated, "He was someone who had all the talent in the world, but he didn't have the commitment to go with it."

"That's sad." He shook his head. "So, did you have a good season?"

"I did okay. I really got comfortable behind the plate as the year moved on, and my offense kept me around for the year. Batting .287 with ten homers will do that, I guess. I threw out fifty percent of the baserunners that tried to steal on me, which is apparently a great stat."

"I'll take your word for it, Mr. Graham. I don't really know much about catching stats. Ten homers is a good number, though."

"I thought so. At eighteen, I was on top of the world. I was getting paid to play baseball, and I was dating the prettiest girl in Texas."

"Did your dad ever come watch you play?"

"Whenever he got the chance, but he worked a lot. Mr. Dillard watched a lot of games. He came and cheered me on at most home games, and a fair number of away games."

"So, he was like a second father to you?"

"He was. He's the person who encouraged me to put my trust in the Lord. Jack was a deeply spiritual man, and an enormous influence on my life."

"Is he the one who got you to become a preacher?"

"The decision was mine, but he had a part in it."

"And you were dating the girl you met at the game the year before? Esther. Your current wife?"

"I was. We just clicked."

"That's funny. My dad said the same thing about my mom. I heard him tell a guy in church once that they just 'clicked.' Isn't that funny?"

"I guess when you know, you just know."

"Did you guys make the playoffs that year?"

"No. We finished with a disappointing 70-83 record. Sixth place. But after the season I had, I was excited for the next season to come."

"What number did you wear?"

"Boy, you really jump around in a conversation, don't you?"

"I just kind of ask when it pops into my head."

Arthur laughed. "I guess I do that too sometimes."

"Dad says it's because I have ADD. Mom says it's okay because all boys, and men for that matter, have ADD. Dad just looks at her and rolls his eyes."

"Your mom's not wrong, and I didn't wear a number on my jersey that year."

"No number? Why not?"

"Because they didn't start putting numbers on jerseys until the Cleveland Indians organization put it on the players' sleeves in 1916. They didn't start putting numbers on players' backs until the New York Yankees did it in 1929."

"Whoa! I always thought they had numbers on jerseys."

"No, not always."

A short time later, Chris came and picked up Lincoln to go home for the day. On the ride home, Lincoln filled him in on today's talk, and by the time they pulled into the driveway, Chris was fully caught up on the 1913 Texas League season.

CHAPTER 3

When they got home, Chris pre-heated the oven and then grabbed a casserole from the refrigerator that Jessica had left them. She had made and put several meals in the refrigerator and freezer for them to eat while she was away. Chris argued he was capable of making meals for the two of them, but she insisted it would be much more convenient for her to supply them with what they needed, because at the end of the workday the last thing he wanted to do was come home and prepare a whole meal for the two of them before baseball practice or games. He knew that what she really meant was that it would not be a two-week period filled with pizza boxes and fast-food wrappers. He appreciated how much she cared about them, and besides, she was a wonderful cook and would leave them with tasty meals that he would just have to pop into the oven. Lincoln sat at the kitchen table and watched him.

"Can't we just get a pizza?"

"Your mother made these meals with a lot of love, and you like her cooking."

"I do, but pizza just sounds good."

Chris smiled. "Yeah, it sure does." He looked down at him. "I'll tell you what. She made enough meals for ten days, which means that she left us to fend for ourselves for a few days. We'll make tomorrow a pizza day. How's that sound?"

Lincoln smiled. "That sounds good."

The timer sounded, and he put the casserole in the oven.

"I'm going to take a quick shower while the casserole cooks, so I need you to make sure that all the stuff you need for practice is in your duffel bag and ready to go after dinner."

"Ok dad. I'm just going to look at the paper first. You know, check the box score of the game. I want to see how Parrish hit."

He watched as Lincoln grabbed the sports section and opened it. Chris smiled.

"The Tigers didn't play yesterday. They don't play again until Thursday."

"Oh, yeah." He gently folded the paper back up and pushed it off to the side. "I guess I'll go make sure my stuff is ready to go."

Chris went and took a shower while Lincoln gathered his equipment. After getting out of the shower, he used half a roll of toilet paper blowing all the drywall dust out of his sinuses. He wore a mask, but so much of it still found its way into his body. He got dressed and went to let Lincoln know that dinner would be ready soon. Lincoln was lying on his bed looking at baseball cards. Chris peeked his head around the corner.

"Ten minutes until dinner's ready, son." He paused. "Looking at your cards?"

"Yeah. Just reading some stats on the back." He flipped a card over. "Parrish had 19 home runs last year."

"He had a good season." He knew Parrish was Lincoln's favorite player. "He's going to be one of the greats if he keeps it up."

Lincoln smiled. "I think so too."

"Ok champ. Start putting those away and wash up for dinner."

"Okay." Chris was turning to leave the room when Lincoln asked him a question. "Can we go to the library on Saturday after the game?"

"The library? Are you feeling okay, Link?"

Lincoln laughed.

"I'm fine. Mr. Graham has me thinking about reading about some of the older players. You know, learning some baseball history."

"I guess we can swing by on the way home. Any player in particular you're thinking about?"

"No, but I'll consult Mr. Graham before we go."

Chris smiled. "Good idea. All right, pal, wash up."

Lincoln put away the cards and washed up for dinner.

Lincoln stood in the batter's box and waited for the coach to pitch. There was nothing he loved more than hitting. He had switched his batting stance four different times already this year, and the one he felt most comfortable with was that of his current hero, Lance Parrish. He stepped out of the batter's box for a second to look over and make sure that his dad was watching. Chris had his eyes focused on Lincoln. The coach threw him eighteen pitches, and he made contact with every one of them. A few went foul, a few dribbled down the first and third baselines, and a few were nice and solid. But the last pitch, that was the one that would be talked about for the next couple of days. Lincoln got ahold of the ball and drove it over the left-field fence. Chris stood and clapped as Lincoln jumped up and down. His coach gave him a thumbs up, and he grabbed his glove and ran toward third base. He looked over at Chris with a big smile on his face. Chris also gave him a thumbs up and smiled back. Phil Michaels, the dad sitting to his left, commented about Lincoln's hitting.

"He's making good contact with the ball. Have you been working with him at home?"

"Whenever I get the chance. I think he's just picking up the game better."

"That's great. I wish Jamie would practice and pick it up better. All that kid wants to do is watch TV and draw comic book people."

"He still might come around. This is his first season, right?"

"It is, but he shows no interest when I try to get him to play catch or hit the ball at home. How long did it take for Lincoln to get interested?"

"I've always been a big fan, so I started taking him to games when he turned six. It's always kind of been our thing, well, until about two years ago. I started my own business and started working a lot more. It's kind of fallen by the wayside a bit, but we still catch a game now and then. He just took to it instantly."

"I guess I never laid that type of foundation for Jamie. My grandfather was a big baseball nut."

He pointed to the older gentleman sitting two rows in front of them. He was tall and very thin and wore a Detroit Tigers baseball cap and eyeglasses that appeared to be from the 1950s. The temperature was roughly eighty-five degrees, which had to be close to his age, and he was wearing a long sleeve flannel shirt and blue jean. The old man stared out at his great-grandson in the batter's box and shouted.

"Come on, Jamie. Make some contact."

They all looked on as Jamie took a swing at the first pitch. He didn't come close to making contact with the ball that was already in the catcher's mitt before he even swung. The coach paused and shouted words of encouragement his way. "That's okay, son. Keep your eye on the ball. You'll get the next one."

Chris stared over at Phil and flashed him a nervous smile.

"With a little practice, he'll get the hang of it."

"I hope so," he responded without conviction. "I have to hit the can. I've had three cups of coffee in the last hour."

Chris gave him a nod and smiled as he climbed down off the bleachers and headed for the bathroom. He watched as Jamie whiffed on three more pitches. The great-grandfather turned around and introduced himself.

"I'm Chet. Jamie's great-grandfather."

Chris stepped down a row and shook his hand.

"I'm Chris. Nice to meet you, sir."

"Your boy has some talent. He hits well, fields well, and has a good arm. I know you said you watched the game quite a bit, but did you ever play?"

"Yes, sir. I played in high school, and for two years in college."

"Why'd you stop? Injury?"

"No. It takes a certain commitment that I couldn't give."

"Didn't you dream of winning a World Series someday?"

"Not really." Chris laughed. "To me, it was just fun."

"Did you get a scholarship to play in college?"

"No. My best friend at the time did. He had aspirations of a World Series ring. I guess I was just along for the ride. I was good enough to make the team as a reserve, but I wasn't a starter. Darren was. He was pro-material."

"Did he ever go anywhere?"

"No. About a year after I left college, he hurt his throwing arm pretty badly. He never really recovered from the injury. Last I heard, he had a wife and three kids and was living in New York, working on Wall Street. He always had a head for finance."

"Some people are like that," he agreed. "So, what kind of business do you own?"

Chris reached into his pocket and pulled out a business card. He handed it to him.

"Carpentry. We do all kinds of work. From additions to renovations."

"Is that what you left college to do?"

He smiled.

"It is. My dad was a licensed carpenter. Growing up, I loved watching him build things with his hands. I didn't realize how much until after my sophomore year of college. I was sitting in my dorm room one day, and it just hit me. Baseball is fun, but it's not my passion. I love building things with my hands. So, I left school and went back home. I started working with my dad and learning the trade. Since then, I have worked with a few different companies and experts that have taught me electrical, plumbing, and all kinds of different skills."

"That's good to know," he stated as he put the business card in his front shirt pocket. "I will recommend you."

"Thank you, sir." He smiled and then paused before asking, "Did you ever play the game?"

"I did. I grew up in Texas and played in the Texas League for a bit."

"Semi-pro ball. You must have been good."

He laughed. "I did okay for myself. I was a decent catcher with above-average hitting. That talent is good enough for the Texas League, but not for the major leagues."

"How did you end up in Michigan?"

"Like you, I knew that baseball would not be my destination. My father-in-law was pressuring me to get a career. Told me I had responsibilities to his daughter and grandchildren. To make sure I took care of them. So, after coming back from a business meeting that he had in Detroit, he told me I should apply for a job at this automotive place. Said it looked to be built to stick around for a while. So, I made my way to Detroit and applied in 1925 to the General Motors Corporation. I put in 40 years and retired in 1965."

"Did you ever regret your decision?"

"No, sir. Not once."

Phil reappeared and took his seat next to Chris. Chet nodded and smiled at Chris, and Chris returned the gesture. Chet turned around and started watching Jamie again.

"What'd I miss?" Phil asked.

"Not much," Chris responded and then added, "Your boy made contact with a couple of pitches."

Phil smiled. "Progress."

"Baby steps," Chris replied.

They both focused on watching the rest of the boy's practice.

3

Arthur and Esther joined hands as he asked God to bless the meal they were about to receive. Pot roast was one of his favorite meals, and no one made it better than Esther

"It smells amazing, my dear," he stated as he looked at her and smiled.

"Then I hope it tastes as good as it smells," she responded.

"I know it will."

He pulled her hand toward him, bent down, and kissed it. She smiled at him.

"How was your day with Lincoln?"

"I don't even need a knife to cut the beef. The fork just cuts right through it."

She laughed. "I'm glad you're enjoying your dinner, but did you hear what I asked you?"

He stopped for a moment and looked at her.

"No. I'm sorry, my love. What was the question?"

"How was your day with Lincoln?"

"It was nice. He seems like a good egg."

"You know you forgot your lunch today?"

"I know, but he brought me a PB&J, and a peach."

"He sounds like a good egg. Should I not pack you a lunch tomorrow?"

Arthur laughed.

"You definitely should. We both agreed to bring our own lunches from now on."

She could tell that Arthur enjoyed the young man's company. Dillard was an only child who shared his father's love for preaching the gospel, but didn't share his love of baseball. They had four grandchildren. Jack, Robert, Alyssa, and William, none of whom shared his passion for the game, and four great-grandchildren, with one on the way, who were too young to even understand the game. Lincoln was somebody with whom he could talk baseball. Someone who loved the game as much as he did. Someone he could teach and tell stories to. At this time in his life, it was a perfect fit.

"Is he going to be back tomorrow?"

"I think so. He didn't say that he wouldn't."

"I'm going to bake some cookies after dinner. You can take some with you tomorrow and share them."

"What kind of cookies?"

"Peanut butter."

"Peanut butter," he whispered as he smirked. "If they make it until tomorrow."

Esther put her fork down and stared at him.

"Arthur Thomas Graham, you will not eat a plate of cookies before tomorrow-"

"I was just pulling your leg, my love." He laughed. "I will take them and share them with the boy."

"Make sure Dillard gets some as well."

"I will, I will."

She reached over and grabbed his hand.

"Are you feeling okay today? Last night you had some heartburn."

Her voice was soothing, and her eyes were full of compassion. There was nobody in the entire world who made him feel so loved. That deep love and support throughout his life made everything he accomplished possible. She was the driving force behind his success on the baseball field and behind the pulpit. God truly blessed him when Esther walked into his life. He reached over and placed his other hand on top of hers.

"I feel good." His smile was sincere. "How are you feeling today?"

"Ditto," she said with a smirk.

They talked about the day's events, the church's renovations, some politics, and, of course, they finished up with Tiger baseball. They cleared the table after dinner, and then she put the dishes away as he pretended to read the newspaper and not nap. When the cookies went into the oven, the house filled with the aroma of peanut butter. Arthur lay in his La-Z-Boy, napping and smiling.

4

Chris smiled as he drove and listened to Lincoln go on and on about practice. He was pumped about hitting one of the coach's pitches over the fence.

"I can't believe it, dad. I really got a hold of that one today!" He shouted, not realizing that he was shouting.

Chris laughed, "You sure did, buddy. That ball went far."

"It did, didn't it?"

"Take me through the at-bat one more time."

Lincoln's smile couldn't get any wider.

"I stepped into the box and dug my feet in real deep, and then I got set. I was staring out at the coach, and he asked me if I was ready." His voice lowered and got intense as he stated, "I gave him the nod." He nodded. "Coach went into the windup and tossed it toward the plate. I gripped the bat extra tight, keeping my eye on the ball the whole time, and as it came across home plate, I swung."

Chris smiled as his son appeared to be quite the storyteller. You could cut the tension with a knife as Lincoln made sure he paused for effect.

"The ball jumped off the bat as I made contact. As I followed through with my swing, I watched as the ball sailed toward the left fielder. Everyone turned to watch as he started running back toward the fence. The ball just kept going. It cleared the fence by at least ten feet." He looked at his dad and gave him a smile and another nod. "A no-doubter."

Chris joined in the fun. "At least ten feet beyond the fence. A homer worthy of Parrish praise."

Lincoln cupped his hands and placed them over his mouth as he mimicked a cheering crowd.

"The coach yelled, 'Home run!' and the crowd went nuts."

"It sure was something," Chris responded. Lincoln started laughing, and his dad joined in. Chris reached over and gave him a playful slap on the brim of his cap. "It felt good to hit that home run, didn't it?"

"It felt great, dad. I love playing baseball. I'm thankful that you and mom make sacrifices so that I can play. Thanks."

For a moment, Chris became speechless. Lincoln was a good kid, and polite most of the time, but recognizing sacrifices, this was something different.

"You're welcome, son." He cleared his throat. "How about a stop at King Kone on the way home? A dinger that far is something to celebrate."

That wide smile came back.

"I'll never say no to ice cream. Thanks, dad."

"Mr. Graham will be happy to hear about your home run tomorrow."

"I can't wait to tell him."

"You like talking to him, don't you?"

"Yeah. He's a nice guy who knows a lot about baseball and how to tell a good story."

"Maybe I'll ask his son if he ever made it to the big leagues. See if the story has a happy ending."

"No...I mean, please don't." He looked at Chris. "It wouldn't be fair to him if we spoiled the ending. According to Mr. Graham, the journey is one of the most important parts."

Chris laughed. "He's right. In every story in my life, I look back and thank God for the journey." He smiled. "So much to be thankful for."

"What about all the bad stuff that happens? Like getting hurt or death?"

"It's all a part of life, Lincoln. Good things happen. Bad things happen."

"But we have Jesus. Right dad?"

"We do. He makes the bad times tolerable. When we're going through those times, He comforts us. We lean on Him to get us through."

"He is our rock." Lincoln smiled at his dad.

"He sure is, kiddo." Chris responded, and then whispered, "Out of the mouth of babes."

"What, dad?"

"Nothing. Let's get that ice cream."

They pulled into the lot of King Kone and parked. Let the sugar feast begin.

CHAPTER 4
Wednesday—July 9, 1980

Lincoln walked up to see Arthur on the bench, feeding the birds. As he sat down, he noticed a book open in Arthur's lap.

"Good morning, Mr. Graham."

Arthur looked up from the book.

"Good morning, Lincoln. How are you this fine morning?"

"Pretty good. You?"

"The same, I guess. How was practice last night?"

Lincoln's eyes lit up, and he could barely contain his excitement.

"I hit a ball so far last night. It was awesome."

Arthur laughed and closed the book. He turned slightly to angle himself toward the young man, to give him his undivided attention.

"This sounds like something I need to hear about in great detail. Start at the beginning and give me all the details. Leave out nothing."

The epic story of the longest home run in history began. Lincoln told the story with such passion and conviction. At one point, Arthur truly believed that a ball hit by Babe Ruth himself could not come within 50 feet of Lincoln's. He stood, and he replayed the epic swing for Arthur, and then once again cupped his hands around his mouth and mimicked the cheering of the crowd. It was truly a sight to behold, and a feat that history would not see again. When he finished, he sat back down and waited for Arthur's response.

"Wow!" was the only word he could get out.

"Pretty cool. Right?"

"Wow," Arthur repeated. "Lincoln, that sounds like one doozy of a home run. I wish I had been there to see it."

"It was awesome," Lincoln shouted in excitement.

Arthur laughed, because when he retold the story later to Esther, he would tell her it was the biggest smile he had ever seen on anyone, anywhere.

"Keep it up and someday I'll see you hitting balls over the fence at Tiger Stadium."

"Wouldn't that be great?" His smile grew even bigger. "We have a game tonight, and one on Saturday morning if you can make it, Mr. Graham?"

"Tonight's too late of notice, but I'll see about Saturday."

"Awesome." He looked down. "What's the book about?"

Arthur handed it to him.

"It's a history of Texas League baseball. I thought you might like it."

Lincoln accepted the book from him.

"You're giving this to me?"

"I am. You can brush up on minor league history and learn some things that you didn't know. Theres a lot of good information in there. I think you'll enjoy it."

"Wow, thanks, Mr. Graham," Lincoln responded as he flipped through the first few pages of the book.

"You're welcome. Are you ready to continue with our story?"

Lincoln closed the book and set it aside.

"Yes, sir."

"Do you remember where we left off?"

"You just finished out the 1913 season. You became a full-time catcher, and you hit 10 home runs that year. Oh, and you were dating Esther."

He smiled. "You're sharp as a tack, kiddo." He tapped his chin. "Okay, let's continue."

2
Fort Worth, TX—May 1914

It was already six weeks into the season, and Arthur had won the starting job. He was batting .375, and his defensive numbers were off the charts. He had caught the last four games in a row, but on this beautiful Saturday afternoon in mid-May, Chet Michaels was given the start. The Houston Buffalos were coming into the matchup red hot, and they had their ace on the mound, Burleigh Grimes. He was a twenty-year-old spitballer from Wisconsin. The major league scouts saw good potential in the young pitcher, so whenever he took the mound, a scout was in the crowd. Arthur was sitting in the dugout talking to Bob Schilling.

"Do you think one will be here today?" Arthur asked.

Schilling stopped oiling his mitt and looked over at Arthur. "One what?"

"Major league scout. You know, because Grimes is pitching."

"I think it's a good possibility. Why?"

"I just wish I was playing. That's all."

Schilling laughed. "So, you think you could catch their eye, do ya?"

"I don't know. Maybe. I've been playing well."

"My advice is just to enjoy the ride. Play ball and get paid for as long as you can, because one day we'll all need to get actual jobs."

"So, you don't think you can make it to the majors?"

He stopped and looked directly at Arthur.

"No. I never did. I'm good at playing baseball, but not great. I know that one day this ride would end. You thought you were going to play major league baseball?"

"Well, yeah. That was the idea."

Arthur dropped his head and stared down at his shoes. Schilling wrapped his arm around Arthur's shoulder.

"You've been dating my sister for almost two years now. She's going to be 18 at the end of this month. My parents are wondering if you see her in your future. She's not getting any younger, you know?"

Arthur looked at him. "I love Esther. She's definitely in my future."

"Then you'd better think long-term, buddy boy. How are you going to support her? And the kids?"

"The kids?"

"Yeah, the kids. You don't want kids?"

"Of course I want kids, but we're still young."

"She's going to be 18, and a month later you'll be 19. I know some people who have one or two kids by that age."

"What about you? You're 21 and not even married yet."

"I've got some prospects, but I've chosen to remain single. You jumped in with both feet. Once you started seeing Esther exclusively, you put a timer on things. All my parents see now is a husband who can give their daughter security, and a bunch of grandchildren."

Arthur gulped and looked straight ahead.

"I didn't realize that."

"Well, that's the situation. Playing Texas League baseball in the summer and working at a hardware store in the off season will not get the job done. You've gotta think bigger…"

Walt Morris walked over and interrupted their conversation.

"Get your gear on, Graham. Michaels is under the weather, so you're catching today."

Schilling looked at him and smiled.

"You wanted a chance to impress the scouts. Here you go."

Morris continued to look at Arthur. "Well?"

Arthur stood up. "Yes, sir, skip."

Arthur headed down toward the end of the dugout to put his gear on. He sat down and started with the shin guards. He looked down toward Schilling, who had resumed oiling his glove. Schilling had a smirk on his face. Arthur finished putting on the rest of his equipment and headed out to the plate. He took up his position behind the plate, and Green started throwing. He really did not like catching for Green. Eighty to ninety percent of his pitches were knuckleballs. You never knew where the ball was going to end up. It might start at the batter's head and end up a foot in front of the plate, bouncing in all different directions. Some knuckleballers were very good and kept the ball catchable, but Green was not. The umpire tapped Arthur on the shoulder.

"Two more and we'll get started."

Arthur flashed Green the number two, and he nodded. After Green threw the second pitch, the umpire yelled, "Play ball."

As Arthur settled in behind the plate, he looked over into the dugout to see Michaels smiling at him. He didn't have the look of someone who was "under the weather." He turned his attention to Green and flashed him the sign. Fastball? No. Curveball? No. Changeup? No, he finally flashed him the knuckleball. Green nodded yes. The first batter for the Buffalos was Dusty Springer. Springer was an above-average hitter, but an absolute bullet on the base paths. If he reached base, he was most likely going to steal second and third on Green. He threw the pitch, and it started above Springer's head but then broke sharply down and to the inside. Arthur caught it right at knee height and perfectly on the black.

"Strike one," the umpire yelled.

Springer stepped out of the box and tapped his cleats with the bat as Arthur tossed the ball back to Green. This time he flashed the knuckleball sign first, and Green gave him the nod. Springer stepped back into the box and got ready for the pitch. Knuckleball number two took the same route, and before the ball could hit Arthur's mitt, Springer laid a slow rolling bunt down the first base line. Arthur leaped out of his crouch and raced to get it. Springer was three quarters down the line as Arthur picked up the ball and gunned it over to first base. The first baseman's mitt popped a millisecond before Springer's foot came down on the bag.

"Out," the first base umpire yelled.

Arthur smiled as he flashed the index finger to his fielders, signifying one out. He scanned the crowd as they cheered, looking for anyone who might resemble a scout. He didn't know what he was looking for, maybe a bright light shining down on a man in an oversized hat frantically taking notes. Arthur went back and took his position behind the plate. The number two hitter grounded out, and number three eventually struck out after many foul balls, a few of which slammed off some of Arthur's body parts, adding to the many bruises the season had provided so far. He walked into the dugout and took a seat next to Michaels.

"How are you feeling, Chet?" he asked with a hint of sarcasm.

"A lot better after watching the beating you took that inning. Better you than me, pal." He laughed.

"What's got you under the weather?" The sarcasm continued. Michaels turned toward him.

"Since you asked so politely," sarcasm returned. "I was helping a neighbor move some of his cattle last night, trying to earn a little extra money, and I fell off my horse. I landed hard on my right hip. It's bruised to where there's no way I can crouch behind that plate for a full game."

"So, if I push on it, you'll feel pain?" Arthur asked.

"If you push on it, we'll both feel pain."

Arthur laughed. "You picked a great day to get hurt. Grimes is on the mound."

"I know. There's a scout out there somewhere."

"You look for him while I continue to chase the ball around. That first half-inning was brutal."

"I'll let you know if I can make him out."

"Thanks."

The game continued, and through seven and a half innings of play, the score was 1-1. Green had settled down nicely, and his knuckleball was finding its way into Arthur's mitt without all the scrambling and bruises. Grimes had given up just two hits all day, both in the same inning. In the fourth inning, Patty started off with a bunt single down the third-base line. The next two batters struck out, which brought Arthur to the plate with a man on first and two outs. In the first inning, he ran the count to three balls and two strikes, fouling off several pitches before finally popping out to the third baseman. He stepped into the box and got ready. He had decided that he was sitting on the fastball up and away. Arthur had studied Grimes over the first three innings and was sure that was his pitch of choice to start this at bat. Grimes went into his windup and

47

delivered. Patty took off from first base. It was a fastball headed up and away. Arthur gripped the bat tightly as he swung. The crack of the ball coming off the bat was loud. It rocketed over the first baseman's head and landed just inside the line. The right fielder was playing more toward center, so the ball made it all the way to the wall and rolled into the corner. By the time he threw the ball back into the infield, Arthur was standing on second with a double, and Patty had crossed the plate to tie the score at one.

In the bottom of the seventh, Arthur stepped into the box and looked out at the mound. Grimes was giving him the stare-down as he took a couple of warm-up swings. He went into the windup and delivered the pitch. It was a fastball that went high and inside. The catcher caught the ball six inches below Arthur's chin. Arthur didn't even flinch. The home crowd booed.

"Ball one," the umpire yelled.

They stared intently at each as the catcher threw the ball back to the mound. Grimes caught it without looking away from Arthur. He never left the batter's box as he took two more practice swings and waited for Grimes' next pitch. Arthur was sitting on a curveball this time. He knew Grimes was playing mind games with him. Brush him back with the fastball and then give him the curve. He wouldn't have it. Grimes went into the windup and then delivered. Arthur stood strong in the box, and as the curveball broke and headed for the outside middle of the plate, he swung with everything he had. There was a loud crack, and the ball jumped off the bat. Everyone watched as it sailed through the air down the left-field line. It had plenty of home run distance but landed just on the wrong side of the foul pole.

"Foul ball, strike one," the umpire yelled.

Arthur was already halfway down the first baseline, willing the ball to stay fair when the call was made. He jogged back to the plate and picked up his bat. He swatted his shoes a couple of times to knock the dirt off, and then stepped back into the box and readied himself. Grimes was staring daggers at him as he waited for the signs from

48

his catcher. When he finally got the pitch he liked, he went into his windup. As he followed through and released the ball, he let out a loud grunt. The ball was moving too quickly for Arthur to get out of the way. He turned his body toward the backstop to avoid the pitch, but the fastball hit him squarely on top of his left foot. Arthur dropped the bat and collapsed in pain. He reached down and grabbed the foot, pulling it into his body. His teammates were already out of the dugout yelling at Grimes.

"That's bush league," Patty screamed.

"You're a hack," Schilling screamed.

It was all background noise to Arthur. His foot throbbed, and his mind was running through every worst scenario possible. Both teams were out of the dugout walking toward each other, screaming. The coaches and umpires were doing their best to keep the situation under control. Arthur felt a hand on his shoulder and heard the calm voice of Jack Dillard.

"Hang in there, Arthur. Everything's going to be all right."

Fifteen minutes later, Arthur was in Dillard's car on the way to the hospital. Both sides had gone back to their respective dugouts, and the game resumed with a new pitcher on the mound. Arthur lay across the backseat with an icepack on his foot. They hadn't taken the shoe off for fear that the foot would swell up. Esther sat in the front passenger seat, turning around occasionally with words of encouragement.

"We'll be at the hospital soon, and they'll fix you right up," she stated softly.

Arthur looked up at her. "It's broken. I know that it's broken."

"So they'll cast it and you'll be good as new in six to eight weeks, kiddo," Dillard chimed in.

"That's half the season," Arthur stated, as his voice cracked.

He covered his face with his hat and tried to hold back the tears. He was still only eighteen, and the need to suppress his feelings hadn't taken over yet. Esther wept for him as they continued to the hospital.

At 7:00 p.m. Arthur was lying in his own bed. Esther and Jack Dillard had just left so that he could get some rest. Arthur just stared at the ceiling. He thought about crying now so that he could get it over with, but he heard the front door close and his father's voice. A few minutes later, Jim walked in and sat down in the chair next to his bed.

"Are you okay, son?" he asked softly.

"Doc says I broke a bone at the top of my foot. It's going to take a while…" He paused for a moment to keep from crying, "to heal."

"But it will heal, Arthur. You'll be back out there playing before you know it."

"I was having such a great season, dad. The scouts were really going to notice me this year."

He smiled and patted his son's forearm.

"You're a young man, Arthur. You'll heal quickly, and then you'll still be a young man when you play again."

"I just…I was really hitting the ball well. The doctor is saying that I'll be out for at least eight weeks, maybe longer."

"The top of the foot is a pretty sensitive area, but if anyone can come back this year, you can."

"Thanks dad. What am I going to do about money while I'm healing? I need to get a…"

"Arthur. Rest, my boy. We can figure everything out in due time. Just concentrate on getting better for now." He smiled. "Was Esther at the game?"

"Yeah. She was worried. She cried on the way to the hospital."

"I bet. She loves you very much."

"I know. The feelings are mutual."

His father laughed.

"I know it is, son. Rest. We'll check on you later."

Jim stood and walked toward the door.

"Dad."

He turned, "Yes."

"Thanks."

Jim smiled at him as he closed the door behind him. Arthur resumed staring at the ceiling. He replayed the at-bat repeatedly in his head. Grimes release of the ball. The crack as the ball hit the top of his foot, and the way he collapsed onto the ground in pain. He could hear his teammates yelling at Grimes, and then the calming voice of Mr. Dillard telling him that everything was going to be alright. Exhausted from the day's events, he finally closed his eyes and went to sleep. No dreams or interruptions. Just sleep.

3
Dillard's Hardware Store—July 1914

Arthur sat on a stool by the cash register. His foot was still in a cast and nestled into a nice homemade boot his dad made for him. The cast would come off in about a week, and they would get an X-ray to see where the healing process was. Arthur hoped he could return to the field this season, but preparing himself for the worst-case scenario. He was deep in thought when the gentleman standing at the counter cleared his throat. Arthur smiled and looked down at the counter.

"Just the gloves and rope for you then?" he asked.

"That'll do." The man replied.

Arthur hit some keys on the cash register to get the total.

"That'll be $3.00, please."

"$3.00?" The man asked. "For gloves and rope?"

"I'm sorry, sir. I meant $.30."

The man put two quarters on the counter.

"That's more like it." He watched as Arthur took the money and fished two dimes from the register. "What happened to your foot?"

"I was playing baseball, and the pitcher hit the top of my foot with the ball."

"That must have been some throw." The man paused for a moment.

"You play ball for Fort Worth, don't you?"

Arthur looked up at him.

"Yes, sir. You've seen me play?"

"I have. You're a good catcher."

"Thank you, sir. Hopefully, I'll get back this season."

The man took his change and picked up his bag.

"Good luck, son."

Arthur smiled and nodded at him as he walked out of the store. Jack locked the door behind him and rotated the open sign to closed. He turned to Arthur.

"Another good day. Thanks for helping."

"Thank you for giving me a job while I recover."

Jack smiled. "You'll always have a job here as long as we're open."

"Thanks…wait…is everything okay, Mr. Dillard? The store isn't in danger of closing, is it?"

"No. Not at all. Were a staple in the community, but small businesses open and close every day. Supply and demand can be a fickle thing, plus some other businesses are always trying to undercut your prices. It's just the nature of the beast."

"Yeah. It sounds rough."

"Do you have a couple of minutes to talk, Arthur, or do you need to get home?"

"I'm in no rush. What's on your mind?"

"Are you hungry?"

"I can always eat."

"Let's go to the breakroom and sit down. I got us a couple of deli sandwiches and sodas."

Arthur hobbled behind him all the way to the breakroom and had a seat at the table. It wasn't a large room, but it was big enough for a table and four chairs. Jack grabbed the food and drinks and had a seat across from Arthur.

"I have something on my heart that I want to talk to you about, Arthur."

Arthur put the sandwich down and looked at him.

"What is it, Mr. Dillard? You know you can talk to me about anything?"

"It's about Jesus."

Arthur breathed a sigh of relief.

"I thought it was going to be about something serious." He smiled and then took a bite of his sandwich. There was a noticeable pause, and he looked up to see Jack staring at him. "I'm sorry. Not that Jesus isn't serious…" he was stumbling over his words when Jack stepped in.

"It's okay, Arthur. I just wanted to ask you about your relationship with Him."

"I know all about Jesus, Mr. Dillard. We learned all about Him in Sunday school and in teen ministry."

"Okay. What can you tell me about Him?"

"He performed many miracles. He's God's only son. Jesus is the savior of the world. He had disciples. He died for us."

"It sounds like you know a lot about Jesus, but do you know Jesus?"

"Isn't that kind of the same thing?"

"No, son, it isn't. Even people who don't believe in Him know a lot about Him. Let me ask you this. Have your parents spoken to you about Him?"

"Yeah. They tell me about all the great miracles He performed and say that He died for us. They asked me if I understood, and when I said yes, they told me I was saved."

"Arthur, knowing about the things that Jesus did doesn't make you saved. Do you even know why it's called being saved?"

Arthur thought for a moment before answering.

"I said a prayer to Jesus to come into my heart, and I was taught to do unto others as you would have them do unto you."

"That's the golden rule mentioned in Matthew chapter seven verse twelve, but being saved is more than saying a prayer and asking Jesus to come into your heart. You must truly believe that He is the King of kings and Lord of lords. He is the Messiah. The one true King."

"How can anyone know that for sure?"

Jim placed his Bible on the table and opened it to the book of Romans, chapter three, verse twenty-three, and explained to Arthur that we are all sinners. Then he flipped over to Romans chapter six, verse twenty-three, and explained that the penalty for sin is death. He then took Arthur to Romans, chapter five, verse eight, and explained to him that while we were still sinners, Christ died for us. Finally, he went to the book of Ephesians, chapter two, verses eight and nine, and explained to him that we are saved by grace, through faith, and not by works. Arthur had many questions throughout the talk, and Jim answered each by flipping to different books and passages in the Bible to show him God's love and guidance to mankind.

"So now that I've explained it to you, does that make you look at it in a different light?"

"Yes. I never realized the extent of His love toward us before. I guess I never realized what it meant to be truly saved."

"Being saved means we live a life that's holy and acceptable to Him. We trust in Him to meet all our needs instead of the world. Our strength is in Him, and we trust in His word to be our ultimate guide. In second Timothy chapter three verses sixteen and seventeen, we are told that all scripture is the inspiration of God, and that it equips us fully to do good works. He saves us from the penalty of sin."

"So, trusting in Him will help me with my foot?"

"Yes. But not in the way you might think. People are under the impression that they can use Him like a genie. He's there to grant wishes. They think that salvation in Christ keeps them from hard times and that financial freedom awaits them."

"But that's not the case?"

"No, son, it isn't. We aren't promised freedom from a rough life, or from financial pitfalls. What we're given is a savior who will be with us through those rough times and financial problems. We have a rock to lean on. He will comfort us and feed our souls. Over the years, I have learned to praise Him for my triumphs, and to lean on Him greatly in my struggles. His unconditional love allows me the freedom to live the best possible life. That's why I share Him with others. I want everyone to experience that amazing grace."

"Wow. I can't believe that He sent His only Son to the cross for me. His love and grace are truly amazing."

"Do you want to experience that amazing grace, Arthur?"

"Yes. I thought I had, but after hearing you explain it to me, I realize I knew of Christ, but I don't know Him."

"Only God truly knows your heart. You can fool men, but you can never fool Him. We can say that we believe, but we are encouraged in First John chapter three verse eighteen to 'love in actions and in truth.'"

"Mr. Dillard, I don't really know how to describe what's happening in my heart right now."

Jack smiled and wrapped an arm around his shoulder. "Can I pray for you, son?"

"Yes, sir, please do," Arthur responded in tears.

"Father in heaven, strengthen this young man in Your name. Please guide him and give him understanding in reading Your word, and on walking the path You have for him. Thank you for loving us so much that You sent Your only Son to redeem us. Bless Arthur and his ministry. In Jesus' precious and holy name, we ask these things. Amen."

"Amen," Arthur echoed. "I'm going to have a lot of questions over the next few weeks, or maybe even months or years."

"I'll be here for you, Arthur. I'll help you along the way, and if I can't answer something, I'll find someone who can."

"Thanks, Mr. Dillard. I can't wait to share this with Esther. If she wants to know more, can I have her talk to you?"

"That would be wonderful, Arthur."

Arthur sat on the bench, staring at the sky. Lincoln grabbed a handful of breadcrumbs and threw some onto the ground.

"So did you play again that season?" he asked.

Arthur turned to him and smiled.

"I did. My foot healed well enough for me to play the last 25 games of the season. I was a little rusty from missing time, and I think a little shellshocked from my injury. I was relegated to back-up duty, but I had found something life-changing that July."

"Jesus?"

He laughed, "Yes, Jesus. That injury really opened my eyes to a lot of things. It made me realize that baseball wasn't the most important thing in the world."

"I know that, but it's pretty important to me."

"It took a fastball to the foot to open my eyes. I loved my family, Esther, friends, and plenty of other things, but baseball was always at the top of the list. I even took God for granted. My parents really set a good example for me, but they just assumed that I was a Christian because I was good at going through the motions. Mr. Dillard made sure that I understood what it truly meant to be a faithful servant of God. At nineteen, I saw our Lord and Savior for the very first time."

"After Sunday school one day, I was eleven. I told my parents that I loved Jesus. They sat me down and explained it to me. He died for my sins and loved me so much. They mentioned many of the things that Mr. Dillard told you. I told them I was ready to have Him be the savior of my life. We prayed, and I accepted Jesus as my Savior. I love to learn about the stories in the Bible, and I talk to Him every day."

"Lincoln, that's wonderful. You learned much sooner than I did. It does my heart good to see such a passionate young man for Christ."

"That's what my mom says. But I still really love baseball too. Just not as much as Jesus."

Arthur laughed. "Me too."

"Did you keep playing baseball?"

"I did. God had a definite plan for my future, and baseball would play a big part in it."

Lincoln smiled. "I was hoping it would."

"After accepting the Lord and studying the Bible for a couple of months, I gave serious consideration to being a pastor. His grace, His mercy, and His love really made a lasting impression on my heart. But...I just couldn't give up on baseball." His thoughts drifted once again, and he took a moment to compose his next words. "1914 turned out to be one of the best years of my life. One that I will never forget."

"What else happened?"

"Well, on December 1, 1914, Esther and I got married."

"How old were you?"

"I was 19, and she was 18."

"Wow! That's young."

"Back in those days, it wasn't. We were so in love, and I knew I wanted to spend the rest of my life with her, so why wait? Mr. Dillard made sure that I had a job at his store in the off-season, and he gave me an advance so that we could buy our first house. Also, after I told Esther about accepting the Lord, she went to church with me and did Bible studies with us at the store after hours. She came to know the Lord that winter."

"Mr. Dillard had an enormous influence on you and your wife."

"That he did. He was a man who genuinely loved Christ, and he shared it with anyone who would listen."

"Hey. Your son's name is Dillard. Is that in honor of him?"

"It sure is. What better way to honor him?"

Arthur looked up to see Chris walking their way from the construction site. He looked at his watch.

"It looks like our time is up for today." He laughed. "Here's an interesting tidbit for you, Burleigh Grimes, the pitcher who broke my foot, is a Hall of Fame baseball player. He won 270 games in the majors and won a World Series ring in 1931 with the St. Louis Cardinals."

"No way. You played against an actual big-league pitcher? And you got a double off him?"

"I did. Another fact about Grimes. He was the last pitcher legally allowed to throw the spitball in major league baseball. They banned it after the 1920 season, but they grandfathered in Grimes and about fifteen other guys."

"The guy actually spit on the ball?"

"Sometimes. They used other stuff as well. Like any type of foreign substance in their glove or on the bill of their cap, or even in their hair. They thought it gave the ball a weird type of breaking action, making it harder to hit."

"Did it?"

"Sometimes. Other times it did nothing. But Grimes was a real gamer. A guy who wanted to win at any cost."

"Baseball is supposed to be fun."

"At your level, yes. But when you look at it as your career. Something happens inside of you. You want to win and win often. That's not a bad thing, but when winning is the only thing you're focused on, things like sportsmanship and integrity take a backseat. That's never okay."

"Yeah. Dad says no one wants to play with a poor sport. We've got kids who slam their bats on the ground when they do badly or throw their gloves and yell at other guys. I don't like playing with them. I saw a kid trip another kid running around the bases before."

"That's what I'm talking about. Play the game with honor and within the rules. Some guys just can't control their emotions."

"Coach will usually sit guys like that down for a bit to cool off."

Chris walked up.

"You ready to go, champ?"

"See you tomorrow, Mr. Graham."

"See you tomorrow, Lincoln, and good luck in the game tonight."

Lincoln smiled. "Thanks."

On the way home, Lincoln filled his dad in on today's conversation. Chris made good on his promise, and they stopped off and picked up a Detroit deep-dish pizza for dinner.

CHAPTER 5

Lincoln had two pieces of pizza and a breadstick. He smiled and looked at his dad.

"That really hit the spot. Thanks."

Chris laughed.

"You're welcome, son. Only two pieces, though. I expected all the pizza would be gone by the end of dinner."

"Two pieces and a breadstick feel just about right to get me through the game without being too full. I'll take down the rest when I get home." He smiled.

"I have to say that's really responsible of you. I'm going to have one more, though. Sitting in the stands rooting for you really makes me hungry."

Lincoln laughed, and before he could respond, the phone rang.

"Can I answer it?" He asked his father.

"Go ahead. I think it's mom calling to wish you good luck at the game."

He jumped up and ran into the living room. He picked up the phone.

"Fisher residence. How may I help you?"

There was laughter on the other end, and then Jessica answered him.

"My baby boy. You sound so grown-up on the phone."

"Mom. I'm not a baby anymore."

"You're my baby." She paused before asking, "Are you ready for the game tonight?"

"I'm ready. Yesterday at practice I hit the longest home run you've ever seen."

"Oh, my goodness. Tell me all about it."

He retold the story of the mammoth blast. Chris watched from the kitchen table as Lincoln passionately described the event. When he finished, he was out of breath and collapsed onto the couch.

"Pretty cool, right, mom?"

"I wish I could have been there to see it. It sounds like it was amazing."

"It was. The only thing Mr. Graham could say was, Wow!"

"Your father told me about Pastor Graham. He's telling you a story while your dad works at the church?"

"Yeah. He played semi-professional baseball in the Texas League back in the early 1900s. He got to meet some great Tiger players. Mr. Graham even got to go up against a Hall of Fame baseball pitcher. He cracked a double off him."

"He did? That's pretty cool. So, you're enjoying spending time with him?"

"For sure. He even gave me a cool book. The history of Texas League baseball."

"Well, Pastor Graham sounds like a neat guy."

"He is, but he's not a pastor anymore. He quit."

"Retired."

"Yeah, retired. Is everything going okay with Grandma and Grandpa?"

"Everything is going well."

"Dad said you had to go because Grandpa got sick."

"He did, but he's feeling much better."

"That's good to hear. Tell them I love them. I gotta go get ready for the game, mom."

"Okay, sweetie. I love you and good luck tonight."

"Thanks, mom, I love you too."

He handed the phone to his dad and went into his bedroom to get ready for the game. Chris sat down in the chair to get comfortable. "Is everything okay with your dad?" he asked.

"He's feeling rough, but the surgery was a success and with some rehab, he should be good as new in a couple of weeks."

"That's great. When do you think you and the kids will come home?"

61

"I'm hoping for only two weeks. Mom really needs my help with getting him back and forth to rehab and motivating him to put in the work. Why, is something wrong?"

"No. I just really miss you…and the kids," he laughed.

She laughed. "I miss you too. I promise that as soon as I can, we'll come home."

"Sorry, I'm being selfish. Take as much time as you need to make sure your parents are okay. We'll be here with some incredible baseball stories when you get home."

"I know you two will. I'll call in a couple of days."

"Okay babe. I love you, and tell the kids I love them."

"We love you too."

He hung up the phone and sat there, thinking. He didn't see Lincoln standing in the doorway.

"You miss her, don't you, pop?"

"I do. But she's doing a good thing in helping your grandpa during a rough time."

"Yeah, she's good like that. I miss her too."

"She'll be home before you know it, buddy. Let's get to the field so you can play some ball. Do you have all your equipment?"

"Yes, sir."

"Then let's roll out."

On the way to the ballpark, Chris noticed Lincoln was reading the book that Arthur had given him.

"Is that book any good?" he asked.

"So far, it is. Right now, I'm reading about Hank Greenberg."

"That was one of the heavy hitters back in the day."

"Mr. Graham mentioned him before. He said that he was part of the story he was telling."

"Hank Greenberg is part of his story? Let me know when he gets to that part."

"Okay," Lincoln responded as he continued to read. "Whoa, he hit a lot of home runs."

"Back then, unless your name was Babe Ruth, that was an amazing feat. Hey, did you invite Mr. Graham to the game?"

"Yeah. He said that he couldn't come today, but maybe on Saturday."

"That was nice of you to ask. Hopefully, he can make it to one of your games. I think he would like it."

"Yeah. I hope it's a game where I smash a home run."

Chris laughed. "Me too, buddy."

2

Esther was in the kitchen preparing a big meal for the family tonight. The whole family was going to be there. Dillard was their only child, but he and his wife Claire had four children, who produced four more children of their own. Arthur walked into the kitchen and wrapped his arms around Esther, who was standing at the stove stirring the sauce.

"That's a lot of sauce. How many are coming to dinner?"

"There are fifteen of us altogether."

"Fifteen," he repeated in shock.

She laughed.

"You make me explain this to you every time. There is our son Dillard, and our daughter-in-law Claire. Our grandchildren, Jack and his wife Jenna, Robert and his wife Carrie, Alyssa and her husband Kenneth, and William. And our great grandchildren, Janice, Joshua, Brenda, and Adam."

"I know there's fifteen of us. I keep hoping to be sixteen. William has to meet somebody, eventually."

"He's 23, Arthur. He has two years of law school left. Let him focus on that right now."

"I had already been married for four years when I was 23."

She turned and looked at him.

"Different times. Besides, you were too afraid to let me get away."
He pulled her in and squeezed her tight.

"Ain't that the truth?" He kissed her on the forehead.

She smiled.

"Robert and Carrie are having number two in a few months. That'll push the number to 16."

"I know. I just want William to find someone so he can have what we have."

"In due time, he will. Now check your meatballs. They smell good, but you don't want to overcook them and dry them out."

"I've been cooking these meatballs for over fifty years. They've been called world famous, you know."

"By who? Janice?"

"Yes. By our very intelligent Janice."

"She's five."

"She's got award-winning taste buds, though."

They both laughed.

"Please check on them."

"I can tell by their very smell when they are ready." He looked into her eyes, and she wasn't buying it. "I think they're ready."

He pulled the meatballs out of the oven and tasted one. The smile on his face told her what she needed to know. He gave her a bite.

"Janice is right. They are world famous."

He smiled and grabbed a platter from the cabinet. He turned the oven off and stacked the meatballs on the platter and covered them with a paper towel. Arthur then placed them back in the oven to keep them warm.

"What time is everyone coming over?"

The front door opened, and Janice came running into the kitchen and wrapped her arms around Arthur's leg.

"Grandpa," she shouted.

He picked her up and gave her a big hug.

"There's my little jellybean, Janice."

She smiled and squeezed him.

"Grandma's here too," Esther stated as she stood behind Arthur. Arthur passed her back, and Janice gave her a big hug. The rest of the family came pouring through the door, and there were plenty of hugs and kisses. Claire and Alyssa helped Esther finish putting all the food on the table, and then everyone took their seats. When they purchased the house in 1940, one thing that Arthur really didn't like was that the dining room was enormous. He told Esther that they could never fill all this space. It was now his favorite room in the house. It was a place where everyone he loved could gather and eat and laugh. He loved watching the family grow over the years. Four years ago, Esther was at an estate sale when she saw the perfect dining room table. It was of old English descent, and it seated 18. Eight on each side, and one at each end. The price was more than right for the table and chairs, but they were in very rough shape. The wood showed signs of weathering, and some chairs required extensive repair. She called their grandson, Jack, to come look at it. He was an aspiring carpenter who loved challenging projects. He told her he could fix it and make it look new. She purchased the set, and he took it to his shop to work on it. Six months later, Arthur came home to the most beautiful dining room set he had ever seen. Jack had done an amazing job, and this table would provide his family with many memories for years to come.

Arthur sat at the head of the table on one side, and Dillard on the other. He looked around to see his family talking and laughing. His heart was content, and he silently thanked the Lord for the blessings He had given him. To his left, Esther took his hand into hers, and they flashed each other big smiles. He cleared his throat, and everyone paused their conversations to look at him.

"Let's thank the Lord for this wonderful meal." He looked at Dillard. "Son, will you do the honors?"

"William asked me if he could say the blessing at dinner tonight," he responded.

Arthur smiled and nodded at his grandson. "William."

The family joined hands as William stood. "Dear Lord. We thank you for your Son, Jesus, who died for us and redeemed us through His blood. Watch over us and continue to guide us as we strive to walk in your ways and honor you by showing others faith, love, mercy, grace, and forgiveness. Please bless this food and the hands that made it. In Jesus' precious name. Amen."

A collective "Amen" followed.

He sat down, and everyone filled their plates with spaghetti and meatballs, breadsticks, and salad. Arthur sat there, staring over at his grandson. A smile on his face. William looked up from his plate to pass the salad and noticed Arthur staring at him. He smiled back at his grandfather. Arthur mouthed the words, "Well done," to him. William mouthed, "Thank you." The passing of the food continued. Food and conversation flowed throughout the night. Later in the evening, Arthur's frustration resurfaced, and he voiced it to Esther.

"I have a house full of my blood, and I don't have one person who watches or likes to talk about baseball," he whispered to her.

"Arthur. Try not to let it bother you so much. You love the game, but they have different passions."

"I get different passions, but they have absolutely zero interest." He crossed his arms and sat back. "Zero."

"What's wrong, grandpa?" William asked.

"Why don't you like baseball, William? You're a red-blooded American male. It should be in your DNA. Baseball, hotdogs, apple pie, and Chevrolet."

William laughed. "That's a commercial, grandpa."

"I know it's a commercial, but it embodies all the things America loves. Baseball being first."

"I don't know. I just never really got into the game."

"I know. None of you did," he responded, shaking his head.

Esther reached over and placed her hand on his arm and smiled. "You still have such a passion for the game all these years later." He placed his hand over hers and looked at her. He sighed.

"I do. I'll never stop loving it because it brought me my greatest achievement in life." He gave her hand a squeeze. "You."

She smiled and kissed his cheek and then rested her forehead on his. As they gazed into one another's eyes, they realized that the room had become silent. They both turned to see everyone in the room staring at them and smiling.

"All right. Shows over," he stated as they separated and went back to eating.

The conversations resumed.

"That's why God sent you, Lincoln," Esther reminded him.

"Yeah, maybe. The kid has a genuine passion for the game and its history." He paused and smiled. "I enjoy talking to him."

"You said he has a game on Saturday. We could have some breakfast and go watch him play."

"I'd like that."

He looked down the table to see Janice staring at him. He winked at her and smiled.

"Maybe I'll play baseball when I grow up, grandpa," she stated as she took a bite of spaghetti.

"Yeah. Well, I'd love to come and watch you play." She gave him a smirk. He looked over at Esther and smiled. "There's hope yet."

CHAPTER 6

Thursday—July 10, 1980

Chris pulled into the parking lot and barely shifted into park before Lincoln was out the door and headed to the bench. "Have a great day, son," he yelled out as he laughed. Arthur was sitting on the bench feeding the birds as Lincoln approached. He stopped for a moment to listen because he could hear Arthur humming, and he tried to make out the song. He smiled, and before he got to the bench and sat down, he started singing. "Jesus loves me, this I know. For the Bible tells me so." Arthur stopped humming and looked back at him.

"You know the song?"

"Jesus loves me. My mom sang it to me as a kid."

Arthur laughed. "It's a classic."

"Did your mom sing it to you?"

"As a matter of fact, she did."

"I wonder how old that song is?"

"1859 or 60. Anna Warner wrote it."

Lincoln stopped what he was doing and looked over at Arthur.

"Is there anything you don't know?"

He thought for a moment. "I don't know."

They both laughed.

"It looks like another nice day," Lincoln stated.

"It does. Now, stop stalling and tell me about the game last night."

Lincoln laughed.

"We won 8-6, and I played great. I had three hits, including a triple, and made four plays at third base."

Arthur smiled. As an adult, you'd say that you had a couple of hits and made a few plays in the field, but young Lincoln knew the exact numbers, most likely because he replayed each of those moments in his head from the time the game ended until this very moment. He took the time to describe to Arthur each hit and play that he made.

The smile never left his face, and he always told his stories with great theatrics. When he finished, Arthur patted him on the back. "Nice job. It sounds like you really had your playing shoes on."

"I did. I had my playing shoes on."

"Do you think you can keep them on for Saturday's game? Esther and I are looking forward to it."

"I'll do my best," came the enthusiastic reply.

"That's all anyone can ever ask of you. Will you be coming back to the church on Saturday? I know your dad has to work at the church at some point."

"No, Eddie's mom is driving us to the game. I'm staying the night at his house on Friday night, so after the game I'm going back to his house to play until my dad gets off of work, so I won't be here Saturday. I hope that's okay?"

"That's fine. Will you be coming back next week to hear the rest of the story?"

"For sure. I'll be back on Monday. I enjoy hanging out with you, Mr. Graham, and talking baseball. Billy's my friend, but like my mom would say, you can only take him in small doses."

Arthur chuckled, "Good, because I enjoy talking baseball with you, too. Speaking of baseball, the Tigers play the Royals tonight. Kansas City has a pretty good third baseman."

"He's the best. I'm a Tigers fan all the way, but he's awesome."

"So, are the Tigers going to win tonight?"

"It won't be easy, but I think they will. What do you think?"

"I agree with you." He tossed the birds some food. "So, where did we leave off?"

"1914 was a big year for you. It started good and then you got injured. Mr. Dillard helped you find Jesus, and you got married. You finished the year as a backup."

"So, on to the 1915 season."

Arthur had claimed the starting job back, but ten games into the season, the team was really struggling out of the gate. They were 1-9 and in Waco to play the Navigators, who were their exact opposite at 9-1. Arthur was at the top of his game. He was batting over .400 and leading the team in RBIs. He was developing a solid reputation as one of the top defensive catchers in the league, and teams were hesitant to steal against the Panthers when he was behind the dish catching. The Navigators were playing great baseball at the moment and had sold out the last three home games. 9-1 was a great start to the season, and it was always fun to watch a winner, but most believe that ticket sales were way up because of their right field addition to start the season. Brooklyn Robins right fielder Casey Stengl was currently on a rehab assignment playing in Waco to start the season. He had injured his left knee to end the 2014 season, and the team wanted to make sure that it healed properly. They thought that starting him in the Texas League, which was considered a Class B league, would provide them with a proper assessment of his progress. Waco was reaping the financial benefits of this decision. The teams finished their warmups, and the umpire was ready to get going. Steve Turner was behind the plate for today's game. Steve had a reputation around the league for his generous strike zone, and as a catcher, Arthur was excited to see him, but as a hitter, not so much.

"Play ball," he yelled.

Arthur hit third in the lineup, and despite his single in the first inning, the Panthers were retired without scoring a run. Stengel was the first batter for Waco, and the crowd stood as he dug into the batter's box. Arthur looked up at him and smiled.

"What are you smiling at?" Stengel asked as he took a practice swing and stared out at the pitcher.

"What's the strike zone like in Brooklyn?" Arthur replied.

Stengel gave a sigh. "The strike zone is the strike zone."

"Okay," Arthur stated as he gave Clark the sign for the fastball, and he nodded.

Arthur was the tallest player on the team until Clark showed up. At 6'2" Arthur was one of the taller players in the league, but Benji Clark was a farm boy from Nebraska, and at 18 years of age, he was already 6'4" 240 pounds. His fastball topped the upper 90s, and his curveball was clearly major league material. He went into his windup and delivered. Stengel watched as the fastball popped into Arthur's mitt, four inches too low and six inches outside.

"Strike one," Turner yelled.

Stengel stepped out of the box and stared at Turner.

"That's not a strike," he stated.

"Strike one." Turner replied.

Stengel looked down at Arthur.

"Now I see," he replied as he stepped back into the box.

"Yep" is all Arthur could say.

He called for the fastball again, and Clark gave him the nod. Arthur set up outside again as Stengel adjusted his stance in the box. The pitch was identical to the first one, and Stengel swung. At the crack of the bat, the fans went nuts. The ball sailed down the right-field line foul. Stengel stepped out of the box and adjusted his grip on the bat. Turner reminded everyone that the count was 0-2. Stengel stepped back in. Arthur looked at Clark and gave him the curveball sign. Clark nodded. He went into the windup and delivered. Stengel was frozen in place as he watched the ball break down and right into the center of the plate.

"Strike three," Turner yelled.

Arthur stood up and smiled as he threw the ball down to third. Stengel looked over at him.

"How tall are you?"

"6'2."

"How tall is the pitcher?"

"6'4."

"Where are they growing you guys?"

"The Midwest."

Stengel laughed as he turned and walked back toward the dugout. Clark struck out the side in the first, and the Panthers headed in to hit. Arthur and Clark sat down next to each other at the end of the bench.

"What was Stengel saying to you?" Clark asked him.

"He asked me how tall I was, and then he asked me how tall you were."

"Why?"

"I don't know. Maybe players aren't that tall in the majors." He laughed. "Hey Benji, do you want to play in the majors someday?" He thought about the question for a moment before he answered.

"I don't know. I guess I'll go wherever God wants me to go."

"How are you going to figure that out?"

"Through prayer and Bible study. I believe He opens and closes doors as we walk through life."

"I'm a new Christian, so I'm trying to learn as much as I can. Can you explain that to me?"

Clark smiled and wrapped his arm around him and gave him a bear hug.

"Congratulations, brother."

"Thanks," Arthur squeezed out as he tried to catch his breath.

Clark released his grip and explained.

"From the time I was able to help my dad on the farm, I just took for granted that I would take over when he couldn't do it anymore. Then, my dad looked at me one day and asked me what I wanted to do with my life. The question shocked me."

Waco made quick work of the Panthers hitters in the top of the second. Walt Morris shouted at them from the other side of the dugout.

"Clark and Graham, can you take the field, please?"

They ran back out onto the field. After a Waco hit, Clark struck out the next batter and then got a double play ball to end the inning.

After two innings of play, the score remained 0-0. Athur and Clark jogged back to the dugout and sat down at the end of the bench.

"Way to recover, Benji," Arthur stated as he put his mitt and mask on the bench next to him.

"Thanks, Arthur," he responded as one of the infielders walked by and slapped him on the knee. Clark smiled and nodded at him.

"You said that your dad's question shocked you?"

He looked at Arthur. "It did. I told him I thought it was my duty to take over for him at the farm." Clark paused and laughed. "He threw his head back in laughter. When he was done, he looked at me and got serious. He said, 'Benjamin, that's what God put me here for, son. Have you asked him why he put you here?' I didn't know what to say. I was ten years old. The thought of God answering a question out loud scared the living daylights out of me."

Arthur laughed. "That would be intimidating."

"Plus, that's just what you do. You take over the family farm. I've grown up in church. I listen to other men talk to their sons, and it's not even up for debate. They will take over the family farm at some point. But my dad believes differently. He sat me down and told me that God has a purpose for every person He created. He discovered his purpose when he was 16. His father, my grandfather, was a farmer. He was dead set on his wanting nothing to do with farming. He was going to make his own mark on this world."

The crowd cheered, and they looked up to see Waco jogging off the field. They grabbed their gear and headed back out. Clark once again threw a scoreless inning, adding two more strikeouts to his total. The crowd would have to wait another half inning before they could see Stengel bat again. It was now the top of the fourth, and the score was 0-0. Arthur and Clark resumed their conversation right where they had left off.

"It turns out that my father's mark was farming. When my grandpa got sick and couldn't keep up with what needed to be done, my dad stepped in and did it for him. For four months, grandpa was bedridden. Dad ran that farm exactly like he did."

"So, your dad realized that maybe farming was his calling?"

"He did. He told me it forced him to see how important my grandpa was to everyone. To them for supporting the family, to others for supplying them with good food, and to the community for charging affordable prices. Plus, it brought him closer to God."

"How?"

"He had watched grandpa for many years get up at 5:00 a.m. He drank a cup of coffee, ate two scrambled eggs, and had some toast with jelly on it. When he finished, he opened his Bible and read a chapter or two and then prayed. When he said amen, he got up and started working."

"How did he know your grandpa did that every morning?"

"Dad fell asleep on the couch quite a bit, and the light in the dining room would usually wake him when grandpa came down. Every single time without fail, he witnessed grandpa do this. He asked my grandma about it once, and she told him that grandpa had been doing that same routine for 25 years."

"That's dedication."

"My grandpa loved the Lord very much, and he passed that on to my dad. So, my dad saw it work for grandpa all those years, so he tried it."

"How did that go?"

"Well," he laughed, "Dad was 16, and very few 16-year-olds like to get up at 5:00 a.m. if they don't have to. So…"

Clark stopped talking, and they looked up to see Morris standing in front of them.

"Arthur, think about taking off your catching gear and stepping into the on-deck circle to get ready to hit. Patty got a hit and is on first, and Anderson has a 1-2 count."

"Sorry, skip."

Arthur removed his equipment quickly and grabbed a bat. He walked into the on-deck circle just in time to hear the umpire yell, "Strike three!" Anderson walked by him with his head down on the way to the dugout. Arthur walked up and stood just outside the batter's box, surveying the situation. Patty was on first with one out. He stepped into the box and dug in. The pitcher went into the windup and threw a fastball high and outside. Arthur watched as it hit the catcher's mitt.

"Strike one," Turner yelled.

Arthur sighed and stepped out of the box. He had forgotten for a moment who the umpire was today. He stepped back in and waited for the next pitch. Patty had a good lead at first. The pitcher glanced over at him before going into his windup. Patty took off for second base. The pitch was a curveball that hit the corner low and to the outside. "Strike two," Turner shouted as the catcher sprang to his feet and threw the ball to second. Patty slid, and his toe just touched the base before the tag was applied. "Safe," was the call by the second base umpire. Patty dusted off his pants and nodded at Arthur. The pitcher got the ball back and mumbled under his breath as he took the mound. His agitation was clear. Arthur nodded back at Patty and stepped back into the box. He went into his windup and delivered a fastball in the dirt. The catcher blocked it with his chest protector, but the ball rolled toward the first base line, and Patty took off for third base. He recovered the ball and turned toward third to see Patty standing on the base, smiling. He called time and walked the ball out to the pitcher. They talked for a moment, and then he returned to his position behind the plate. Arthur was now looking at Patty on third with one out and a 1-2 count. The next pitch was high and inside, and he held his breath as he waited for Turner's call. "Ball two," he shouted.

Arthur breathed a sigh of relief. He stepped out and took a moment to compose himself. He stepped back in and waited for the next pitch. The pitcher went into his windup and delivered a curveball inside that had to be blocked by the catcher to keep the ball from going to the backstop. Arthur backed away from the plate in case Patty was coming home, but the catcher recovered the ball in enough time to keep him on third. The ball went back to the mound, and Arthur took a deep breath. He stepped back into the box and

75

readied himself. He felt that their strategy was to come back inside to go for the strikeout. Arthur looked out at the mound as the pitcher went into his windup. The pitch was a fastball, low and outside. Arthur kept his head down on the ball, adjusted his swing, and followed through. The ball sailed down the right-field line and headed to the corner. Arthur was already rounding first as he watched Stengel leap at the last second and make a snow cone catch near the base of the rightfield wall. In one motion, he hit the wall, spun around, and threw the ball to the cutoff man. Patty tagged and scored from third for the first run of the game, but a dejected Arthur slowly jogged back to the dugout. He sat down next to Clark and started putting all his catcher's gear back on. Clark slapped him on the back.

"That was a great hit, Arthur."

"Yeah, but an even better catch," he replied.

They both laughed.

"All I know is that you staked me to a 1-0 lead."

He smiled, "You're welcome."

"Plus, there's a reason he's a major league baseball player. I'd say after this series he'll go back to Brooklyn. That knee looks healed."

"Yeah, no hitch in his giddy-up on that catch."

They both laughed again.

Arthur put his last piece of equipment on, and it was time to go back out. As they exited the dugout, he looked at Clark.

"We'll pick up where we left off when we go back in."

Clark nodded and jogged toward the mound.

The bottom of the fourth saw Stengel lead off the inning. He took a couple of practice swings and then stepped into the batter's box. Stengel looked out at Clark and watched as he nodded to accept Arthur's sign. He gripped the bat and dug in as Clark went into the windup. It was a fastball that was high and inside. Stengel pulled his hands in and swung. He just managed to get a piece of the ball and fouled it behind the plate and into the crowd. They scrambled for the ball, and a lucky fan stood up and held the ball over his head as the crowd cheered. Arthur got another ball from the umpire and threw it out to Clark. He looked over at Stengel.

"A bit late on the fastball."

Stengel smiled at him. "I've got two strikes left." Before he stepped back into the box, he looked down at Arthur, who had dropped into his crouch behind the plate. "Aren't you the one who hit that easy fly ball to me last inning?"

"That would be me. Thanks for catching that. It gave us a 1-0 lead."

Turner chimed in. "If you ladies have finished catching up, can we get back to the game?"

Stengel stepped back into the box. Clark got the signal and went into his wind-up. Another fastball high and inside. Stengel timed this one perfectly, sending it down the leftfield line and into the corner. When the ball came back into the infield, he was standing on second base with a leadoff double. Three more hits and a walk later, the 4th inning ended with Waco holding a 2-1 lead. Arthur and Clark sat back down at the end of the bench.

"Tough inning, Benji. Shake it off. We'll get em back," Arthur encouraged him.

"They had some good at-bats. The hits don't make me half as mad as the walk does."

Arthur patted his knee.

"There's plenty of game left. We still have some hits to get out of our system."

"I'm counting on it," Clark replied as he smiled.

"You said that your dad hated getting up early."

"He did. But he got up at 5:00 a.m. every single day and mimicked the old man's routine. Before he knew it, he was reading the Bible just before bed too. He said that those stories came to life for him. Working the land and seeing God's incredible creation really gave him a deep appreciation for farming. The way he tells it, he fell in love with two things that year. God and farming,"

"So, when you say that you'll go where God wants you to go, you're waiting for him to show you like he showed your dad?"

"Something like that. I just think that you have to maintain a daily relationship with God and have the patience to wait on him to show you his plan."

"So, in those four months, your dad saw his future?"

He laughed. "In those four months, my dad could see that farming could be his future. Until that point, he had completely ruled it out, but my grandpa's illness forced him to see differently."

"So, when your grandpa started working the farm again, did your dad help more?"

"He did. He also continued his Bible studies in the morning and at night. Dad concluded that farming was God's calling for his life, and even though there are tough days and seasons, he hasn't regretted that decision one bit."

"So, your future could be in farming or baseball?"

"Or something completely different. My dad has shown me that the Lord has a plan for all of us. We just need to be fully open to it."

"How do you have that kind of patience?"

"Ask any farmer and he will tell you that one of the key ingredients to the success of any farm is patience."

Arthur sat back and thought about what he had said. Patience was just one of those traits that he didn't feel anyone had a grasp on. He was so deep in thought that he didn't realize the inning had ended and his team was taking the field to start the bottom of the fifth. Clark reached the top step of the dugout and looked back.

"You coming, Arthur?"

Arthur looked up and smiled. "Patience, Benji, patience."

They both laughed. The fifth went smoothly for Clark, and he set down the side in order. The rest of the day belonged to the pitchers. Three Waco pitchers combined to give up six hits and two runs. Clark pitched a complete game, giving up six hits and three runs. Arthur walked over and sat next to a dejected Clark.

"You pitched a great game, Benji. They just got a couple of timely hits."

"I know, but a loss still stings."

"I get it. Look on the bright side. Stengel only got one hit off you, and you struck him out twice. A major league ballplayer, and you got him twice."

Clark smiled. "I did, didn't I?"

"You did." Arthur smiled. "Hey. Would you like to come over for dinner sometime so we could talk more about the Bible?"

"I'd like that, Arthur."

"Good. I'll talk to Esther and get it set up."

The 1915 season saw the Panthers finish in third place at 81-72. Arthur finished the year with a solid .287 batting average, 27 home runs, and 87 runs batted in. He also finished the year in the top three in defense for his position. He wasn't approached by any scouts throughout the season, so when it ended, he went back to working at Dillard's. Everyone in America was on edge and monitoring the war in Europe. It had been over a year now, and it appeared as if no resolution was in sight. The fear was mounting that the United States would have to get involved, and that meant sending young men overseas to die.

3

"You had such a great year, Mr. Graham. How come no scouts asked you to try out?" Lincoln asked as he stared at him.

"I don't know, kiddo. I guess that's just how it goes. Some guys get breaks, and some guys don't. I guess I just figured that it wasn't my time yet."

"Did your friend Benji ever get looked at?"

"When Stengel got back to Brooklyn, he told them about Benji. He said he felt the kid had the right stuff to make it on a major league roster. So, a scout came down a week later and watched him pitch a game. He struck out ten and pitched eight scoreless innings. We won the game 4-0. A week later, Benji was pitching for their AA affiliate in the international league. The Rochester Hustlers."

"Did he make it to the big leagues?"

"He sure did. They brought him up toward the end of the year. Can you guess who he pitched against?"

"The Detroit Tigers," Lincoln yelled with enthusiasm.

Arthur laughed.

"You guessed it, kiddo. He pitched three innings in relief and gave up only one run. His greatest moment of the day came in his second inning of relief. On a 3-2 count with the bases loaded, and the score tied at three, he reached back and threw a fastball right by one of the greatest players to ever play the game."

Lincoln was sitting on the edge of his seat, and his eyes were as wide as saucers as he asked with a raised voice, "Who was it, Mr. Graham?"

Arthur smiled as he maintained a long pause for dramatic effect. He leaned in and whispered, "Ty Cobb."

"That is awesome." Lincoln stated in disbelief as he leaned back in his seat.

"That is awesome," Arthur responded. "Benji told me he was so shocked that he stood in place frozen until one infielder running in slapped him on the shoulder and congratulated him."

"Ty Cobb. Wow."

"That's exactly what I said. Ty Cobb. Wow."

"Did you and Benji remain friends? I know he was supposed to come over for dinner."

"We did. As a matter of fact, I usually talk to him once or twice a month. He's living up north in a city called Manistee."

"So, what happened to his major league career? Did he win a World Series or go to the Hall of Fame?"

Arthur smiled and looked at him.

"No, but he played two more years in the majors. He went up against some of the greatest players to play in any generation, and he did well against them. He got to pitch in the World Series against the Red Sox in 1916."

"Did he win?"

"They lost the series four games to one. In the second game in Boston, the game went 14 innings before the Sox won 2-1. Benji pitched the eighth through the eleventh. Four scoreless innings, striking out five batters. Benji had great stuff."

"He got to pitch in a World Series. That's what dreams are made of." Lincoln's voice trailed and he stared off into the distance.

Of all the things to love about youth, this is what Arthur loved most. The appreciation of a dream come true. The look on Lincoln's face was priceless at that moment.

"It sure is, Lincoln. Benji looks back on those years with fondness and is grateful that God included those years on his journey."

"So what happened? Why didn't he keep pitching?"

"After two seasons of playing major league baseball, he said that his heart just wasn't in it anymore."

"How can your heart not be into baseball? It's like the greatest game ever."

Arthur laughed.

"He told me he felt closest to God when he worked on the farm. He enjoyed playing baseball, but he loved farming. A couple of years away showed him that."

"Is he still farming today?"

"No, he's 84 now. His grandson has taken over. These days he does a lot of reading and fishing."

"It's pretty cool he got to play in a World Series."

Arthur smiled. "It is." Arthur scratched his chin and thought for a moment. He looked over at Lincoln. "I've been a little selfish with your time, Lincoln."

"How do you mean, Mr. Graham?"

"I'm pretty sure that I could have told you this story in a few days instead of dragging it out until the end of next week. You'd probably rather go to your friend's house next week and play."

"Billy's my best friend, but he doesn't know squat about baseball. I like hearing about the good old days of baseball. You're a great storyteller, and besides, so far it seems like you've led an interesting life with some interesting people in it."

Arthur turned and wiped a tear from his eye. He cleared his throat and turned back around.

"Thank you, Lincoln. They truly were the good old days of baseball, and I really think you're going to like how this story ends."

"It sure looks to be heading that way, Mr. Graham," Lincoln smiled. "Plus, me and my dad talk about it on the way home, and I think he's really interested in seeing what happens."

"Two audiences. That's a lot of pressure."

They both laughed, and each grabbed a handful of breadcrumbs. They tossed them on the ground and watched as the birds devoured them.

"My dad and I want to go to the Hall of Fame one day," Lincoln stated out of the blue.

"That'll be a nice trip," Arthur added.

"Have you been?" he asked.

"No. I know plenty of people who have, and they all seem to like it."

"Cool."

"Do you know who was the very first player inducted into the baseball Hall of Fame?"

Lincoln thought long and hard before answering, "Babe Ruth."

"That was a great guess. Ruth and Honus Wagner tied for second, but our man Ty Cobb won first place.

He smiled. "A Detroit Tiger is number one all-time."

"Yep. No one played the game like Cobb. He could do it all. Over 4100 career hits. I don't think anyone will break that record."

They spent the rest of their time talking about his game on Saturday, the Tigers game tonight, and who made the best pizza in Detroit.

CHAPTER 7
Friday—July 11, 1980

Lincoln and Chris sat at the kitchen table eating a bowl of Kellogg's Frosted Flakes cereal before they left for the church. Chris watched as his son shoveled it in without coming up for air.

"This isn't a contest, son," he joked.

Lincoln looked up at him.

"I'm trying to finish them before they get soggy. It's gross when they get soggy because there's no crunch, and it feels like you have a mouth full of mush."

Chris laughed.

"I guess I can understand that." He took a sip of coffee. "I've been thinking about what you told me on the car ride home yesterday, and I still think that it's so cool that Ty Cobb was the first player ever inducted into the Baseball Hall of Fame."

"Yeah. It's awesome."

"Arthur is like a walking baseball encyclopedia."

"He knows a lot."

"His son, Dillard, seems like a sharp guy. He doesn't know a ton about baseball, which is surprising, but he's knowledgeable about construction and building."

"Mr. Graham says none of his family is really into baseball. That's why he enjoys talking to me."

"I guess that answers my question."

"He knows a lot about God, too."

Chris laughed. "I should hope so."

"He was impressed with you and mom teaching me about Jesus and faith and all."

"Well, it's important that you know Jesus, not just know about Him."

Lincoln looked over at him. "That's what Mr. Graham said."

"I wish you listened to your teachers this much. You would be a straight-A student."

Lincoln smiled. "Maybe if they related things to baseball, I would." They both laughed. Chris looked at his watch.

"We have to get going. Don't want to be late." He looked over at Lincoln. "You finished?"

He wiped his mouth with his sleeve, grabbed his bowl, and stood up. "All done."

They both walked their bowls over to the sink, rinsed them, and then placed them on the sink.

Arthur was standing in front of the bench when Lincoln walked up. He was spreading the breadcrumbs from side to side.

"Good morning, Mr. Graham."

Arthur turned to face him.

"Good morning. You seem chipper."

"I got a good night's sleep."

"That's important. Did you watch the game last night?"

"I sure did. I got home from practice at the start of the second inning."

"Not a fun game to watch."

"They didn't have the bats going last night. You can't win them all."

"Ain't that the truth? Brett had another great game, going 3 for 5 with 2 RBIs. Kansas City looks tough."

"Yeah. Parrish was 0 for 4. He had an off game, but we'll bounce back tonight against the Sox."

"At a boy, Lincoln. I like your confidence."

"Mr. Graham, me and my dad were talking on the way home from practice last night, and he told me that the guy you were talking about, Stengel, was a big deal. He said that he had won a bunch of World Series."

"He did. Nine, to be exact. Two as a player, and seven as a manager with the Yankees."

"Nine! Whoa!"

"That's what happens when you have players like Mantle, Ford, and Yogi Berra. No other manager has managed five World Series wins in a row."

"And you played against him." Lincoln's smile covered his face.

"Don't be so amazed yet. This story has a lot of plot twists you're going to like."

"I can't wait to tell all the guys at school this year, and my science teacher, Mr. Brush. He's a huge baseball fan. He's from New York and always talks about the Yankees."

"They had some glorious years. I guess if you had to name an organization with the most iconic names, New York would be right up front."

Arthur took a seat on the bench, and Lincoln sat down next to him. He grabbed a handful of breadcrumbs and tossed them onto the ground.

"What was your favorite subject in school, Mr. Graham?"

"I always liked English. We got to read a lot of books. I enjoy reading. You?"

"I like to read, but I kind of like history the best. It's neat hearing about past events."

"What's your favorite?"

"I guess I like to read about all the different inventions created over the years, and I like the Old West."

"Cowboys and Indians are cool."

"Yeah." He smiled. "Did you like history?"

"I did. Until I was a part of it." His voice trailed off as he spoke.

"Yeah, but you're the best kind of history. Baseball." That smile returned.

Arthur left the topic alone. The boy was only twelve and didn't need to hear about the carnage of war. He changed the subject.

"On to the year 1916."

Fort Worth, TX—September 1916

Esther sat in the stands and watched as Arthur and the Panthers were wrapping up the 1916 season. Arthur was hoping for a breakout season to impress the scouts, but he had a very up and down year. His defense remained solid, but his batting stats for the year dropped in every category. It was the last day of the season, and the Panthers currently sat in fifth place with a 71-74 record. The Beaumont Oilers were their opponent today, and with a record of 77-68, they weren't much better. Esther had called Jack Dillard earlier in the day to ask if he could come out and watch the game. Arthur had seemed stressed lately, and it had been a while since they had done their weekly Bible studies. Three months, to be exact. Either he had a game, practice, or invented some excuse to miss. This wasn't like Arthur. She felt that his focus wasn't on God anymore, but on baseball and baseball alone. Esther continued to read and study without him and even made sure she attended church every Sunday. Her faith and knowledge grew, and she feared Arthur had seen God as an afterthought. She watched as Arthur took some practice swings in the batter's box. In the top of the first, the Oilers scored three times to take a 3-0 lead, so the Panthers were already facing a hill to climb. Arthur looked up into the stands and gave her a smile before he walked to the plate. She smiled back and waved. It didn't take long for him to swing and miss at three straight pitches, and as he walked back toward the bench, he slammed his bat on the ground. He yelled and screamed as he disappeared into the dugout. This was not like Arthur. She tried to smile as a few of the wives looked her way, but all she could do was smirk.

"Good pitch sequence," a strange voice next to her stated.

She turned to her left to see a distinguished-looking older gentleman sitting next to her.

"I'm sorry, sir. Did you say something?" she asked.

He looked at her.

"No, I'm sorry. I was thinking out loud again."

She laughed. "Do you often think out loud?"

"I do. It's a pleasure to make your acquaintance. My name is Denton. Denton Young."

"It's nice to meet you, Mr. Young. I'm Esther Graham, but please just call me Esther."

"And I would prefer you call me Denton." He smiled and nodded at her. She smiled and nodded back. "Are you a fan, Esther, or do you know someone in the game?"

"My husband is the catcher for the Panthers."

"The gentleman who just struck out?"

"Yes."

"You probably thought that I was talking about him a few minutes ago when I was thinking out loud. I'm so sorry. A friend of mine asked me to come watch the game today and evaluate the pitcher for the Oilers. They think he might be the right fit for their organization."

"Are you a scout?"

"Heavens no. He just wanted my expert opinion on this one guy."

"Oh."

"You sound disappointed. Did I say something wrong?"

"No, Mr. Young, I mean, Denton. My husband, Arthur, has been trying to get to the big leagues for a couple of years now, and for a moment, I just thought that maybe God sent you to make that happen."

"I'm sorry, Esther. I really know very little about hitting. I just know about pitching. How long has Arthur been playing in the Texas League?"

"This is his fifth year now. He just turned 21 in June."

"Well, he's a young man. If he keeps working hard, then I'm sure he'll get his shot."

"I hope so."

He observed the look of worry on her face.

"When I talk to my friend, I'll have them look at Arthur next season. They can always use a good catcher. Is he any good?"

"He's very good. One of his teammates told me just the other day that he was one of the top three catchers in the league. He said that 'Nobody can steal on him.'"

"That sounds like a very good defensive catcher. How does he hit?"

"Last year he hit .287 with 27 home runs."

"Wow." He scratched his chin and thought for a moment. "What about this year?"

"His numbers are down," she laughed nervously. "But he still has 18 home runs."

"I promise I'll mention him to my friend."

"Thank you." She smiled and then asked out of curiosity, "So, what are your thoughts on the pitcher?"

"He's got some decent stuff, but I think he needs a little more time before he makes the jump to the next level."

"I don't mean to be annoying, but may I ask how you came to that conclusion?"

"You're not annoying at all. I like when someone takes an inside interest in the game."

He turned toward her fully and explained to her the reason for his assessment. As Arthur stood behind the plate waiting for the inning to start, he couldn't help but notice that his beautiful young wife was talking in great detail to a handsome gentleman. He was so focused on them he failed to hear the umpire several times. Arthur felt a tap on his shoulder. He turned to see the umpire staring at him.

"Today. Please."

"Sorry," he stated, embarrassed.

The Panthers didn't fare any better in the top of the second either. Four runs and a pitching change later, they found themselves down 7-0. It was a long half inning, and when they finally came into bat, Arthur looked in the stands to see Esther talking with Jack Dillard, not the stranger from before. The Panthers spent less than ten minutes sitting down before they were out of the dugout and back on the field. The last game of the year started out rough and got no better. Beaumont won the game 13-3. The only bright spot for Arthur is that he ended the day two for four with a home run and two runs batted in. After the final out, Arthur walked onto the field and stood near the third baseline. He was taking in the field one last time for the year. He closed his eyes to envision better days.

"Excuse me, Mr. Graham." He heard a voice that made him open his eyes. He turned and looked to his right. Standing in front of him was the gentleman that Esther had been talking to in the stands earlier.

"Please call me Arthur. What can I do for you, Mr.?"

"Young. You can call me Denton, though."

The man smiled.

"What can I do for you, Denton?"

"I just wanted to say that you played an excellent game."

"Thank you," he smiled. "We were a little flat today, though."

"It wasn't the team's best effort, but you looked comfortable in the batter's box."

"Thank you again, Denton."

"Can I ask you a question?"

"Sure."

"You faced the starting pitcher three times today. You struck out on three pitches, singled, and then hit a towering two-run homer. What is your impression of him?"

"You mean what did I think of him as a pitcher?"

"Yes. I would like your expert analysis, please."

Arthur sighed and paused for a moment.

"When I faced him for the first time, I was way too eager. They had just gone up 3-0, and I tried to hit the ball as hard as I could. To tell you the truth, two of those three pitches were balls. The second time, we were down 8-0. I took my time. On a 2-2 count, he threw me a low-90s fastball that I took the other way for a hit."

"How was his fastball?"

"Honestly. Not very impressive. In the three at-bats, I saw it six times. All probably in the low to mid 90s with little movement."

"What pitch did you hit for the home run?"

"A curveball. He telegraphed the pitch, so I knew what was coming."

"What did he do to telegraph it?"

"He sets up differently on the mound when he throws the curveball. With his other pitches, he pitches from the middle of the rubber. When he throws the curve, he takes a half step to the third base side."

"When did you figure that out?"

"Right around the third inning. I like to watch the pitchers from opposing teams to see if I can pick up on anything that can give our team an advantage."

"You think like a manager and observe like a scout."

He laughed. "I don't know about all of that. I just love studying the game. Are you a scout?"

"No. I love the game too. I was just doing a favor for a friend today." He smiled. "If you don't make it to the big leagues as a player, you'd be a heck of a scout."

"Well, I hope to do it as a player first. But if that doesn't work out, then maybe I'll explore other options."

"It's something to think about." He extended his hand to Arthur, and they shook. "The best of luck to you, Arthur. I hope to be rooting for you someday."

"Thank you, Denton. I hope you are too."

They shared a laugh, and then Young exited the field and walked toward the parking lot. Arthur stood there for a couple of more minutes and then walked back to the dugout.

He gathered his gear and met Esther and Dillard by the bleachers. She gave him a hug, and he kissed her on the cheek. He shook Dillard's hand, and the two of them sat down. Esther excused herself to go talk to a few of the other players' wives who were waiting for their husbands.

"Tough day out there for the team, but you were swinging the bat well," Dillard opened the conversation.

"Yeah, but I felt off today. Really, the last month or so. I don't know what it is."

"Do you have anything weighing on your mind? Any recent problems at home or on the field?"

"Home is great. I haven't performed this season like I wanted to, but I don't feel like that's it."

"How is your walk with God going? You haven't really been to church or our Bible study in a few months."

This annoyed Arthur. "My walk with Him is fine."

"When you accepted Him as your Lord, you made a commitment to build a relationship with Him and serve Him."

"I know what I did, Mr. Dillard."

"Maybe you feel off because that relationship has taken a backseat to everything else, and He isn't a priority anymore."

"Mr. Dillard, I really don't feel like talking about this right now. I just want to go home and rest. I'm tired, sore, and mentally exhausted."

Dillard smiled. "Okay Arthur. Call me when you feel like talking. If you don't, then I'll see you at the store in a week."

"Thanks."

"Tell Esther I said goodbye."

He gave Arthur a smile and a slap on the shoulder and then left. Esther was watching from a distance, and when she saw him leave, she excused herself from the other wives and walked back over to him.

"Did Jack leave already?"

"Did you ask him to come and talk to me?"

She looked at the ground. "Yes."

"Why did you do that, Esther? The last thing I wanted on the last day of a crummy season was to get lectured on my…"

"Lectured! That man has been like a second father to you and has always been there for you. What did you say to make him leave?" She was angry.

"I told him I didn't feel like talking about anything right now. I'm tired, sore, and I just need some space to think."

"Some space? To think? About what, Arthur?"

"I don't know. Everything. I just want to rest. Can we go home so I can rest? Please."

"Fine."

She stormed away. Patty was walking by and started laughing.

"Somebody is sleeping on the couch tonight." Arthur just sighed and picked up his equipment and followed her.

3

Lincoln took a bite of his apple. "She sounded really mad."

Arthur laughed. "She was."

"Why were you angry with Mr. Dillard?"

"Because I had lost focus on what was important, and he held me accountable for it."

Lincoln had a puzzled look on his face. "Accountable?"

"He knew I was feeling a bit off because I allowed baseball and other outside factors to take me away from my daily relationship with God. I was mad at him for pointing it out to me, and mad at Esther for calling him because I knew he would point it out to me."

"Isn't that what friends do? When they see something hurting you, they try to help."

"We lose sight of the help when we let pride get in the way. Suppose you were struggling at the plate. You were in a slump and didn't get a hit in your last 50 at-bats. One of your friends was suddenly trying to tell you how to stand or hold the bat. How would you feel?"

Lincoln thought about it for a moment.

"I'd probably be mad at him because he was trying to tell me what to do."

"That's pride. When you're too proud to let someone help you. Jack saw that in me that day. He didn't give up because he loved me and wanted to see me happy. He knew the only way that was going to happen was to reestablish my relationship with God."

"I'm assuming you did."

"I did, but it took me a lot longer than it should have."

"How much longer?"

Arthur sighed and looked off into the distance.

"About three years."

Lincoln stopped eating the apple and looked at him.

"That's a long time."

Arthur continued to stare off into the distance, and his speech was low.

"Pride took hold of me and held on for a long time."

Lincoln put his hand on Arthur's shoulder.

"It's okay, Mr. Graham. It eventually let go."

Arthur smiled and patted the young man's hand.

"It never fully lets go, son. It lies dormant in your body and rears its ugly head occasionally. The only way to manage it is to maintain that close relationship with our Lord." He scratched his chin. "Let's see, where were we? Ah yes. The 1916 season was rough but not disastrous. I went to work for Mr. Dillard a week later."

"Did that guy ever tell his friend about you?"

"What guy?"

"The one that Esther was talking to. You know, the one who asked you about the pitcher after the game?"

"Oh yes, that fella. Denton Young."

"Yeah, Denton."

"He might have, but no one ever contacted me. A fun fact about Denton Young. His nickname was Cy."

"Cy Young?"

"The one and only. I knew he looked familiar when we were talking, but I was so mad that I didn't realize it until later."

"You met a lot of famous people playing in Texas, Mr. Graham."

Arthur laughed, "I sure did. What do you know about Cy Young?"

"I know he has more wins than any other pitcher in baseball history.

He's in the Hall of Fame. What else is there to know?"

"Very good, young Lincoln. He is the only pitcher with over 500 wins. 511, to be exact. He also has the most losses of any pitcher in Major League Baseball with 315. He pitched for 23 seasons and won the World Series once."

"Whoa! One time. That almost doesn't seem fair."

"It's a team sport, kiddo. You can be the very best at what you do in a team sport, but if the rest of the team doesn't perform, you don't win."

"I guess so. He still won a championship. That's cool."

"Yep. He also retired with a lot of records, and he showed future generations that perseverance pays off."

"Did you get any of these guys' autographs?"

Arthur laughed.

"No, but I got my picture taken with quite a few of them."

"That's a scrapbook I'd like to see."

"I'll make sure you see it."

"Awesome."

"One more fact about Cy Young that may surprise you. He was elected to the Baseball Hall of Fame on the second ballot."

"Not even on the first try?"

"Nope. Crazy, right?"

"I'll say."

Arthur looked up to see Chris walking their way. He looked at his watch.

"It looks like our time is up today."

"I'll see you tomorrow at the game. Right?"

"Yes indeed. We're looking forward to it."

"Great. Well, see you in the morning, Mr. Graham."

Arthur tipped his cap. "See you in the morning."

CHAPTER 8
Saturday—July 12, 1980

Lincoln and Chris made their way to the field from the parking lot. Lincoln looked up to see Arthur sitting in the stands, and what he assumed was Esther sitting next to him. He broke away from his father and ran toward them. Arthur saw him and waved. He ran up to where they sat and stopped right in front of them.

"Mr. Graham, you came," he stated with a big smile on his face.

"I told you I would. You didn't believe me?"

"I did, but I also know that people say a lot of things they don't mean, just to shut kids up," he stated with a big smile on his face.

"If I say it, I mean it."

"He does have a big smile," Esther stated as she stared at Lincoln.

"You must be Esther," Lincoln stated as he held out his hand. "It's nice to meet you."

She smiled as she shook his hand and returned the sentiment. "It's nice to finally meet you, Lincoln. Arthur talks about you nonstop. He's very impressed with how much you know about baseball."

His smile grew even wider.

"Mr. Graham has taught me a lot. It's so cool that he's met so many great players." He looked over at Arthur. "Mr. Graham, did you know that Cy Young pitched 749 complete games in his career?"

"Really. I did not know that. Thanks, Lincoln, you've taught me something today. How did you know that?"

"Dad got me a book from the library about Hall of Fame pitchers." He shifted his focus to Esther. "Did you know who you were talking to that day?"

"I didn't. I just knew he was a nice man named Denton."

"Well, I've gotta go warm up. I'll see you after the game."

Before either of them could say anything, he was already gone and with his teammates on the bench. Esther looked over at him.

"You knew that about Cy Young."

"I did, but he was so excited to tell me about it."

She reached over and held his hand.

"You old softy."

"Sometimes," he stated as he patted her hand.

Chris walked over and sat down on the other side of Arthur.

"Good morning, Mr. Graham. I'm glad you could make it."

"We're excited to see him play." He leaned back slightly and introduced his wife. "This is my wife, Esther."

Chris leaned forward and smiled at her.

"It's very nice to meet you, Mrs. Graham."

"It's nice to meet you, Chris, and call me Esther, please."

"Okay, Esther. Lincoln has really enjoyed hanging out with your husband this week."

"Arthur has enjoyed his company as well. Are you a baseball junkie?"

"Not as much as Lincoln, but I still like the game, and I love watching him play. I know he would love nothing better than to play great today because the two of you are here."

"I'm sure he'll do great." She smiled. "So, your wife is still away?"

"Yeah. She's still at her parent's house helping. Hopefully, just one more week, but I know she'll stay until she feels comfortable that they are both able to do well without her."

"She sounds like a wonderful daughter."

"She's a very caring person. I don't know where our family would be without her. I know I'd be completely lost."

"She's the glue that keeps your family together," Arthur inserted himself into the conversation. He continued, gently squeezing Esther's hand, "We couldn't manage without these amazing women in our lives. God is good."

Chris smiled as he looked at the two of them.

"So true," he agreed. "God is good."

"What position is Lincoln playing today?" Esther asked.

"Third base," Chris answered. "He asked to play catcher, but the coach told him, 'Maybe next week.'" He looked at Arthur and smiled.

Arthur smiled but didn't say a word. He just watched as Lincoln took some ground balls and threw them over to first base.

The game started, and Lincoln was batting third in the top of the first. Arthur watched as Lincoln took some warmup swings in the on-deck circle. The leadoff hitter walked, and the second batter was in the box with a 2-2 count. The pitcher delivered a swinging strike, and the number two hitter walked back toward the team's bench with his head down. As Lincoln made his way to the plate, he patted the hitter on the helmet and said something to him that made him smile. The hitter returned to the bench and received some high-fives from his teammates. Lincoln dug into the batter's box, took one practice swing, and then did a windmill with the bat before getting set and staring out at the pitcher. The first pitch was low and away, ball one. Lincoln repeated the process. The second pitch was high and outside, ball two. Lincoln again repeated his process. Arthur smiled. At age twelve, Lincoln already had a routine. In their conversations, they had discussed good hitter counts, and a 2-0 count with a man on first was one of them. He watched as Lincoln dug in deep and repeated his process. The next pitch came in across the heart of the plate, and Lincoln didn't miss it. The barrel of the bat came through and made solid contact with the ball. It rocketed off his bat and shot down the third-base line. The crowd cheered, and he was off to the races. The run from first came all the way around to score, and he was standing on second base with an RBI double. He looked over at his dad and then at Arthur and pumped his fist.

"That's a boy, son," Chris shouted out to him at second.

Arthur looked over at Esther and smiled. "The kids got game."

She smiled and gave his knee a pat. One of the true joys in life was seeing the ones you love genuinely happy, and she could tell that he was. Arthur was a devout man of God, a devout family man, and a great lover of the game of baseball. From the moment she met him, it was apparent that baseball would forever remain a big part of who he was. Sitting here next to him at this moment, she could see the sparkle in his eye as a twelve-year-old boy blasted a line drive double down the line.

"He reminds me of a young George Brett," she answered.

Arthur turned toward her and smiled. "You might be right."

Chris was eavesdropping on their conversation and couldn't help but produce a smile of his own. It was clear. They were meant for each other.

The games at this level only went for seven innings, but it was a very enjoyable seven innings worth of baseball. In the end, Lincon's team won 6-2. He batted three times and went 2 for 3 with two doubles and two runs batted in. He made some great plays in the field with no errors. At the end of the game, the teams lined up and gave each other high fives. The coach had a brief meeting with them and then turned them loose to go home. Lincoln walked up to them with a big smile on his face. Chris gave him a hug.

"Great game, buddy."

"Thanks, dad." He looked up at Arthur. "Those game shoes were on today."

Arthur and Esther laughed.

"I'll say they were," Arthur replied.

"You played a great game, Lincoln," Esther stated.

"Thanks," he smiled.

His friend Eddie yelled at him from the parking lot. "Come on, Link."

"Well, I'd better get going. Thanks a lot for coming to the game today."

"It was our pleasure, Lincoln," Arthur replied as Esther nodded in approval.

"I'll see you on Monday." He turned and gave his dad a hug. He ran toward the parking lot to leave with Eddie's family.

Chris yelled in his direction. "Make sure you listen to his parents, and not too much junk food, please."

Lincoln just threw a hand in the air and waved without even turning around. They all laughed. Chris turned to Arthur and extended his hand. Arthur took it and they shook.

"Thank you both for coming to the game today. It meant a lot to Lincoln."

"We were happy too," Esther responded for both of them. Arthur smiled and nodded.

"Well, I guess I better get over to the church and get to work."

"I'll see you over there after lunch," Arthur stated.

"Will Esther be joining you today?" He asked.

"Heavens no. Feeding those birds is Arthur's scene. I'm going to do a little shopping," Esther responded.

"I'm not feeling too good, Esther. Maybe we should stay home," Arthur stated as he winked at Chris.

Chris laughed.

"You can't take it with you, Mr. Frugal. Go feed your birds, and I'll try to keep it under a million," she shot back.

Arthur just smiled and shook his head. That moment made Chris aware of just how much he missed Jessica and the kids. They said their goodbyes and left the field.

2

It was now 2:30 p.m. and Arthur had just thrown the last of the breadcrumbs on the ground. He smiled as he watched the birds share the bounty. It seemed like a good time to leave today. Just as he was about to get up from the bench, Chris came around the side and sat down next to him.

"The birds are lucky to have a good friend like you. You keep them fed and happy," Chris stated.

"They remind me a lot of a congregation," Arthur responded. "You feed them the bread of life, and they will keep returning to get more."

Chris smiled. "Thanks again for coming to Lincoln's game this morning. It was nice to meet Esther as well."

"We were so happy to do so. You and your wife are raising an exceptional young man. In just the short week that we have spent together, I have learned so much about him, and I've done most of the talking."

"That's a miracle in itself," he laughed. "Thank you for saying so. When Jessica took his brother and sister to go help her parents, I thought he would be extremely bored and, in that boredom, he would be, well, for lack of a better word, a pest. He has really enjoyed his time with you."

"The feeling is mutual. How are you doing without Jessica at home?"

"I miss the living daylights out of her, but this project has kept me busy."

"It's true what they say. 'Absence makes the heart grow fonder.' How is her dad doing?"

"According to her, he's responding well. She thinks she'll be able to come home in a week, maybe a week and a half, tops."

"That's good to hear." He turned to look over his shoulder at the construction. "How long are you staying to work on it today?"

"I think my part is done. Those guys are just finishing up a few things and should be done by 4:00 p.m." He paused before continuing. "Your son Dillard told me you were in the Army during WWI."

"I was."

"Lincoln has been keeping me up to date on your story, and I know you're about to enter the 1917 season. When did you go into the Army?"

Arthur turned to face him.

100

"I would not tell him about my military service or the war, if that's what you're afraid of? I was going to tell him I played some of the season and then got called off to serve, and then pick up with the 1919 season."

"Oh no, Arthur, I'm sorry. I didn't mean to offend you by insinuating that you were going to. I just figured you might want to share that part of the story with me. Dillard made it seem like it was pivotal in your decision to enter the ministry. I knew you wouldn't expose the boy to the stories of war."

"Do you really want to hear an old man tell that story, or are you just being nice?"

"I really want to hear the story. So far, it's been fascinating and interesting. Baseball seemed your inevitable path, but something in that war changed that path. I really want to hear it."

The kindness in his eyes convinced Arthur.

"There are only four people who have ever heard it. My parents, who have gone on to be with the Lord, Esther, and Dillard."

"I don't mean to pry…"

"You're not. No one else has ever asked. After my experience in the war, I questioned God's path for my life. I was sure that baseball was my destiny, but it changed the way I looked at things. When I finally gave it all to Him, He gave me a reward that was so unimaginable and so amazing that it humbled me to my very core."

"Will I hear that part of the story today?"

Arthur smiled.

"No, I'm afraid not. But you will hear it from Lincoln, eventually."

"You know my wife Jessica got her degree in English. She wants to be a novelist someday. I think she would be interested in telling your story."

Arthur laughed. "There are many more interesting things in the world to read about."

"I'm not sure there are."

"Well, maybe a discussion for another day," he laughed some more.

"Maybe," Chris agreed.

"Okay, let's get started. From April 1917 to July 1917, I was red hot. I was batting over .350 and hitting with power. I had 19 home runs. Word on the street was that a few teams were scouting me for a promotion."

"With those numbers, I'm not surprised."

"Then, Uncle Sam pulled my name. I was off to war."

"You were drafted."

"I was. They were drafting males from the ages of 21 to 30 to start."

"Esther must have been terrified."

"She was scared, as was I. But when your country calls, you answer that call. The silver lining for Esther and me was that I was sent to Camp Bowie, which is just outside of Fort Worth, to train. We spoke on the phone and wrote to each other often, praying that the war would end before I would have to see active involvement overseas. During my training, I became good friends with a young man from Oklahoma. I say young, but we were the same age at 22. We were a part of the 36th Infantry Division. He was in his last year of seminary."

"I thought ministers were exempt from the draft?"

"Ministers, yes. Students, no. His name was Tom Colson. He looked like a linebacker, but he was soft-spoken and always made you feel that he genuinely cared about what was going on in your life."

Arthur smiled. "That's because he did."

"He sounds like someone I would want to be friends with," Chris responded with compassion in his tone.

"You definitely would want him as a friend." Arthur paused for a moment and reflected silently on his friend. He cleared his throat and then continued. "Anyway, when he found out that I had given my life to the Lord, we started doing a prayer and study group together. One in the morning and one in the afternoon."

"How early was the one in the morning?"

"0500 hrs. We had to be up and ready to train at 0530, so he usually read a verse to us, explained it, and then we prayed. In the afternoon, it was usually at 1900 hrs. We discussed a passage in more detail, and then we prayed. We started out with just a handful, but by the end of the first month, there were 30-plus men meeting in the morning and at night. In the last month, even the drill sergeant joined in."

"I guess a lot of men were looking for something to believe in and keep them safe."

"They absolutely were, and because of Tom, they found the peace that they were looking for. I wasn't lying when I told you he was soft-spoken, but when he talked about the Lord, his passion was clear. I can't even put a number on the souls he helped lead to Christ during our time together in the service."

"He inspired you to preach?" Chris asked.

"He had a profound impact on my life. He really drove home the point that the only way to lead a truly impactful life for Christ was to have a daily relationship with Him through Bible study and prayer. It doesn't matter what your profession is. Do it for His glory. Whether you play baseball, build houses, teach, fix cars, or whatever, let people see His grace and love in you. Some people think only ministers can make an impact for Him, but there are so many stories out there of everyday people shining His light for the world to see."

"That's what my parents taught me. God wants a close, intimate relationship with each of His children. In cultivating that relationship, He promises He will always be with you. I can't tell you how many times I have had to lean on Him. But I can tell you one thing. I never, ever feel alone in this life."

"It sounds like they did a great job. I'm assuming they also took a serious approach to setting an example through their actions?"

"Oh yeah. Our family life was extremely normal, but there were arguments and disappointing events, but they always modeled love and forgiveness. I can say with extreme confidence that our house served the Lord. Jessica and I feel the same way. We do the best we can at modeling Christ and teaching our kids His grace and love."

Arthur smiled. "I see that in Lincoln."

"Thank you, Arthur." He smiled. "So, Tom awakened your inner pastor?"

"He got the needle moving in that direction." He laughed, "Until then it was baseball or nothing."

Chris winked at him. "It's a great game."

"Anyway, Tom and I were like brothers. He confided in me, and I in him. He had a rough childhood, which led to some poor decisions. When he turned 18, he told me he got into a car accident. His anger was out of control at that point, and he jumped out of his car, meaning to do the other driver harm. The driver of the other vehicle was a pastor at one of the local churches in the area, and instead of letting his anger take over and do something he would regret, he listened as the man told him about the loving mercy of God. It was the domino that started his journey of faith, eventually leading him to seminary."

"God places His children where they're needed."

"Indeed, he does. So, we trained together day in and day out for over a year. Then it came time for us to put our training to the test."

"You were called to active duty?"

"We were. Have you ever heard of the Meuse-Argonne offensive?" Chris looked at him with wide eyes and an open mouth.

"The history books say that it was the turning point in the war."

"It was, and it was also a turning point in my life. On August 1, 1918, we were called to France. We had additional training through September and then joined in the battle in October."

3
October 16, 1918—Montfaucon-d'Argonne

It was during the second phase of the battle that Arthur and Tom found themselves pinned down behind a small church in the town of Montfaucon, France. Casualties on both sides were mounting, but the allied powers were being pushed back instead of moving forward. Tom looked over at Arthur, and at that moment, time seemed to stand still. Bullets weren't whizzing by their heads, bombs weren't exploding, and buildings weren't crumbling. As they stood against the small church, their backs to the wall, Tom looked over at Arthur and smiled.

"Sometimes life really doesn't turn out how you thought it would, eh, Arthur?"

"I did not see this coming."

"The whole time I was studying to be a pastor. I never gave one thought to standing here at this moment in time. But God is so good."

"So good? How can you make that statement at this very moment?"

"I'd make that statement at any moment. His love is purer than anything this world has ever produced. We may not always know why things happen, but when you trust in an all-powerful God who has nothing but unconditional love for His creation, you trust in His will to always manifest itself."

"Can we just concentrate on getting out of this mess, please?"

Tom took a quick peek around the corner. He could barely see through all the smoke and dust. He watched as his company attempted to advance against the German front. Corporal Cruz was sprinting to a position of cover when he dropped to his knees and fell face first onto the ground. He was a son, a brother, a husband, and a father of three. He died at the tender age of twenty-eight. Tom put his back against the wall again and closed his eyes.

"Father, please be with his wife and children. He was a good man and one of your eternal soldiers."

Arthur looked up at him. "We're not going to make it out of this, are we, Tommy?"

Tom looked down at him.

"I don't know the answer to that, Arthur, but I know that your testimony and faith in Christ help lead a lot of these men to eternal life when they leave this world."

"Tommy, you're the one who faithfully led a Bible study daily so that…"

With one hand, Tom shoved Arthur as hard as he could and sent him flying in the opposite direction. "Grenade!" He shouted and fell onto it.

4

Arthur sighed. "I woke up in the hospital three days later. The explosion sent me into the wall of the church. I had a head injury, and they had operated on me and removed shrapnel out of my thigh, side, and left forearm."

Chris placed his hand on Arthur's shoulder. "I'm so sorry that happened to you."

"He would have been a great preacher, but his path ended on the battlefield. I know that at that moment he was trying to give me the credit for all the work he had done. He was that generous. He didn't want me to leave this world thinking that I had done nothing with the life that God gave me. That was just who he was."

"Did he have a wife? Kids?"

"No, he was married to the Lord's work." Arthur smiled and then he sighed again. "But I had to tell his parents and his siblings. It was one of the hardest things that I've ever done."

"I can believe that." His kind words and gentle tone were welcome.

"As I lay in that bed recovering, I thought about all the Bible studies and lessons that he taught us. While I recovered, I read God's word and prayed all hours of the day and night. By the time I was being released from the hospital to go back home, God showed me what He wanted me to do."

"Preach?"

"Preach…eventually," he laughed. "Once or twice a week, Tommy had me lead the study. At first, I was awkward, I stuttered, and I was just plain overwhelmed. But after a few weeks, I got into a groove. I

106

not only enjoyed leading the study, but I also loved all the prep work that went into it."

"So, when you got back, you went into the ministry full time?"

"No. There was one thing that still had a powerful hold on me."

"Baseball."

Arthur laughed, "Baseball. I was just drawn to it. The ministry was calling my name, but I looked for any little sign that told me I should play baseball."

"Like what?" Chris asked.

"It was easy. A few days after I woke up, I prayed God would give me a sign. Let me know that preaching His word was my path. I had no sooner opened my eyes and saw Hall of Fame pitcher Christy Mathewson sitting in a chair by my bed."

"In France?"

"Here was a man who played 17 seasons in the majors, retired after the 1916 season, and out of pure patriotism, signed up to serve his country."

"That's dedication. How old was he when he went to France?"

"He was 38 years old."

"He held a passion for baseball and for his country." Chris smiled.

"He did. In my head, I assumed I was supposed to be a professional ballplayer, even though quite a few players served their country during the war." He looked at Chris. "Sometimes we impose our own will rather than follow the Lord's." He smiled. "We also forget that He see's the bigger picture, and we don't."

"It's tough to let go when you really set your heart on something."

"Yes, it is. Anyway, when my injuries were better, they shipped me home. I got back home in February 1919."

"So, you could play the 1919 season?"

"My injuries kept me from playing until July of that year, but even when I was ready to return, I didn't have a job. They had moved on to someone else. I had been gone for two years."

"Did you see that as a sign to go right into the ministry?"

Arthur laughed, "No. Which, according to my logic, it should have

107

been. Esther and I had a long talk about it. She could see that I still really wanted to play baseball, but I think in her heart she knew what God had planned for me."

"Smart lady."

"Yep. So, she proposed I continue to play baseball, but in the off season I would go to the local Bible college and take classes toward a degree in theology."

"So, what did you do for the rest of the 1919 season?"

"I worked at Dillard's until the following spring. I enrolled at The College of the Bible that fall to take classes."

"But you returned for the 1920 season?"

"I did. God loves us and allows us to choose our own path. It doesn't mean He will not bless our alternate path. It just means that we won't get the ultimate fulfillment He has planned for our lives, and His purpose, if we choose that path instead of His."

Chris smiled, "If you leave your heart open to Him and constantly seek His path, then I believe your alternate path will change course to line up with His."

Arthur laughed. "So, you've heard my story, then?"

They both shared a laugh. Chris looked at his watch and then looked back at the sight. One of his workers was motioning toward him, requesting his presence.

"Thank you for sharing this part of your story with me, Arthur. I know it wasn't easy, but it is part of a story that Lincoln and I are thoroughly enjoying." He stood. "It appears as though I'm needed."

"Thank you for listening."

CHAPTER 9
Monday—July 14, 1980

As Arthur pulled into the parking lot, he noticed Chris's truck was already there. He slept a little later today. He stepped out of the car and into the bright sun. Arthur was wearing a charcoal gray fedora with a black band, a white dress shirt, black dress pants, and black penny loafers. He grabbed his cane and started toward the church. He waved to Chris and the crew as he passed by, and as he approached the bench, he saw no sign of Lincoln. As he got closer, he noticed a set of feet protruding from one end of the bench. He cleared his throat, and Lincoln sat up. Arthur laughed.

"Did I startle you, young Mr. Lincoln?"

"A little." He rubbed his eyes. "We got here early, so I figured I would relax until you got here."

"I thought maybe you'd changed your mind about coming back this week."

"No way. I really want to hear the rest of the story."

"Did your dad tell you we talked on Saturday after the game?"

"Yeah, he said you told him about some war stuff."

"I did. They drafted me in July 1917, and I served until February 1919.

"He also told me that before you got drafted, you were hitting .355 with 19 home runs."

"I was."

"If that wasn't getting you looked at, I don't know what would."

"They were looking, but then duty called."

"That really stinks, Mr. Graham."

"To us it does." He smiled as he patted Lincoln on the shoulder. "But when we commit to serving God, we trust that everything in his plan for us ultimately serves the greater good."

"Is that what you were thinking at the time?"

"Heavens no. I was thinking, this stinks." They both laughed. "But looking back, even though it was very painful, I now know it was one of the greatest blessings in my life."

"What if you never find out why something horrible happened to you or someone you love?"

"That's the tough part. We must trust, even when we don't see. In the book of John, chapter twenty, after Jesus appears to some of His disciples and they share the good news, Thomas refuses to believe unless he sees the imprint of the nails in Christ's hands. After Jesus lets him see and feel the imprints, Thomas believes. But Jesus tells the disciples in verse twenty-nine, 'Blessed are those who have not seen and yet believe.'"

"Is that where the phrase 'Don't be a doubting Thomas' comes from?"

Arthur laughed, "It is."

"So, when you came back in February 1919, did you play again?"

"No. I was nursing some injuries, and by the time I was healthy, they had replaced me on the roster with another catcher."

"Ouch. I'm assuming you eventually played again because the story can't end there."

"You assume correctly. The guy who replaced me was okay at the plate, but he was not very good defensively. So, when the 1920 season rolled around, I got my job back."

"How old were you?"

"I was 24 going on 25."

"You were young enough to still have some gas in the tank."

Arthur spoke, but had to place a hand over his mouth to conceal a smile. He waited a few seconds and then responded. "Thank you."

"You're welcome," he replied without looking up from feeding the birds. He stopped feeding and looked at Arthur. "Did you ever play against Babe Ruth?"

"Unfortunately, I did not. That would have been cool."

Lincoln smiled. "Real cool."

"Did you know that in 1920 the Yankees purchased Babe Ruth from the Red Sox?"

"I can't believe they ever let him go."

"Nobody can. But a fun fact that most youngsters don't know is that he was used more as a pitcher for Boston, then a power hitter."

"I read he pitched, but I didn't think that he was any good at it."

"From 1914 until 1919, the Babe had 49 home runs for Boston. In that same span, he had 89 wins as a pitcher, his best year coming in 1917 when he won 24 games."

"Wow. How come they didn't use him more as a hitter? He hit a lot of home runs for the Yankees."

"659 to be exact. The Babe could really put em in the seats, and out of the yard."

"It doesn't make sense to get rid of a player like that."

"No, it doesn't, and since the Red Sox sold the Babe, they haven't won a World Series. People say that they haven't won because of the 'Curse of the Bambino'".

"My dad said something about that. Do you believe in the curse?"

Arthur laughed, "No. I don't believe in curses." He looked at Lincoln and raised his eyebrows. "But it is strange that they haven't won in over sixty years, especially after winning the World Series in 1912, 1915, 1916, and 1918."

"That's a puzzler," he stated as he shook his head. "Mr. Graham, do you think God cares about baseball? I mean, who wins and who loses? Does He have a favorite team?"

"I would say no. God doesn't really care about baseball, or any sport."

"But God has to care. He cares about everything," he responded in desperation.

"I don't think He cares about the sport, but I know He cares about the players."

"But the sport is important to them."

"There are a lot of things that are important to us that aren't important to God. People care about money, fame, status, and all kinds of things that aren't important to Him. But He always cares about His people. He created us and loves us unconditionally."

"But if He loves us and likes seeing us happy, then it makes Him happy when a Christian baseball player or team wins the World Series."

"That's true, but what about the other team that loses?"

Lincoln thought for a moment and then answered.

"I don't know. I know He loves them, but...I don't know."

"I don't either, but His purpose is always fulfilled no matter what. Both the winning side and the losing side have players who trust in Him to guide them. We don't know why He allows one to win over the other. But through winning a championship or losing one, it brings character. God might use that character to show the individual, or others, the path to His ultimate purpose for them. Do you understand?"

"I guess I do, but it really stinks being on the losing end."

"I will not disagree with you there. Over time, the loss stings less and less, but you'll never forget it."

"I hope He likes seeing me on the winning side of things," Lincoln remarked.

Arthur erupted in laughter and rubbed the top of his head.

"So do I, Lincoln, so do I."

Lincoln smiled and looked over at him.

"So, in 1920, were you back with the Panthers?"

"I was, but some things had changed since I had been gone. The Panthers were now a minor league team for the Detroit Tigers."

"No way!"

"Yes way. In 1919, the Tigers tapped into that Texas League talent pool, and they decided the best way to do that was to have a team in Texas."

"That's so cool. So, did you get your starting job back?"

"I blew them away at the tryouts. Morris not only told me I hadn't lost a step, but he said I was better than before."

"You must have really worked out a lot."

"In the fall and winter, when I wasn't working at Dillard's, or studying for tests or doing homework, I was working out." He rubbed his chin and shook his head. "Poor Esther was the one who suffered the most. We had very little time together."

"She probably missed you a lot."

"She was my rock. Esther never complained once. Whenever I went to her and apologized, she would say, 'You're doing what's best for this family. We all have to make sacrifices.' I was just being selfish. I should have quit playing baseball and worked on becoming a pastor, but it was burned into my brain that I was meant to play ball. She was very understanding. Still is."

"Maybe you were meant to do both."

He looked at Lincoln and smiled.

"That's what I was thinking. Anyway, I completed my first year at The College of the Bible." He paused and looked at him. "That's the college I went to for theology. Did I tell you that?"

"No, but my dad did. He filled me in on some details from your talk on Saturday."

"Oh, very good. I had good grades, but now it was time to focus on baseball."

2

Fort Worth, TX—August 1920

110 games into the season, Arthur was struggling. His defense held strong, but his offense doomed him to a backup role. The new starting catcher was a veteran who had played parts of three seasons in the majors. Jake Skubal was now 33 years old and desperately trying to get back to the show. He was above average offensively, with good power numbers, and played average defense. The Tigers had four catchers on their current roster. Two veterans, who weren't really lighting the world on fire, but were experienced, and two who were younger at 25 and 23. Clyde Manion, the 23-year-old, was hitting .275 in 32 games, and showed promise in both offense and defense. Arthur knew that going into the season, he would have a

good chance of getting called up if he could just duplicate the start of his 1917 season. Missing two and a half seasons certainly took its toll on his play. He wasn't sleeping all that well, and he felt his reflexes suffered because of it. But he was playing the game he loved, and he felt confident that it would come back to him.

On a very warm August evening, Arthur was getting ready to catch the second game of a doubleheader against the Wichita Falls Spudders, the new affiliate for the Pittsburgh Pirates. His teammates were in the field warming up as he sat on the bench at the end of the dugout. He sat there, just staring off into the sky. The surrounding noises were muted, and his mind drifted to the last time he had seen his friend Tom. Their backs were against the wall. There was gunfire all around them, but he heard Tommy's voice clear as a bell. "God is so good." Arthur smiled as a single tear rolled down his cheek. He felt a hand grab his, and as he came out of his trance, he looked to his right. Sitting next to him in the dugout, holding his hand, was Esther. She didn't say a word. She just looked straight ahead. He cleared his throat and squeezed her hand. She turned toward him. "Are you okay, Arthur?"
"Yeah," he got out. "Some days are tougher than others."
"Is there anything I can do for you?"
"No, it's just something I have to work through."
She smiled and then kissed his cheek.
"I'm always here if you need me."
He smiled, "I know you are. Thank you."
Morris yelled from the infield as he walked toward the dugout, "Alright, let's bring it in."
Esther got up and left the dugout as Arthur put his catching gear on. He closed his eyes. And whispered, "God, please clear my head and help me focus. Thank you." He finished getting his gear on and ran out onto the field and took his position behind home plate. The top of the first went quickly. It only took five pitches to record three

outs. As he made his way into the dugout, Morris read off the first three batters' names.

"Patty, Jacobs, and Graham."

Morris had him batting third tonight, so he hustled into the dugout and took off his equipment while the first batter strolled to the plate. By the time he grabbed a bat and made his way to the on-deck circle, Jacobs was jogging back from first after grounding out. He bypassed the circle and made his way to home plate. He took a couple of practice swings and then settled into the box. Jimmy Zinn was pitching tonight. The big right-hander had a great fastball and a lively curveball. He was 16-8 with a 2.15 ERA. Arthur had zero hits against him this season in eight at bats. Zinn nodded to his catcher and then fixed his gaze on Arthur. Arthur stared back at him and watched as he went into his windup. "Curveball" echoed the voice inside his head as Zinn followed through and delivered to the plate. Arthur rocked back in his stance and waited for the ball to break. Just as it came over the center of the plate, he took a step forward and swung. The loud crack made those who were paying attention to other things turn their heads toward home plate. The ball leaped off the bat and sailed through the air toward left field. The fielder never even thought about moving as he watched the ball sail over his head and land in the back of the stands. A no-doubt homer that made the crowd erupt. Arthur trotted around the bases as Zinn continued to stare out into left field. As he rounded second base, he looked into the stands to see Esther standing with the rest of the crowd, cheering and celebrating the long blast. He smiled and gave her a wink. His teammates welcomed him back to the dugout with smiling faces and hearty congratulations.

"You hit that thing a mile," Patty yelled as he slapped him on the back.

Arthur made his way to the end of the bench and started putting his gear back on. Where did that voice come from? He was just standing there minding his own business when out of nowhere, "curveball" popped into his head. He smiled, closed his eyes, and whispered under his breath, "Thank you, Lord."

"Did you say something, Arthur?" Jarvis, the backup catcher, who was sitting nearby, asked.

"No. I was just thinking out loud," he responded.

"That was one heck of a ball you hit. Almost like you knew exactly what he was about to throw."

Arthur smiled, "Thanks."

He finished putting on his equipment and made his way back onto the field. The second inning was uneventful for both teams. Even though the Panthers put together a couple of hits, no runs came across the plate. In the top of the third, the Spudders leadoff hitter sent a line drive over the head of the shortstop into left center for a base hit. As the home plate umpire cleaned off the plate, Arthur watched as the runner and the third base coach stared each other down. Arthur then looked out at his pitcher, who was kicking dirt away from the front of the mound, trying to get it situated to his liking. He squatted back behind the plate and just before he gave the sign, the voice in his head returned, "Pitchout." He went down on one knee and looked around. The umpire stepped off to the side and looked down at Arthur.

"Are you alright, son?" he asked.

Arthur looked up at him with confusion in his eyes and asked, "Did you hear that?"

"Hear what?" he asked back.

Arthur then looked up at the batter in the box. It was Joe Nichols. They had played together for a couple of years, and Arthur had seen him in Dillard's a few times.

"Did you hear that, Joe?" Arthur asked.

"I heard nothing, Artie. If you're asking me if I heard what pitch he was going to throw, I missed it. Can you repeat it for me?" Joe asked with a smile on his face.

The umpire chuckled and then shouted, "Play ball."

Arthur resumed his position behind the plate and looked out at

Sears. He gave him the sign for the pitchout, and he nodded in agreement. Sears went into the stretch and checked on the runner. As he went into his motion, the runner took off for second base. He threw a fastball wide. Arthur came out of his stance and, in one fluid motion, caught the ball and gunned it down to second base. The runner was sliding in just as Patty caught the ball and slapped the tag on him.

"Out!" the umpire yelled.

Sears looked back at Arthur and gave him a thumbs up. Arthur, looking shell-shocked, finally gave him one back. The top of the third ended when the next two batters popped out and struck out, respectively. In the bottom of the third, Arthur came to the plate with a man on first and two out. He took two practice swings and then stepped into the box and stared out at Zinn. Arthur watched as the pitcher and catcher tried to get on the same page, but it ended with the catcher calling time and heading out to the mound for a conference. It wasn't a long chat, and he made his way back to the plate and took up his position. Arthur stepped back into the box and stared out at Zinn. Zinn checked the runner and then went into his windup. "Fastball" echoed the voice inside of his head this time, and Zinn followed through and delivered to the plate. Arthur gripped the bat tightly and, as the fastball came into the upper left corner of the strike zone, he connected. The ball once again jumped off his bat and sailed through the air. The right fielder watched as the ball came toward him down the line. He turned and ran back toward the fence, watching as the ball kept rising. When he made it to the fence, he looked up to see the ball strike the foul pole. The crowd erupted once again as Arthur jogged around the bases for his second home run of the day. The dugout welcomed him with smiles and high fives, and more than a few "Attaboys." He made it to the end of the dugout and put his equipment on. He then stood and turned toward the stands. Esther had a big smile on her face as she waved and blew him a kiss. He smiled and threw his hand up to simulate catching the kiss. He then slapped it onto the side of his face. After three, his team led 3-0, compliments of Arthur. Sears walked over and slapped him on the back.

"You're single-handedly trying to get me the W today," he said with a smile.

"I guess I'm just having a day, that's all," Arthur responded.

"Well, keep on having it," Sears stated as he made his way up the front steps to head toward the mound.

Arthur finished putting on all his equipment and made his way to the plate. The next two and a half innings flew by. Not a lot of excitement, but going into the bottom of the sixth, the Panthers held a 3-1 lead. Arthur was due up first in the inning. He hurried into the dugout and quickly removed his gear. He walked over to the bat rack and stopped. Arthur reached out and placed his hand on the barrel of the bat he wanted, but then just stood there. He closed his eyes and talked to the Lord silently. "I don't know what's going on, Father, but thank you for your loving-kindness right now. Please keep me humble, so that I may always honor you and not myself."

"They're waiting for you, King Arthur," Morris stated as he stood to the side of Arthur.

"Sorry," he replied.

He selected his bat and walked out of the dugout toward home plate. He wasn't prepared for what was about to happen. The crowd rose to their feet and cheered louder than anything he had ever heard. Arthur stopped and looked up into the stands. He had a lump in his throat the size of Texas right now. Arthur gave them a salute in appreciation, and they got even louder. He looked at his teammates. They were clapping and cheering as well. As he walked toward the plate, he looked out at Zinn, who was staring him down. He took a couple of practice swings and settled into the box. Zinn was still staring him down as he got ready. Finally, he took his place by the rubber and took his eyes off Arthur to look at his catcher. As he went into his windup, Arthur gripped the bat tightly. Just as he was coming through to deliver the ball to the plate, the voice in Arthur's head echoed, "Duck." Zinn released a fastball that was very inside and head high. Arthur dropped his bat as he fell backwards onto the turf. The catcher missed the ball and hit the backstop behind him. There was a collective "boo" that echoed through the stadium as Arthur was picking himself up off the ground.

"Ball one," the umpire yelled.

Arthur dusted himself off, picked up his bat, and stared out at Zinn. He took two practice swings and then took his place back in the box. The crowd cheered. Zinn looked in at him and smiled. He took the mound again and got the signal. He went back into his windup and delivered. "Duck," the voice echoed once again. The fastball came in waist high and almost a foot inside again. Arthur jumped, bent at the waist, and threw his backside out as far as he could. The ball missed him by less than half an inch as it smacked into the catcher's mitt. The crowd's boos were even louder as the umpire took a step to his right and pointed at Zinn.

"One more like that and you're out of here," he yelled.

Zinn smiled and nodded his head to let the umpire know he understood. The crowd continued to boo as Zinn received the ball back from his catcher and stood on the mound. Arthur took a deep breath, took two practice swings, and then stepped back into the hostile zone that he once knew as the batter's box. He stared out at Zinn, who was staring back at him with a big smile on his face. Zinn nodded to his catcher, set, and then went into his windup. Arthur watched closely as he came through and delivered the ball to the plate. "Curveball" came the echo. Arthur gripped his bat and waited for the ball to break across the plate. The ball broke perfectly in the dead center of the dish. Arthur reached back with every bit of power that he could muster, and as the bat came through the zone, the connection was solid. The crack of the bat was loud but could barely be heard above the roar of the crowd. Zinn just dropped his head and closed his eyes. He knew exactly where that ball was going. Arthur hadn't even touched first base before the line drive cleared the left-field wall. The crowd noise was deafening as he rounded first and headed for second. He glanced over to the mound to see Zinn, still

119

bent over at the waist, staring at the ground. As he rounded second base, he looked into the stands to see Esther staring back at him. Her hands were covering her mouth, and the wives next to her were clapping and smiling in her direction. As he rounded third and headed toward home, the crowd cheered even louder. When he finally reached home plate, he stood directly in the center, looked up into the sky, pointed a finger toward the heavens, and softly whispered, "God is so good."

3

He stopped speaking for a moment and sat there staring down at the birds. He was thinking about Tommy. Arthur smiled.

"Mr. Graham, are you okay?" Lincoln asked.

"I am." He cleared his throat. "That's the only time that I ever hit three home runs in a game."

"It sounds like it was awesome."

"So awesome."

They both laughed.

"Did you get up to the plate a fourth time?"

"I got up with one on base and two outs in the eighth inning."

"No home run though?"

"Zinn was out of the game, and the new pitcher didn't want any part of me that day. He walked me intentionally, which really upset the crowd."

"I bet. They wanted to see number four. It must have felt good to have all those people cheering for you so loudly?"

"It's a feeling that's hard to put into words. I guess the only way to describe it is that it made me feel like the most important person in the world."

"It sounds like you might have needed a pick me up that day."

Arthur laughed, "I really did."

"How do you explain the voice you were hearing before the pitches?"

"Years of experience would be my guess. I believe I developed good instincts and subconsciously recognized some of the pitchers tells." Arthur laughed. "Some might have been guesses as well."

"I bet Esther was proud of you."

"She was. She made me my favorite supper that night to celebrate. Liver and onions."

Lincoln leaned back against the bench and crinkled his nose.

"I thought you said you were celebrating. That doesn't sound like a celebration meal."

"What's your ideal of a celebratory meal?"

"I don't know. Cheeseburgers, fries, and a chocolate shake. Fried chicken, pizza, steak, anything but liver and onions."

"Have you ever had liver and onions?"

"Once, when we visited my grandparents. My dad barely ate his."

"I guess it's not for everybody," he laughed. "Esther is a superb cook, though."

"I don't know if anyone is that good of a cook to make liver and onions taste good," he crinkled his nose again as he said it.

Arthur laughed. "Did you know that Ty Cobb's favorite meal was liver and onions?"

"It was?"

"Yep. He said it was rich in minerals and protein. He attributes it to being a big factor in helping him to become the all-time hits leader in baseball."

"Disgusting." He shook his head. "I'm glad it worked for him, but I think I'll try to find another way of getting hits."

Arthur slapped his knee and laughed.

"You could always try hotdogs and ice cream like Babe Ruth."

Lincoln smiled. "That's more like it."

"You know it's important to eat well, don't you? Too many sweets will slow you down."

"My mom makes sure that I eat the right foods, but she's a good baker too. So, she also makes sure that I get my fair share of sweets. She says that I'm young and can 'work it off.' Eventually it'll go right to my thighs, or something like that."

Arthur continued to laugh and shake his head.

"I guess moms know best," he responded.

"That's what she says, and when she looks at my dad, that's what he says, too."

"I have no doubt," Arthur replied with a smile. "Okay, where was I?"

"You were about to finish the 1920 season."

"Oh yeah. 1920 wasn't great for me, except for the three-home run game. Wait. What time is it?"

He looked at his watch. It was 11:45 p.m. "I told Esther I would be home by noon today. We have some antique stores to go to."

"Why?"

"Because she likes antiques, I don't know." He looked down to see that he still had half a bag of breadcrumbs. "Here, take this and finish feeding the birds."

Lincoln took the bag. "Thanks."

"We'll pick this back up tomorrow. Have fun at practice tonight."

"I will. See you tomorrow."

"See you tomorrow."

Arthur was sitting on the bench feeding the birds as Lincoln came running up and plopped down on the bench next to him. This sent the birds into flight and startled Arthur.

"Geez Louise!" Arthur exclaimed.

"Good morning, Mr. Graham," Lincoln replied.

"Where's the fire, son?" Arthur asked.

Lincoln laughed.

"There's no fire. I'm just excited to tell you about practice last night."

Arthur turned toward him.

"Oh yeah. What happened that's got you so charged up this morning?"

"Two dingers! I hit two in practice last night. Over the fence. Gone."

Arthur laughed. "I know what dingers are. Remember my story from yesterday?"

"They weren't in a row, but I was in practice last night remembering the story, when I just felt this surge of energy."

"I'm glad I could be such an influence on you."

"It was so awesome. I couldn't wait to get here this morning and tell you."

"I can tell. Your excitement level is through the roof."

Lincoln looked beyond Arthur to the other side of the bench.

"What's that?" He asked as he pointed to the baseball bat leaning up against the bench.

"Oh that? It's a bat," he replied.

He threw some crumbs onto the ground. They sat in silence for a moment.

"Why do you have a bat?" Lincoln finally asked.

"I got it for a friend," Arthur replied with a smirk

"Did you get me a bat, Mr. Graham?" Lincoln asked without trying to contain his excitement.

"Esther and I were at the antique shop yesterday, and she purchased a lamp for the end table that sits in the corner of the living room. Apparently, this lamp was owned by the poet Emily Dickinson…"

"What about the bat?" Lincoln interrupted. Arthur stopped his story and looked over at him. Lincoln looked away to avoid eye contact. "I'm sorry, Mr. Graham. I'm just really excited about that bat."

"I know you're excited, but it's rude to interrupt someone when they're talking."

"I know. My mom and dad get mad at me all the time for doing it."

"Then why do you keep doing it?"

"I don't know. I just get so excited that I can't help it. I try to remind myself that it's not polite, like my mom says, but I just can't help it."

"Do you want me to finish the story or just tell you about the bat?"

"I really want to know about that bat, but you should finish the story. I'm sorry. I'll try hard not to interrupt again."

Arthur smiled. "Like I told you before, the story helps build anticipation. If it were just a common story about my getting you a bat, then I would get right to it. I tell the story the way I do for a couple of reasons. First, because it's a good story, and second, it'll give you something to talk about if anyone asks you about the bat."

"Plus, if I see Mrs. Graham, I can ask her how she likes her famous lamp."

"Now you're getting it, my boy. Some stories give you conversation pieces for a later date. I mentioned Emily Dickinson for a reason. Where was I? Oh yeah. The lamp belonged to Emily Dickinson. She was a famous poet who lived in the mid to late 1800s. The store's owner was vacationing in Massachusetts when she came across the lamp at another antique store in Amherst. Unfortunately, the store is closing, and the owner decided to part with the lamp as a way of clearing everything out before she moved."

"Was it expensive?"

"Esther loves to haggle, and there's nobody better at it. She got it at a good but fair price. Anyway, as we were leaving the shop, I noticed we were only a few blocks from Tiger Stadium. We drove over to the park, and I said hi to an old friend. He invited us in so I could talk to some of the old timers who remembered me. On the way up to the owner's office, I ran into some of the current players who were just finishing a workout. They were very kind. We shared some stories, and I told one of them that your favorite player was Parrish. He had me wait for a second as he went into the locker room. A short time later, Mr. Parrish came out of the locker room and handed me a bat that he signed."

"He autographed a bat and gave it to you. Sorry. I did it again," Lincoln blurted out.

Arthur laughed, "That's okay. That was the part you were supposed to get excited about. He gave me the bat and shook my hand. We talked for a bit. He's a delightful fellow, by the way, and then Esther and I left."

Arthur handed him the bat. Lincoln immediately looked at the barrel of the lightly stained bat and saw the signature in blue.

"Whoa," was all he got out.

"He was very knowledgeable not just about the history of the game, but about Tiger baseball. He was happy to sign the bat for you."

"Thank you so much, Mr. Graham. This is the best gift I've ever gotten."

"You're quite welcome, Lincoln. Are you going to use it to hit or hang it up somewhere?"

Lincoln looked up at him as if he had lost his mind.

"It's going on my wall. Maybe my dad can build a case for it."

"You don't want to hit with a big leaguer's bat?"

"No way. Breaking it would crush me."

Arthur shrugged his shoulders. "Suit yourself."

"You would use it?" He asked.

"Maybe at least once. He's probably taken batting practice with it or even used it in a game a time or two."

125

"You think so?"

"Sure."

"I'll think about it." He returned to smiling from ear to ear as he stared at the signature. "It's still the coolest gift ever."

"I'm glad you like it. Okay, are you ready to get into the story?"

"One second, please."

Lincoln stood and walked over to a safe place in front of the bench. He looked down at the ground and spit. He shuffled his feet and cleaned out a spot in the box. Lincoln looked straight ahead while he did a couple of windmills with the bat. He got into his stance, positioning his hands down toward the base of the bat while the barrel hovered above his head. He held this position for a few seconds before taking a stride forward and swinging with all his might.

"Crack! The ball jumps off the bat and the crowd goes wild," Lincoln yelled as he mimicked the cheering crowd. "That ball is way back. It's gone! It's a home run! And a fan from Garden City, Michigan, caught that one." Lincoln gently set the bat down and held his arms in the air while he jumped up and down.

Arthur sat on the bench, clapping and laughing. "Ernie couldn't have said it better himself," he responded as he continued to laugh.

Lincoln picked up the bat and jogged back over to the bench and sat down. A king-sized smile on his face. "I hope one day he's saying that about me for real," he stated as he held the bat in his lap.

"I hope so too," Arthur responded.

"Okay, Mr. Graham. I'm ready to start the 1925 season."

"We're going to speed things along a bit. I'm going to cover multiple seasons today so that we can get to the bread and butter of the story." He observed Lincoln's confusion. "The whole reason I started telling it."

Lincoln smiled and nodded, "Oh."

Fort Worth, TX—September 1925

It was the last game of the season, and the Cats were about to finish in first place again. It would be their seventh season in a row. Morris had them playing great baseball, which is why the Tigers took them on as their minor league affiliate. The last five seasons had been tough for Arthur. His defensive game was still solid, but his offensive numbers were like a roller coaster. In the last five seasons, his stats were below average, and the Tigers kept finding younger catchers who always had a great season from year to year. This season he was hitting .215 with 11 homers. He was the backup to a 19-year-old who had put together a solid season. He was hitting .312, with 26 home runs, and 73 RBIs. At 30, Arthur was now seen as the veteran catcher who filled a roster spot because of his experience and stability. Most of his teammates over the years were promoted, traded to other teams, or moved on to other professions. Today, against the Houston Buffaloes, Arthur was starting. His counterpart was nursing an injury, one that Arthur felt a 19-year-old should never have, so that he would be the Cats backstop. He was standing off to the side, stretching, when he heard a familiar voice calling to him.

"Arthur, Arthur, Artie." The voice yelled from behind the fence down the third-base line.

Arthur smiled as he turned to see Mike Patty leaning up against the fence. He was wearing a suit and holding a pad and pen. He walked over to greet his old friend and teammate.

"Patty. You come here to get your spot back?" Arthur asked.

He laughed, "No. I'm a scout for the St. Louis Cardinals. They wanted me to come here today to see how our single A players were progressing and maybe see if the Tigers had any talent we might want to trade for." He winked at Arthur. "You still chasing the dream, buddy?"

"Still chasing."

"You'd make a good scout. I could put in a good word for you."
Arthur smiled and looked down. "No. That's okay. I still like the
thrill of the game, and besides, I'm close to getting my theology
degree."
"What are you gonna do with that?"
"Preach."
"Artie, you've got baseball in your blood. Come be a scout, or
maybe even a coach."
"Maybe in a few more years." He laughed nervously. "Well, I'd
better get back to the dugout. We're about to start soon."
"It was good seeing you, Artie. Goodluck."
"Thanks. It was good seeing you too, Patty. If St. Louis needs a
subpar, good-natured catcher, then let me know."
Patty smiled. "Will do, pal. Take care of yourself. Tell Esther I said
hi."
"Did I tell you I'm a father?"
"No kidding? When did that happen?"
"July."
"Well congratulations. Boy or girl?"
"Boy. We named him Dillard."
"Well, give my very best to Esther and Dillard. I'll see you around,
Artie."
"Thanks. See you around, Patty."
Arthur turned and made his way back to the dugout.

Arthur checked the lineup just before the game started and saw that
he was batting ninth. He sat down on the bench and put on his gear.
After he got everything on, he leaned back, closed his eyes, and
softly whispered a quick prayer.
"Lord, please help me today to give my best. Thank you for
allowing me to play a game that I truly love. Thank you. Amen."
He opened his eyes, grabbed his mitt, and took the field. The Cats
played admirably that day, and Arthur caught a great pitching
performance by the 18-year-old phenom that the Tigers were

bringing along slowly. What the organization was noticing was that Arthur had a great way with their young pitchers. His experience and gentle nature were an impressive combination. That day, the young phenom held the Buffaloes to one run on three hits, while striking out ten in a complete game performance. Arthur had studied the Buffalo hitters well and made all the right calls behind the plate. His strategy and defense were once again brilliant, but at the plate, he was 0 for 3 with three strikeouts. The season ended, and Arthur found his way back to Dillard's.

3

"You must have been pretty down in the dumps?" Lincoln asked.
"I had my moments, but with all the great people in my life reminding me of God's love and grace, those moments passed quickly."
"That's good. My mom always says that if we dwell too much on the bad stuff in life, it'll drive you crazy. 'It's the devil's way of sending you into a tailspin.'" He stated emphatically as he pointed at nothing. "She also says, 'Don't let the devil catch you staring at a problem that you can fix by talking to Jesus on your knees,'" he laughed. "I don't know what that means, but it's funny when she says it."
Arthur smiled. "I think what she's trying to say is that it helps us to avoid temptation. Sometimes we struggle over the right decisions, and if we stare too long, our sinful nature makes the choice our godly nature should have made. She wants you to pray and seek the Lord's guidance instead of eventually giving in to the wrong temptation."
Lincoln thought about that for a moment.
"I guess that makes sense." He turned to Arthur. "Was it like that when you were trying to decide to keep playing baseball?"
Arthur smiled. "I never thought about it, but now that you say it, it

kind of was. I knew I wanted to preach, but I also really wanted to play baseball. In my head, my plan was to be a big leaguer for ten to fifteen years and then go to the pulpit. That had to make God happy. Right? But the problem with that plan is that it was the plan I devised. I knew in my heart that the right plan was to follow His plan for me, and be happy to do it."

"It seems like it all worked out. You got to play baseball for a while and then became a preacher."

"It worked out because I eventually allowed myself to relax and listen. To let His will be done, not mine. I fought it for a very long time, as you'll see."

"My mom also says, 'Don't cry over spilt milk.' I think it means you have to clean it up and move on."

Arthur laughed. "Are you sure you're twelve?"

Lincoln smiled and nodded yes. "Did you ever get your starting job back?"

"Not really."

"But you continued to play baseball for a while? I mean, you didn't quit after the 1925 season, did you?"

"Heavens no. Like I said, I'm going to fast forward a little here, so just stop me if you have questions. Okay?"

"Okay."

"From 1926 to 1929 I continued to play for Fort Worth. They remained the Class A affiliate for the Tigers through the 1929 season. The next few years flew by in a blur of bus rides and dusty fields, and before I knew it, it was 1930. Heading into the 1930 season, two things happened. The Tigers dropped Fort Worth as their major league affiliate, and I was turning 35 in June of that year, and I had never even come close to getting a taste of the majors. My window was closed or closing quickly."

"Did Fort Worth move its team?"

"No, but the Tigers had made Beaumont their new Class A affiliate. It was still in Texas, but it was just over three hundred miles away."

"But you could keep playing for Fort Worth if you wanted to?"

"Esther and I talked about it. If I would not play for a major league affiliate, I would quit playing."

"But what about your dream of playing in the majors?"

"In my mind, that's all it would ever be. A dream. I was a husband and a father. My priority was taking care of my family."

"Did you keep working for Mr. Dillard?"

"When the season ended at the end of 1929, I went back to the hardware store and continued to work for him. He was always very supportive and kind to Esther and me. I had also started interning at a local church that fall. I was to graduate from The College of the Bible with a theology degree that spring, after ten years of work; and Pastor Blount, our home church pastor, invited me to be his understudy."

"So, you were leaving baseball to be a full-time pastor?"

"Baseball made that choice for me." He smiled. "It was an excellent opportunity to learn from one of the best pastors anywhere. He would mentor me, and when it was time, I would find my church to lead."

Lincoln scratched his head. "I thought there was more baseball in this story."

Arthur moved forward without addressing his concerns.

"It was a very busy fall and winter for me. I worked full time at the hardware store, and part time at the church, because the internship didn't pay, so I still had to work at Dillard's making money."

"Did you try to make the team at Beaumont?"

"I couldn't ask Esther to pick up and move just to play another season in the minors. We had an established life here. It wouldn't be fair to take her away from family and friends."

"I guess not."

Arthur laughed. "But she was always looking out for my interests, not her own. When I graduated at the end of April 1930, I got a phone call from Del Baker. He was a backup catcher with the Tigers from 1914 to 1916. Then he decided he liked the management aspect better. He was one of our coaches with Forth Worth for the last two years before he got hired as the manager for Beaumont to manage the 1930 season." He stopped talking for a moment because he noticed Lincoln looking up at him with a big smile on his face. "What are you smiling at?"

"Nothing. It seems like your baseball career isn't over yet," he stated as his smile grew wider.

Arthur laughed, "I guess it wasn't time to hang up the cleats just yet. He told me that his backup catcher got hurt and was out for the season. He hoped I was interested in coming to Beaumont to fill in for hopefully the rest of the year."

"What did Esther say?"

"She told me to go. When I tried to make excuses, she wouldn't have it. Two days later, I was in Beaumont."

"Did she go with you?"

"No. We had a house in Fort Worth. She stayed there with Dillard, and I made sure that I sent the checks home as soon as I got them. Mr. Dillard had a good friend who lived in Beaumont, and they let me stay there at no charge. Well, he said no charge, but I have a feeling that he paid them while I stayed there."

"How long did it take you to get back into game shape?"

"Physically, I was still in good shape. I just had to re-acclimate myself to baseball after being off for the winter and first part of the spring. By the end of May, it was like I had never left."

"Did you play good that season?"

"I hit .285 with 10 home runs and played very well defensively."

"Did they think about calling you up?"

"If they did, they said nothing to me about it. Anyway, Del asked me to stay on for the following season as well."

"Because of your stats?"

"Because I was a veteran presence in the clubhouse, and because he liked me." Arthur smiled. "I didn't care why. I just knew I was playing baseball again."

"What about your family and the church?"

"The season ended in September. We were 68-84, so we missed the playoffs. When I got back home, I told Esther they wanted me back next season. Del was good enough to get them to give me a contract for the next two seasons."

"What did she say?"

"She said, Okay, we have to sell the house and move because she wasn't spending another summer without me."

"What about the church?"

"I told Pastor Blount that we were moving to Beaumont. He wished us the best of luck and told us he would pray for us on our journey. He was a kind and godly man. The hardest part was telling our parents that we were taking their grandson away from them."

"Yeah. They probably weren't too happy about that. Where did you live? Did you buy a house?"

"We found a nice little house close to the field. Mr. Dillard bought our house in Fort Worth and decided to rent it to a nice family. His kindness knew no end. Our families ended up being a lot more understanding than we gave them credit for."

"Did you move right away?"

"No, there was no need of it. I worked at Dillard's until the beginning of March, and then we moved. It didn't take us long to get settled in. Beaumont was a pleasant town, and Esther made some good friends. I also found a very nice little church there, just five minutes down the road. The local pastor was looking for some help, so I signed on in the off-season to do whatever needed to be done at the church. Anything from preaching a Sunday sermon to cutting the grass or doing general maintenance."

"Did you get to preach a lot?"

"Not a lot, but I gained some valuable experience. Anyway, in the 1931 season I played in roughly 47 games. I hit .273 with 8 homers." Arthur smiled. "It was fun, but the 1932 season was a season to remember. That year, the Exporters featured a future Hall of Famer in Hank Greenberg."

"I remember him from the book you gave me. He liked to hit home runs."

"Boy, did he. Hammerin Hank is what they called him. He hit 39 homers that year, and we went 100-51 and won the league championship. One of the dominant pitchers during that time was Lynwood 'Schoolboy' Rowe. He won 19 games for us and led the league with a 2.34 ERA. The Tigers called both up for the 1933 season."

"So, how did you hit that year?"

"A little better than the year before, .279 with 10 homers."

"Still no call-up?"

"No. I was 37 now, and they were content to let me mentor the younger players."

"So, after you played your two years, what happened? Did they extend your contract?"

"They liked what I was doing, so they gave me another two years. In 1933 my numbers were like the previous year, and they had two young prospects who they were really excited about in camp for the 1934 season."

"So, were you the third catcher?"

"They made me a player-coach that year. It's also the year they signed Mickey Cochrane to catch and manage the Tigers. He is one of the best players ever to have played the game."

"I've heard his name before."

"He was an exceptional talent, and one heck of a nice guy. He had already won two World Series championships in Philadelphia for the A's in 1929 and 30 and won the AL MVP in 1928. The city of Detroit was excited to have him."

"Was he a home run hitter?"

"No, he was good for extra-base hits, and he hit for average and RBIs. He also knew how to manage a good game behind the plate, and the pitchers loved him. I met Mickey at the beginning of the 1934 season. He made his way to Beaumont to get a look at the players and staff. Being catchers, we clicked right away. He stayed with Esther and me for a couple of days and picked my brain about the team constantly."

"Did you ask him what it was like to win a World Series?"

"You bet I did. He said it was one of the best feelings in the world. We talked so much shop during the two days he stayed with us. He was surprised that I hadn't seen the majors."

"Did you tell him he could help you get there?" Lincoln smiled.

Arthur laughed, "No. I told him about the two young prospects we had. He didn't like that they were both 18 and 'green.' He wanted a veteran to back him up in Detroit because he thought we had the juice to win it all that year." Lincoln's smile grew bigger, and before he could ask, Arthur answered it. "No, he didn't bring me up in 1934."

"Who did he get to back him up?"

"Ray Hayworth. He was 30 and had five seasons under his belt. Ray was a good catcher, and one of the guys I played with and mentored in the minors."

"Were your numbers better than his?"

"They were similar, but he was eight years younger. Cochrane liked him, so he didn't see the need to change things. Anyway, Mickey went back to Detroit, and when the season started, I was still in Beaumont."

"I'm sorry to hear that, Mr. Graham. I really thought this story was leading to you getting your shot in the majors."

Arthur laughed. "Don't give up hope yet, young Mr. Lincoln." He patted his knee. "Where was I? The 1934 season was a good season for the city of Detroit. As a player, Mickey won the AL MVP again and led the Tigers to the World Series against the St. Louis Cardinals. They dropped the series 4-3 after being up 3-2, but things looked promising for them to go back in 1935. I didn't play as much in the 1934 season, but I still hit and fielded well enough to be kept for the 1935 season as a player-coach."

"How did the two catchers you were mentoring do?"

"Good. They played nearly the same number of games and had very similar numbers. Rudy York hit .278 with 15 homers, and Gabe Weaver hit .272 with 12 homers. York was very good defensively. As a matter of fact, the Tigers called him up in 1937, and he was a mainstay for them behind the plate for ten seasons."

"It sounds like you were a good teacher, and you got to rub elbows with a lot of talented players."

"God certainly blessed me in my baseball career, even though at the time I felt I was dragging my heels in doing what He made me to do."

"It seems like you were doing what He wanted you to do."

Arthur scratched his head. "I think you might be right. Unfortunately, in those days, it seemed like I was a little more self-serving than God-serving." He smiled. "Even though I felt I was delaying His path for me, He gave me the biggest wink of all in the winter of 1935. One evening in early February, there was a knock at our door. It was around 7:00 p.m. and we had just finished dinner. I opened the door to find Mickey Cochrane standing there. The surprise on my face must have been clear, because he laughed and patted me on the shoulder. I invited him in, and Esther took Dillard to his bedroom to read him a story as Mick and I talked."

"Was he offering you a job to be a coach on the Tigers?" He blurted out in excitement.

Arthur laughed, "Patience, my boy. He told me that Ray had some serious family issues that he had to deal with. He thought Ray was going to miss at least half of the season that year. Mickey told me he was very impressed with how I played the game, and even more impressed that I had kept myself in great physical condition. He was also very surprised that I had never gotten a shot to play at the major league level. He asked how old I was going to be this season. I told him I was going to turn 40 in June. He leaned forward in his chair and asked me, 'How would you like to come to Detroit and be my backup for the 1935 season?'"

"Oh, my gosh, Mr. Graham! No way! He asked you to play for the Detroit Tigers?" Lincoln shouted. "I thought maybe a coach, but no way!"

"I was speechless. I couldn't get the word yes out of my mouth. That's when Esther came running from the bedroom shouting, 'Yes, yes, yes, he'll do it.'"

"Awesome," he shouted so loud that a few of the construction crew looked their way.

"I almost broke down and cried in front of him. He told me that even if Ray came back at any point in the year, I could stay with the club for the entire 1935 season. He told me that if I needed help finding housing, he would help me out. Mickey pulled a contract out of his bag and handed it to me. He said he had to get to the hotel, but he would stop by the next day to discuss it. We shook and then he left."

"Do you have a copy of that contract, Mr. Graham, and can I see it?" Arthur laughed. "You'll see it, along with a lot of other cool things. After he left, Esther and I sat at the kitchen table staring at the contract. With tears in her eyes, she said, 'You did it.' I told her we did it, and then she gave me a big hug. I was completely overwhelmed at that moment. I celebrated with her, and when she went to bed, I sat in the living room in silence and thanked God for His blessings. I will never forget that day as long as I live."

"If that happened to me, I don't think I would forget it either."

"The next day Mickey stopped by around 3:00 p.m. and we went over the contract over pie and coffee. Of course, I signed it and thanked him over and over throughout our conversation. The team had already reported to spring training in Lakeland, Florida, but he told me to report by March 1st. The irony was that in 1933, they held spring training in San Antonio, Texas. Esther and I had some things to figure out for the upcoming season."

"Like where to live," he laughed.

"That was a big one. Luckily, we had Mr. Dillard. When I called and told everyone the good news, everyone was over the moon happy, but he was the one who offered to come and help us with whatever we needed."

"Mr. Reliable."

Arthur laughed, "Ain't that the truth? By March 1st I was in Lakeland practicing with the team, Esther and Dillard stayed in Texas while Mr. Dillard was completing a deal on a nice house he had found on the west side of Detroit, and by opening day on April 17, 1935, we were completely situated."

"He was a man who got things done."

"Mr. Dillard was very polished and efficient in almost everything he did."

"Did he ever get married and have kids of his own?"

"No. I don't know why. He would have made a great dad. He was a father figure to me. The only reason I can think of is that he worked a lot. I mean, he was at the store every day from open to close, unless he was at church."

"Did you ever ask him why he didn't have a family of his own?" Arthur laughed. "He said that we were his family, and I was okay with that."

"Yeah, but you guys moved to Detroit and left him back in Texas. He must have gotten lonely."

"He had the store and church, and we talked often on the phone. Mr. Dillard always seemed genuinely happy. I guess that's why I never really questioned it."

"I suppose not." He scratched his head and smiled. "I can't believe you made it to the majors, Mr. Graham. That's so awesome. You worked really hard. The majors!"

"Thank you, Lincoln. Sometimes I wanted to give up, but in Romans, chapter five, verses three and four, He encourages us that, 'Tribulation produces perseverance; and perseverance, character; and character, hope.' I believe strongly in perseverance, but I faltered in my hope. Sometimes it felt like all of that hard work was a weakness."

"How do you mean? I thought it was a good thing to keep working at stuff?"

"It is a good thing, but sometimes you can let it take over your life and miss out on something special that God has planned for you."

"Do you feel that way? It's kind of confusing."

"I know it is." He tapped his chin as he thought and then asked Lincoln, "Have you ever heard the phrase, 'You can't see the forest for the trees?'"

Lincoln shook his head and answered, "No."

"It's a phrase that explains a lot. You see, sometimes you get so focused on one thing that you can lose sight of the bigger picture." He looked over at Lincoln, who had a very confused look on his face. "I was so focused on getting to the majors, I was losing track of all the important things around me. God's direction for my life, my wife's, and the life of my child. I was only thinking of my happiness, what I wanted, and what would make me feel complete. The majors or bust. I'm sure I missed some valuable lessons along the way."

"I think I get it. The majors were the trees, and all that other important stuff was the forest. Is that right?"

"You've got it."

"But the saying really doesn't make much sense."

"How so?"

"You say that 'You can't see the forest for the trees,' but aren't the trees the forest?"

Arthur threw his head back and gave out a loud, joyous laugh.

"That is a very good observation, Lincoln. But the forest is more than just trees. It's got a complete personality. It has trails, streams, rock formations, caves, animals, and so much more. Don't miss out on all of that because of the trees."

Lincoln smiled. "I guess that makes a lot more sense. Thank you for helping me to understand that, Mr. Graham."

"What good is all of this knowledge if I don't share it?" He winked at him.

Lincoln smiled back and then clapped his hands together and rubbed them.

"Now, let's get to that major league baseball career."

Arthur laughed as he looked up to see Chris walking toward them.

"It'll have to wait until tomorrow."

Lincoln turned around to see his dad.

"Are you done for the day? You have nothing else you have to do?" Chris laughed.

"Did I come at an exciting point in the story?"

"Mr. Graham was just about to talk about his first year in the majors with the Detroit Tigers," Lincoln blurted out.

"Wow!" He looked at Arthur. "You were a Detroit Tiger? That's very impressive, Arthur. What year?"

Arthur smiled. "1935."

"1935." Chris tapped his chin and thought. Finally, his face lit up, and he spoke. "That was the year…"

Arthur cut him off.

"That I played for the Detroit Tigers."

Chris smiled.

"Come on, son. You can fill me in on today's story on the way home."

"Okay. See you tomorrow, Mr. Graham." He gave Arthur a hug. "I don't know if I'll get much sleep tonight."

"Have a good practice tonight, and I'll see you in the morning."

As the two of them made their way to the truck, Chris noticed Lincoln was carrying a baseball bat.

"Did Mr. Graham give you a bat? It looks kind of big."

"Yeah. Lance Parrish signed it."

"Really?" Chris asked, surprised.

"It's all part of today's story," he stated as he smiled at his dad.

Perseverance Rewarded

Chapter 11
Wednesday—July 16, 1980

Arthur hummed as he threw more breadcrumbs onto the ground. The birds came from all directions and landed on the ground to consume their breakfast. A few scattered and a few fluttered their wings, but remained as Lincoln came running up to the bench and plopped down next to Arthur.

"Good morning, Mr. Graham?" He shouted as he grabbed a handful of crumbs from the bag and threw them onto the ground.

"Geez. Are you trying to give an old man a heart attack?" He stated as he grabbed his heart.

Lincoln laughed. "No. I'm just really excited to hear the story today, and to tell you that at practice last night, I hit a couple of balls with the bat you gave me yesterday."

"You did? It didn't break, did it?"

"No," he laughed. "I only hit a couple of balls with it, but they were solid. I made sure that I used the side he didn't sign."

"Why only a couple?"

"It's too heavy for me right now. Plus, I didn't want to take a chance of breaking it."

"It takes a lot to break those bats, but I don't blame you. I wouldn't want to take a chance of breaking it either."

"Dad said that he is going to build me a case for it."

"That's nice."

"Yeah. The guys at practice were jealous. I didn't let them use the bat, but I let them touch it. That made them happy."

Arthur smiled.

"Are you ready to get into the story?"

"I've been waiting for this all night."

"Okay then. Let's get started."

Lincoln turned toward Arthur and rested his elbows on his knees and his chin on top of his folded hands.

142

Navin Field, Detroit, Michigan—April 17, 1935

Arthur walked out onto the field and stood just in front of the home team's dugout. He started in right field and slowly scanned all the way to the left field corner. A slight breeze blew and ruffled the blades of grass in front of him. He closed his eyes for a moment and let the breeze wash over him. The air filled his nostrils with the smell of fresh-cut grass, rich soil, and chalk. He smiled. He could hear the murmur of the crowd and feel the excitement of another season about to begin. This time he wasn't in the hot Texas heat, working to get noticed by a major league team. He was standing on the major league baseball field of the Detroit Tigers, soaking it all in.

"Arthur."

He continued to smile and look out over the field.

"Arthur," the voice stated a second time.

He looked to his right to see Mickey standing there. He didn't speak. Mickey smiled as he tried a third time.

"Arthur."

"Yes...Mick...Sorry...I," he stuttered.

"Don't apologize, Arthur. I get it." Mickey paused as he looked out over the field. "It's beautiful. Every year I'm thankful that I get the opportunity to play this game." He looked back at Arthur. "So, I understand when someone takes the time to drink it in."

"I've been playing baseball for over twenty years now, but I've never seen or felt anything like this."

"I felt the same way the first time I stepped onto a major league baseball field. Are you ready?"

"I am," he smiled.

Cochrane tapped his chin with his index finger and smiled.

"You're starting today."

"Mickey, I'm the backup."

"Not today. Get your gear on and warm up, Tommy." Arthur stood still, stunned, not moving. "Arthur. Get the lead out."

"Yes…sir," he finally got out.

Arthur ran back to the dugout while Cochrane made his way over to change the lineup on the official scorecard. He penciled Arthur in as the starting catcher, hitting in the number two spot in front of Charlie Gehringer. He handed the card back to the umpire, Jim Decker.

"Are you alright, Mick?" Jim asked.

"I feel great, Jimmy. Why do you ask?"

"Because you ain't starting."

"A good manager goes with his gut. This kid's got it today." He smiled.

"Kid? He might be older than everybody on this field." Decker laughed.

"Arthur's 39, Jimmy. How old are you?"

"I meant players, and even some coaches. I'm what you would call more experienced."

Cochrane laughed. "Well, today I'm going with more experience. So, take it easy on him, will ya?"

Decker laughed and slapped Cochrane on the shoulder. "Whatever you say, Mick."

Cochrane handed him the card and walked back to the dugout. He gathered the players together and stood on the top step. "All right, boys, listen up. Last year we were close. That's behind us now. This is a new day and a new season. We have the same team, except for a couple of key additions." He leaned forward, and his voice intensified. "This year we ram it down everyone's throat and see this thing through to completion. What do you say?"

The team cheered loudly and slapped each other as their adrenaline spiked. They trusted their leader, and they vocalized their support of his words. He motioned with his hands for everyone to settle down and pulled Arthur to the top step with him.

"Graham is going to lead us onto the field today. It's his MLB debut, boys, so let's try to get him a win."

More cheers and chanting from the team filled the dugout. Cochrane turned to Arthur.

"Go out there and do what you've been doing for twenty years." He smiled. "The game is the same."

Arthur nodded and smiled back. "Thanks, Mick."

Cochrane gave him a little push, and he started running for home plate with his teammates following. The crowd erupted as their Detroit Tigers took the field for the first time in the 1935 season. When he reached the plate, Decker handed him the ball.

"Give him some warmups and let's get started."

"Yes, sir," Arthur responded as he took the ball from him.

He threw the ball out to Bridges, slid his mask into place, and crouched behind the dish. The atmosphere was electric. After a few pitches, Decker told him it was time to start. He flashed the number two to Bridges, and he nodded. After the second pitch, he sprang up and threw the ball to Gehringer at second. He watched as they threw the ball around the horn. He took a deep breath and silently prayed.

"Lord, thank you for allowing me to be here today. Please be with me as I represent you in all that I do. Amen."

"Play ball," came the shout from Decker as he cleaned the plate. He crouched down and looked over at Greenberg at first. Hank punched the inside of his glove and pumped his fist at Arthur. Arthur smiled and nodded. He looked up as the White Sox hitter stepped into the box. Rip Radcliff smiled down at him as he took some practice swings.

"Arthur," he nodded.

"Rip," Arthur acknowledged back.

He gave Bridges the fastball sign, and he nodded in agreement. He wound up and delivered a beautiful ball that touched the black on the inside lower corner. Decker shot up his arm and yelled, "Strike one!"

The 1935 season was officially underway. The top of the first was uneventful, and Chicago went down 1-2-3. Arthur made his way to the dugout and removed his gear. Greenberg came over and sat next to him.

"Well, rookie, how did it feel?" Greenberg asked with a big smile.

"Like no other inning I've ever played before," Arthur shot back.

"All right, let's see what you can do at the plate."

Arthur stood. "I need some of the Greenberg magic."

Greenberg grabbed the barrel of Arthur's bat and pulled it in toward his lips. "You give this man a hit. You hear me?"

They both laughed.

Arthur pulled the barrel up toward him. "I'd listen to him if I were you."

He stepped into the on-deck circle and watched as Jo Jo White, the Tigers speedy centerfielder, took a couple of pitches from White Sox pitcher, Sam Jones. With the count at 2-1, White sent a slow roller down the third-base line. Chicago third baseman Jimmy Dykes ran in and scooped it up and threw a perfect ball that hit the first baseman's mitt just before White's foot came down onto the bag.

"Out," the first base umpire yelled.

Arthur stepped to the plate with no one on and one out. He took his customary two swings before stepping into the box. The White Sox catcher, Luke Sewell, looked up at him as he got settled in.

"Aren't you a little too old to be a rookie?" He asked.

Without looking down, Arthur answered, "Isn't your pitcher 42?"

"Yeah, but he's been playing for over twenty years."

"So have I," he responded.

Sewell just shrugged as he gave Jones the sign. Arthur gripped the bat tightly as he waited for the pitch. He watched as the curveball broke down and ran outside.

"Ball one," Decker shouted.

Arthur stepped out and adjusted his shoulders. He took a couple of practice swings and was right back in the box. He stared out at Jones and dug in. Jones once again received the sign from Sewell and gave an approving nod. He went into his windup and delivered. Arthur watched as the fastball hit the catcher's mitt low and inside.

"Ball two," Decker shouted.

This time, Arthur stayed in the box and took his practice swings as Sewell tossed the ball back to Jones. Jones caught the ball in disgust and then grimaced as he took his place back on the mound. He shook off a few signs before he and his catcher landed on the same page. Arthur gripped the bat and leaned in as Jones delivered. He watched as the slow curve broke down and ran over the middle of the plate. He took a stride forward and made contact. The ball leaped off his bat and over the head of Jones, shaving the top of his cap. The line drive made its way onto the outfield grass between second and short, giving Arthur his first career hit in his very first major league at bat. The crowd erupted as Arthur reached first, and both Cochrane and Greenberg stood on the top step of the dugout, clapping and cheering for him. When the ball made its way back to Jones, Cochrane called time, came out of the dugout, and motioned for the ball. Jones threw the ball to his catcher, who flipped it over to a waiting Cochrane. He looked over at Arthur standing on first base, held it up, and smiled. Arthur tipped his cap to say thank you, and the game resumed.

The Tigers lost their home opener 7-6. Arthur played the entire game and finished 1 for 4, with his lone hit coming in that first at-bat, but he threw out a baserunner attempting to steal second base in the sixth inning. In the locker room after the game, Mickey presented Arthur with the ball from his first hit.

"Thanks, Mick," Arthur humbly stated as he took the ball.

"You never forget your first hit." He slapped Arthur on the back. "You played a great game today. Tommy really felt comfortable with you behind the plate."

"Thanks. I just wish we could have won."

"You can't win em all. It's a long season, and this team was built for the long haul. Mark my words, we'll get plenty of W's this season, and you'll be on the catching end of a lot of them."

Arthur smiled. "That sounds good to me."

Cochrane slapped him on the back again and then stepped up onto the bench nearby. "Listen up, boys!" He paused, and they turned their attention toward him. "Today we played hard, but we didn't get the results we wanted or deserved. Tomorrow is a new day, and we will get those results. Go home, take it easy, reset, and come back tomorrow ready to punch these yahoos right in the mouth."

The team nodded in agreement as he stepped down from the bench. Arthur looked around the locker room and saw his teammates smiling and jostling one another. Charlie Gehringer walked by, and they made eye contact.

"Nice hit out there today, rook," he stated as he smiled and winked.

"Thanks," Arthur responded as he smiled back.

He finished showering and getting dressed and was out the door to get home to Esther so he could tell her all about his experience. He was flying so high right now he thought nothing could top this. As he exited the stadium to go to his car, he was approached by a young boy and his father.

"Excuse me, Mr. Graham," the young man stated.

Arthur smiled and dropped to one knee to look him in the eyes. "What can I do for you, son?"

"Can I get your autograph, please?" He asked as he handed him a ball.

"You certainly can," he responded as he took the ball.

Arthur reached into the inside pocket of his jacket and pulled out a pen. The only piece of advice that his new teammate Goose Goslin had for him when they met was, "Always carry a pen." When he asked why, Goslin laughed and responded, "You'll see." He now knew why. He smiled as he autographed the ball.

"What's your name?"

"Ryan…Ryan Kirk, sir."

"You want to be a ballplayer someday, Ryan?"

"More than anything."

"How old are you?"

"Eight. I practice every day." He smiled and then added. "When I'm done with my chores."

Arthur looked up at his dad.

"That's a good man. Always make sure you get those chores done first."

The dad smiled at him as he squeezed his son's shoulders.

"Yes, sir."

Arthur handed him the ball back.

"Keep up the good work, Ryan. I hope to be seeing you on this field someday."

Ryan gave him a big smile and then lunged forward and hugged him. Arthur laughed as he hugged him back.

"Come on, Ryan, I'm sure Mr. Graham would like to get home and relax after a long day on the field," his father stated.

He pulled away from Arthur and returned to his father. He stood smiling as he stared at the signature on the ball.

"What do you say, son?" His dad asked him.

"Thank you. Thank you so much, Mr. Graham," he cheerfully replied.

"You're very welcome, Ryan," Arthur responded as he stood.

He watched as the father grabbed his son's hand, and they walked down the street. The boy held the ball in his other hand, refusing to take his eyes off it. Arthur smiled and walked to his car.

3

He looked over at Lincoln and smiled.

"That was a good day. Sometimes I remember it like it was yesterday, and other times, it seems like it was a million years ago."

"I can't believe you played major league baseball. You were a Detroit Tiger."

Lincoln looked as if he had stars in his eyes.

149

"You look how I looked staring out at that field for the first time in 1935."

"It's just so…"

"Unbelievable," Arthur finished his sentence for him.

"Yeah. Unbelievable."

"I look back on it now and thank God for the opportunity to live out a boyhood dream. I was playing with and against Hall of Famers who were way more talented than me, but here I was, rubbing elbows with them."

"Does it make you mad it took you so long to get there? It seems like you deserved to be there a lot sooner."

He turned and looked at Lincoln.

"If it's one thing that whole process taught me, it's that if I was going to trust in God's power, I had to trust in his timing. Ecclesiastes 3:1 states, 'To everything there is a season, A time for every purpose under heaven.' I think about that verse, and that day on the field, every time I want to rush God into a decision."

"I don't like waiting for stuff."

Arthur laughed.

"Nobody does, but what if God let me choose when my big-league dreams came true? When I was 18, 22, or even 25?"

"That would have been great."

"In theory, yes. But what if it had changed one aspect of my life that made me who I am today?"

"Like what?"

"Maybe I miss out on meeting Esther, which means I miss out on having Dillard. If I rush God's plan, then maybe I have one or two very sub-par seasons, or get hurt in my first major league game, never to return. Maybe I never met Mr. Dillard, or any of the other people who have helped shape my life to what it is today."

"But maybe you become one of the best players of all-time. People stand in line just to see you or get a picture with you. Your records are so good they'll never be broken."

He put his hand on Lincoln's shoulder.

"I am grateful for the life God chose for me. When I look back on all that has happened, I now realize that I wasn't waiting for Him to make a decision, He was waiting for me. All I had to do was trust Him."

Lincoln scratched his head and looked puzzled.

"Isn't everything God's decision?"

"God gives us the free will to make our own decisions. He ultimately knows what decisions we are going to make, and where we will end up, but He lets us choose the path of how we get there. Does that make sense to you?"

"I think so." He scratched his head some more.

"Think about it like this. Walk from here to the Upper Peninsula."

"Whoa! That's a long walk."

"That's right. It is a long walk. Think about that walk as if it's your life. As you walk, you come to a road that splits off and goes in different directions. You come to a point in your walk where you have three different paths to take, but all lead to the same place. You have a decision to make. God is leading you down a certain path. One that will get you to your destination a lot sooner, and it's the path that He has chosen for you to take so you can accomplish His work in your life in His time. You follow me so far?"

"Yeah. I understand. Go on."

"But one of the other two paths looks more enticing. Without praying and asking for His direction, or maybe you prayed and asked, but you took one of the other paths, anyway. It delays His will for you by one, six, ten, twenty, or even forty years."

"Forty years! That's forever."

"It would seem like that." He scratched his head. "I know of one character in the Bible who delayed God's purpose for him for close to forty years."

"Moses?"

"Very good, young Lincoln. Moses didn't return to Israel to lead God's people into the Promised Land until he was eighty years old."

"That's a long gap."

"Some have gone longer, some shorter."

"So, we eventually get to where we're going, but it just takes us longer to do it, and our actions can change things along the way?"

"Yes. God lets us know in Jeremiah chapter twenty-nine verse eleven, 'For I know the plans I have for you, declares the Lord, plans to prosper you and not to harm you, plans to give you hope and a future.'"

"I think I understand now. His plan for our lives is the one we should follow. But even if we stray, we can always come back to Him, and He will guide us back to that plan so we can get where He intended us to be?"

Arthur turned to face him.

"My boy, you are a quick study. Yes. That is exactly what I am saying to you. I made decisions based on what I wanted rather than on His direction." Arthur smiled. "But He still blessed me with grace beyond my wildest dreams."

"You got to play major league baseball, and you still got to do preaching." Lincoln smiled.

Arthur laughed. "Yes, I did. Baseball was awesome, but I have never been happier than when I am behind a pulpit delivering His word to His people. I could have been doing that a lot sooner, but I took a slight detour." He laughed. "But your mom is right."

"She often is."

Arthur chuckled.

"There is no use crying over spilt milk. When we get to where we need to be, we need to press forward and give it everything we've got without letting the past keep us there."

"Why did they call him 'Sad Sam Jones?'"

Arthur smiled and answered, "Because a reporter thought he always looked sad when he was on the mound pitching. He won three World Series. Which I'm assuming made him happy."

"Cool. Why did they call the one guy Rip? Was that his real name?"

"I'm not sure. I think it was because he rarely struck out. He always made contact with the ball."

"Do you still have the ball? You know from your first major league hit that day?"

"I do. It's in a box with all my other things from my baseball days." Arthur looked up to see Chris walking toward them. "Here comes your dad. We'll pick this up tomorrow."

"Okay, Mr. Graham. See you tomorrow."

He ran to meet his dad, and Athur gave him a wave. Chris smiled and waved back. He could tell Lincoln was talking a million miles a minute because Chris was nodding his head and laughing.

It was 7:00 a.m. and Arthur sat on the edge of the bed, clutching his chest as Esther slept soundly. He closed his eyes and drew a deep breath. He held it for a few seconds and then exhaled. Arthur opened his eyes to see Esther standing in front of him. It startled him, and he laughed.

"You move like a cat, my dear," he stated as he continued to laugh.

"Arthur, what's wrong?" She asked with a look of concern on her face.

"It's nothing, my love. Just a few gas pains."

His answer did not convince her.

"It might be, but let's get dressed and go make sure."

She sat down beside him and placed his hand in hers.

"Please don't worry, my love. I believe the chili from last night is just hanging around a little longer than it should."

He patted her hand, trying to reassure her.

"If this were me, would you want me to go to the hospital, or sit on the edge of the bed and do nothing at all?"

He thought for a moment. "I…"

He started to speak and the belch that left his body was one of the loudest and longest they had ever heard in their entire lives. When it was over, they looked at each other and laughed like they had never laughed before. His hand was no longer clutching his chest. He was wiping the tears from his eyes as he continued to laugh. Esther did the same as she reached over on the nightstand and grabbed some Kleenex. She handed him a couple, and they spent the next few moments wiping their eyes.

"I'm so sorry," he stated as he continued to dab his eyes. "That was very unexpected."

"I almost patted your back. You probably would have knocked me off the bed," she responded.

154

They laughed some more.

"My love, I haven't laughed like that in a long while. I feel much better. My pain is gone."

"I wish my sense of smell was gone for the moment," she responded, barely getting it out as the laughter started up again.

He laughed again as well, and he put his arm around her and drew her close. They laughed a little longer, and then he kissed her on top of the head.

"I thank God every day for bringing us together. I love you so very much, Esther."

She wrapped her arm around him.

"I love you too, Arthur. I couldn't imagine a single moment on this earth without you."

They sat on the edge of the bed holding each other, reminiscing about some of their favorite memories together over the last 65 years of marriage. When they finished, they faced each other, and he placed his hand on the side of her face.

"You have given me a lifetime of love and laughter. God is so good."

"I will not argue that point."

He smiled. "Miracles do happen."

"Don't ruin the moment, Arthur."

He laughed and caressed her face.

"I am only joking, but you know this."

"I do. Let's have a little breakfast before you go to see Lincoln."

"I could stay home today if you'd like? We could take a walk. Go to the park."

"You just got to the juicy part of your story. It wouldn't be right to leave it like that."

"You want to go back to bed after I leave?"

"Yes."

Arthur chuckled and kissed her again.

Arthur was feeding the birds when Lincoln came running up and sat down. The birds had gotten so used to this that they didn't even scatter. They just continued eating.

"Good morning, Mr. Graham."

"Good morning, Lincoln. How was your game last night?"

"Good. I went 2 for 4 and we won."

"Five hundred. Very nice. Did you play third?"

"Yep. Nothing got by me. One ball took a weird bounce and hit me in the shin, but it didn't hurt too badly."

"That's good. You've gotta keep the ball in front of you. Nice job."

"Thanks. So, what happened in the second game of the season?"

Arthur smiled. "I guess we're going right into it, then?"

"If you don't mind? My dad and I are itching to know what happened in the second game."

Arthur laughed.

"The second game of the season, we won 5-4. Mick caught that game and looked great, but over the next six games, we would only win one."

"Did you catch any of the other games?"

"I was behind the plate when we played Cleveland at home in the sixth game. We lost 5-0, and I went 0 for 3 with two strikeouts."

"I hate striking out. The season isn't starting off so good."

"No, it wasn't, but a huge turning point to our season would come in the ninth game in Chicago."

3

Comiskey Park—Chicago, April 25, 1935

"It's the bottom of the ninth here at Comiskey with the Tigers and White Sox tied at eight," announcer Ty Tyson informed the radio audience. "The Tigers tied the game on a solo home run by

Greenberg in the top half of the inning. Coming to the plate to lead off the inning is left fielder Al Simmons. A two-time World Series champion, Simmons has hit the ball well today."

On the field, Simmons stepped into the box and stared out at the Tiger pitcher, Clyde Hatter. Cochrane flashed Hatter the signs, and they agreed on fastball high and inside. Hatter went into his windup and delivered. The ball caught more of the plate than either Hatter or Cochrane wanted it to, and Simmons jumped all over it.

"Simmons connects on the pitch and sends it on a line down into the leftfield corner," Tyson's voice going up an octave.

Tiger left fielder Goose Goslin sprinted to the corner and scooped the ball with a backhand just before it got to the wall. He instinctively turned and threw the ball to Gehringer at second base. Simmons slide beat the throw, and Cleveland started the inning with the winning run on second base and no one out.

"Simmons was sprinting out of the box and ended up on second with no one out. He had 36 doubles last year, and this is already his fourth of this season." Tyson shuffled through his papers. "The Tigers are on the verge of starting the season 2-7 after falling just short in the World Series last year."

The next two batters struck out, and it looked like Hatter and the Tigers were battling to take the game into extra innings. Shortstop Luke Appling stepped to the plate next. He wasn't known for his power, but he was a contact hitter. Cochrane called time and walked to the mound.

"Let's walk this guy, Clyde," Cochrane suggested. "Appling is more likely to put the ball in play and get the run in from second. Dykes is up next. He's having an off day."

Hatter seemed to stare past him as he talked. He was staring at Appling, who was wearing a smug look on his face. He would later tell the team that he thought Appling had winked at him.

"Clyde, are you hearing me?" Cochrane asked.

Hatter then focused his gaze on Cochrane. "No," he finally answered.

"No," Cochrane repeated.

"I'm striking him out and wiping that smug look off his face."

"Clyde, this isn't the time to let pride enter the equation. Let's go after Dykes and take this thing into extra innings, giving Hank and Charlie a chance to get us a much-needed win."

"No. I can get this guy."

Cochrane turned and looked over his shoulder to see both the umpire and Appling looking out at them impatiently.

"Don't make me regret this," he stated as he handed the ball to Hatter. "If we're going to get him on anything, it's going to be curveballs."

"I can blow it by him, Mick…"

Cochrane cut him off. "Curveballs."

Hatter nodded like he understood, and Cochrane made his way back to home plate.

"Can we finish the game now?" The home plate umpire asked sarcastically.

Without saying a word, he kneeled behind the plate, and Appling stepped into the box. Cochrane flashed the curveball sign, and Hatter nodded. He went into the stretch and then checked on Simmons at second. He had a moderate lead off the bag but was being held close by Gehringer. Hatter went into his windup and delivered a curveball low and outside.

"Ball one," the umpire yelled.

Appling stepped out of the box, and Cochrane threw the ball back to the mound. Hatter walked around the mound. He finally took his place on the rubber and stared in at Cochrane. He flashed the curveball sign, but Hatter shook it off. Cochrane could feel his blood boiling as he emphatically flashed the curveball sign again. Hatter again shook it off. Gritting his teeth and clenching his jaw, he flashed him the fastball sign. Hatter nodded. Cochrane showed he wanted the ball high and inside, but when Hatter delivered to the plate, it was right at the belt and on the outside black. Appling swung and made solid contact, sending it down the right-field line.

Pete Fox, the Tigers right fielder, got a great jump on the ball and was scooping it up as Simmons was rounding the bag at third. Fox had a cannon for an arm and bypassed the cutoff man, firing the ball into the plate. It was a perfect one-hopper to Cochrane. He caught the ball and turned to face the runner, but his left cleat was stuck in the ground and wouldn't let him turn fully to brace for the impact. Simmons lowered his shoulder and with full force ran into the waiting Cochrane. Both men flew backwards and landed hard on the ground. The ball came out of his glove and rolled past the umpire, who was looking down at the plate. Simmons landed just in front of home plate, but the momentum sent him rolling over the plate, almost taking out the umpire.

"Safe," he yelled.

"He's safe and the White Sox win it," Tyson yelled into the radio as he watched the scene unfold. "Wait a minute. Cochrane is still down on the ground, and he appears to be clutching his left leg."

Cochrane was holding his left knee and in obvious pain as the team ran out to check on him.

"Folks, Mickey Cochrane is still down on the ground, holding that left leg as the White Sox players continue to celebrate." Tyson stated. "Losing the American League MVP from last season would be a serious blow to their chances of winning the pennant, and an even bigger question on the minds of all Tiger fans is, 'Who is going to be this team's catcher?'" Tyson paused for a moment to take a sip of water. "The soon to be 40-year-old rookie who has eight major league at bats? No matter how you slice it, the Tigers are in big trouble if Cochrane is out for any extended period." Arthur stood and watched as the coaching staff helped Cochrane stand, but he was in obvious pain and couldn't put any weight on his left leg. He looked at Cochrane's face, which told the real story. His season was over.

Arthur looked at Lincoln.

"Mickey was the heart and soul of that team. Sure, we had some great Hall of Fame players, but Mick was the spark plug that ran the engine. He was a genuine leader."

"Was he hurt for a long time?"

"He would miss the entire season."

"That's awful, Mr. Graham. He was so close the year before, and now an entire season was gone."

"Unfortunately, that's how life goes sometimes, son."

"I don't know what I would do."

"You would eventually move forward, and so did Mick. Being the leader that he was, it didn't take him long to realize that he had a team to manage. He couldn't help us with his physical skills, but he knew he had the knowledge to train us for the long season ahead."

"He still managed the team?"

"Of course he did. He had a job to do, and he did it. He missed the next series in Cleveland, and our third-base coach, Del Baker, managed the team. Del was a former Tiger, and the guys liked him. We lost two out of the three games, which sent our record to 3-9 on the season."

"Were you the starting catcher now?" He asked with excitement.

"Del started Frank all three games in Cleveland."

"I thought Mr. Cochrane had you as his backup?"

"He did, but Del liked Frank better. He went with youth."

"That's not right. You paid your dues. You worked hard to get there…"

Arthur placed his hand on Lincoln's shoulder because he could see that he was getting worked up. "It's okay, Lincoln. Mick met us in St. Louis for the next series and put me into the starting lineup."

"Mick's a smart man."

They both laughed.

"When no one else did, he had confidence in me. I can't explain why, but he did."

"Mr. Graham, you of all people should know that it was what God wanted."

Arthur smiled. "That's a very astute observation. If I were going to continue to hold on to the game of baseball, then He was going to give me my shot."

"I'm glad He did," Lincoln said with a smile.

"So am I."

"What was wrong with Mr. Cochrane's leg?"

"He tore some stuff in his knee. Real bad. He had to have surgery in a couple of weeks after the incident, but in the meantime, he was going to manage his team. He made them slap a brace on it and then drive him to St. Louis."

"Was he mad at that Simmons guy for causing the injury?"

"No, he knew it was part of the game. He said he would have done the same thing. His cleat just got stuck, and that's why he got injured. Al visited him at the hospital after the game. He said he was sorry, and Mick forgave him."

"Cool. Was Al a good player?"

"He was. As a matter of fact, both Al and Appling are Hall of Famers." Arthur laughed. "Al felt so bad about the injury that he came to Detroit and played the 1936 season with the Tigers."

"No way?"

"It's true."

"Did Mick come back the next season?"

"He did, but he only played 44 games. It had nothing to do with the knee. He had other health issues." Arthur paused and thought about his old friend, who had given him the opportunity to live out his dream. "Let me tell you about the St. Louis game."

Sportsman's Park, St. Louis - April 29, 1935

Mickey Cochrane leaned on one crutch as he addressed his team in the dugout. "Listen boys. What happened to me was a fluke. It's nobody's fault. It's just part of the game. Moving forward, you have a catcher who is more than capable of leading this team day in and day out. For some unknown reason, he sat in the minors when he should have been in the majors, starting behind the plate a long time ago." He paused as Greenberg and Gehringer voiced their support for Arthur. "I look at every one of you and know that this team can not only get back to the series but can give this organization and city its first championship."

The dugout roared with cheers and celebration. The fans in St. Louis looked around the stadium to see where the noise was coming from, after all, the game hadn't even started yet.

"Let's give these fans something to boo about," shortstop Billy Rogell shouted.

The Tigers pumped their fists and high fived each other as they cheered and agreed with Rogell. Cochrane ended on that note and gave out the lineup. Arthur was catching and batting second, and fan favorite Tommy Bridges was on the mound.

"Mickey Cochrane is back with the team here in St. Louis as the Tigers take on the Browns in the first of a two-game set. The Tigers are 3-9 to start the season and need a win badly. Cochrane has decided to start Graham behind the plate, so it looks like he is going to lean on the 39-year-old rookie to step in and take his place." He paused for a drink of water. "Those are some big shoes to fill."

Arthur was due up in the top of the first inning. He reached on a single to rightfield and scored on a Gehringer double in the next at bat. The Tigers jumped all over the Brown's starter in the second inning and put four on the board to take a 5-0 lead after two. The combination of Bridges and Graham was working well. They were now getting ready to bat in the top of the eighth inning. Bridges had struck out seven, and Arthur had thrown out two baserunners attempting to steal. He stood on the top step of the dugout as Brown's pitcher Jim Walkup finished his warmup throws. Jo Jo White walked toward the batter's box to get the inning started. He was getting ready to make his way to the on-deck circle when Mickey rested his arm on his shoulder.

"How are you feeling, Artie?" he asked.

"Pretty good, skip."

"You look comfortable behind that plate. I think ole Ty Cobb himself would have a hard time stealing second on you."

"Thanks Mick. That means a lot coming from you."

"Let me finish." He smiled. "I can see that you feel good behind the plate. No question. What I want to know is how you feel at the plate?"

"A little unsure, if I'm being honest."

"What are you unsure of?"

"I'm just scared of letting the team down."

"So, you're scared. Not unsure."

"I guess you could say that."

"What are you so scared of?"

"Letting the team down. Scared of striking out. Scared of not coming through."

Cochrane turned and faced the team.

"Do any of you guys expect anything from Graham at the plate?" Some shook their heads no while others verbally told Cochrane no. He focused his attention on Arthur. "Arthur, relax. I have seen you hit, and I can tell you that you're a much better hitter when you are relaxed. This team will look to you to catch a good game and give encouragement. They look to other guys to bring the offense. So, just relax."

Arthur smiled. "I can do that."

White singled up the middle, and Arthur made his way to the batter's box. He was one for three on the day with two strikeouts. He stepped one foot into the box and paused before stepping in fully.

Arthur looked up into the heavens and smiled, thanking God silently for allowing him to play the game he loved at the highest level, and for people like Mickey, who motivated him to be his best. He stepped into the box and took two practice swings before he set himself and stared out at Walkup. White took a modest lead off first and watched as Walkup pitched out of the stretch. Arthur was sitting fastball on this first pitch and was surprised when the curve broke across the center of the plate.

"Graham looked like a deer in headlights on that pitch," Tyson stated as he laughed. "I think he even thought about bailing out of the box, judging from his body language."

Arthur did think about bailing out. It was a great curveball. Arthur stepped out of the box and shook his head. He looked out at Walkup, who was smiling as he got the ball back from the catcher. He took a deep breath and reset. Arthur stepped back in and waited until Walkup got the sign he was looking for. Arthur assumed he was going to get another curveball after the embarrassing way he looked on the last pitch. He went into his windup and delivered a fastball inside and low.

"Ball one," the umpire shouted.

He stepped out and looked over at the dugout. Cochrane was standing on the top step, pushing both hands toward the ground and mouthing the words, "Relax." Arthur nodded and then stepped back into the box. He decided he was going to sit on a curveball. Whether it came on this pitch or the next one, that's what he was going to do. White took a slightly bigger lead at first than before. Walkup came to a pause and stared at him. Arthur gripped the bat tightly and waited for the pitch. Just as the pitcher went into his motion, White took off from first. The fastball came across the plate belt high and on the outside corner.

"Strike two," the umpire yelled.

The catcher popped up and threw the ball to second, but White slid in ahead of the tag. The second baseman threw the ball back to the pitcher, and the Tigers had a man on second with nobody out in the inning. Arthur had a chance at an RBI now. White finished dusting himself off and Walkup took his place back on the rubber. He stepped back into the box and waited for the next pitch. Walkup nodded as he got the pitch he wanted and then went into his stretch. He glanced over his shoulder at second to see where White was and then focused his attention back on Arthur. Walkup then came through and delivered the ball to the plate. The curveball started three inches behind Arthur before it broke and came across the inside middle of the plate. Arthur didn't miss. He came through and met the ball with the barrel of the bat, making solid contact. The ball leaped off the bat and headed for the left-field corner. Everyone in the dugout became silent as they jumped up and leaned over the railing to watch the ball. White was between second and third, jumping into the air and waving his arms frantically for the ball to stay fair. Arthur jogged toward first, the bat still in his left hand, as he watched the ball continue to hook into the corner. The ball glanced off the foul pole and landed in the seats.

"Home run," the home plate umpire screamed as he made a circling motion with his right hand.

Arthur leaped into the air and pumped his fist with his right hand as he ran toward first, releasing the bat from his left hand three quarters of the way down the line. He gave the first-base coach a spirited high-five as he rounded the bag and headed to second. As he rounded third base, he looked into the dugout to see the boys still hanging over the rail, yelling and clapping. He finally touched home, and when he got to the top step of the dugout, Mick was there to congratulate him before he went through the parade of handshakes and slaps. He sat down at the end of the bench, looking out toward left field, panting and smiling from ear to ear.

"Feels good, doesn't it?" Cochrane stated as he took a seat next to him.

"It feels great. Is this how your first home run felt?"

"Oh yeah. It's a rush like you've never felt before. Welcome to the club," he stated as he slapped his knee and headed back to his place at the front.

Arthur shook his head and whispered to himself, "Thank you, Lord." He finished putting on his equipment for the bottom half of the eighth, but ended up taking it off again before the inning was completed. The Tigers scored nine runs in the inning, and he batted twice, with a home run and a walk to his credit. The Tigers won the game 18-0.

6

"18-0. Whoa," Lincoln stated in disbelief.

"You said it. We went into that two-game series in St. Louis with a chip on our shoulder. The next day we won 11-3. They were glad to see us go."

"Did you hit another home run the next day?"

"Mick put the kid in to catch. He played a good game."

"Wait. Were you two just going to rotate for the rest of the season?"

"No, he told me after the St. Louis series that I was the starter. The only way he would take me out was if I asked, or we were playing a doubleheader. It gave me a lot of much-needed confidence."

"Cool. So what happened next?"

"We played like the team that went to the World Series the year before. Watching the way Mickey dealt with his injury was inspirational to the entire team. He didn't let it get him down at all, and if it did, he didn't show it. He chose to move forward instead of wallowing in self-pity."

"So, he put the team above himself."

"Yes, he did, and no one appreciated it more than I did. I needed that encouragement more than anyone, because I had some big shoes to fill."

"I'll say you did. The guy won the league MVP the year before, but like you always say, Mr. Graham, God puts you places for a reason."

Arthur laughed.

"He sure does, Lincoln. No one was more grateful to Him for that than I was."

"So, did you start to win again?"

"We did. You remember we started out 2-9?"

Lincoln shook his head yes. "Yep."

"We went 6-2 in the next eight to go to 8-11. I played five games in a row, and in that stretch, I went 9 for 21 with two home runs, and threw out six out of eight guys trying to steal."

Lincoln just stared at him with a look of admiration on his face. "That's awesome, Mr. Graham."

"The only word I can use to describe it is blessed." He smiled as he looked up into the blue sky. "And Esther was so supportive. She took care of so much around the house and did so much just so I could live out my dream. I thank God every day for that woman."

"Yep, she's a real peach," Lincoln stated as he threw the birds some crumbs.

Arthur laughed and ruffled his hair.

"You know one thing that I was proudest of during that 6-2 stretch?"

Lincoln looked up at him and asked, "What?"

"I threw out Jimmie Foxx twice trying to steal a base."

Lincoln looked at him, confused.

"Was he a good player?"

Arthur laughed.

"I'm sorry, son. I forget that you're only twelve sometimes. Jimmie Foxx was an outstanding baseball player. He started playing in the majors when he was only 17 years old."

"Whoa! He must have been good."

"He was. He played for 20 years. Jimmy won the World Series twice, the league MVP three times, was a nine-time all-star, and won a Triple Crown."

"What's a Triple Crown?"

"It's a very rare feat for a baseball player. It's when you lead the league in home runs, RBIs, and average in the same season. Only 18 players in the game's history have done it until now."

"That's cool. And you threw him out twice trying to steal?"

"Yep. In fairness to Jimmy, stealing bases wasn't his strong suit. In his 20-year career, he stole less than 100."

"So what? You threw out a Triple Crown winner."

Arthur laughed. "I guess I did. I like the way you think, kid."

"Thanks, Mr. Graham. I like the way you tell a story."

"Here comes your dad. Tomorrow we'll start out with the next series against the Yankees and a Mr. Lou Gehrig."

"I've definitely heard of him. I can't wait. See you tomorrow, Mr. Graham."

Lincoln gave him a big hug and then ran to meet his dad. Arthur smiled.

"See you tomorrow, Lincoln."

Chapter 13
Friday—July 18, 1980

It was 5:00 a.m. and Arthur was already out of bed and at the kitchen table enjoying a cup of coffee, a hard-boiled egg, and some wheat toast. He had his Bible open to the book of 1 Timothy, chapter two. This Bible belonged to his grandfather. It was comically large in print because his grandfather's eyesight was so bad, but now Arthur could appreciate it. He loved to read the pages that had notes from his grandfather, and over the years, he added plenty of his own. He took a sip of coffee and refocused. Arthur read verse four softly to himself.

"Who desires all men to be saved and to come to the knowledge of the truth."

This passage always hit him in the heart. He held back tears as a lump developed in his throat. Arthur closed his eyes and said, "Thank you, Father." He opened them and then ran his fingers over the note his grandfather had written by the verse. "Our God is an awesome God." On one special trip to Rome, Arthur was standing in front of the Colosseum with Esther and a team from his church. He placed his hand on one of the outer walls. He closed his eyes and prayed for all the innocent blood that had been shed in the arena, and something profound came over him. Arthur opened his eyes and then walked over and stood on a nearby bench. He preached to no one in particular, and before he knew it, he was surrounded by groups of people listening to him speak about the grace of God. Arthur talked about Christ's crucifixion and resurrection, and the sacrifice of the Apostle Paul to bring that message to the Gentiles at the cost of his own life. He ended his sermon with two verses that sum up God's unconditional love and grace toward us all. 1 Timothy 2:4, and 2 Peter 3:9 which states, "The Lord is not slack concerning His promises, as some count slackness, but is long suffering toward us, not willing that any should perish but that all should come to repentance." He looked out at the silenced crowd and reminded them that Jesus was coming back, but that God's eternal love for us delayed His return so that all His children could repent and know His glory. When he was finished, he stepped down off the bench, wiped his brow, and then sat down. He doesn't remember the exact number of people who were there that day. A hundred and fifty, maybe two hundred. But he remembers the sixteen people who approached his team and gave their lives to the Lord. He ran his fingers over his grandfather's note again. "Our God is an awesome God." A phrase that stayed at the front of his mind for his entire life.

It was now 7:30 a.m. in the Fisher household, and Lincoln sat in his bed with his back against the wall. Chris opened the door to wake him up.

"Lincoln, it's time…" He stopped when he saw him. "What's wrong, son?"

Lincoln looked over at his dad.

"Nothing. I was just thinking."

Chris came in and sat down on the corner of the bed.

"About what?"

"Do you read your Bible in the morning or do any type of devotions when you get up?"

"I don't. Usually, I sleep as late as I can and then get up in just enough time to grab some breakfast and then head out the door."

"Do you pray before you leave?"

Chris thought about lying to his son at this moment. He knew that reading the Bible and praying were important to a close relationship with God, but he had neglected both.

"I'm too ashamed to answer that question, son. I've been neglectful of both for some time now."

"That's okay, dad. Mr. Graham says that it's never too late."

He smiled, "I suppose Mr. Graham is right. What's got you thinking about this today?"

"I don't know. I just woke up early on my own, and it popped into my head. Then I prayed and asked Jesus to keep my family safe and asked Him to help me be a better person."

"Did you feel better after you prayed?"

"Yeah. I did. It made me feel like God was really listening to me. It made me feel closer to Him."

"That's what reading the Bible and praying do, buddy."

"I can see why Mr. Graham does it every morning. It's a great way to start the day."

Chris laughed.

"You know you can talk to Him throughout the day."

"Mr. Graham? I know."

"No," he laughed. "God. You don't have to bow your head or close your eyes to talk to Him."

"You just talk out loud. Won't people think you're nuts?"

"You talk to him in your head." Lincoln looked confused. "For example, when I'm working on a project and I'm trying to figure out the best way to do something, I take a minute to stop and pray in my head, 'Lord, please give me the knowledge to do this right.' That's praying."

"So, every time you talk to God, it's praying?"

"Yes. Even when you're just making a statement and not asking for something. Communication with Him is intimacy and closeness that He desires from us. Does that make sense?"

"I think so. What's an example of a statement to Him?"

"For one, praising Him. When I do a job that really makes the customer happy, I'll get into my truck to drive away and take a moment to say, 'Thank you, Lord, for helping me to make my customers happy.' I often say thank you to Him for your mom and all of you guys."

"Okay. I understand now. So, when I get a hit and I'm standing on base and I think, 'Thanks God for helping me get a hit,' that's talking to Him, and it makes Him happy?"

"Yes."

"Cool."

"I want you to know that we should still make time each day to read our Bible and pray to Him, because it's important."

"I know. Mr. Graham taught me that. He says that our prior…prior…prior…"

"Priorities?"

"Yeah, priorities are things that show what's important to us."

"That's right, and God should be at the top of that list."

"That's what he said."

Chris smiled and then looked at his watch.

"Let's go grab a bowl of cereal so we can continue this conversation at the table."

2

Lincoln walked up and sat down on the bench next to Arthur.

"Good morning, Mr. Graham."

"Good morning, Lincoln."

"Check this out," Lincoln stated as he smiled.

He pulled out a paper bag that he had hidden in his jacket. He opened it and showed Arthur a bag full of breadcrumbs.

"You brought your own bag today. Does your dad know you wasted all that bread?"

Lincoln laughed.

"He bought a new loaf at the store yesterday, and this was what's left of the old loaf. He said I could feed it to the birds because it was going to expire tomorrow."

"I guess they eat like kings today," Arthur stated as he smiled.

"I can see why you like feeding them. It's relaxing."

"Plus, it's a good way to get rid of old bread."

They looked at each other and laughed.

"I talked to my mom last night," he stated as he threw a handful on the ground.

"Oh yeah. That's nice. How are things going with your grandpa?"
He asked as he turned toward him.

"Good. She said that he is doing his rehab everyday now without a fight, and that grandma is doing good at getting him to do it."

"That sounds like real progress. Did she say when she would be home?"

"Next week."

"Are you excited to see her and your brother and sister?"

He smiled, "Yeah. I miss them. Dad said our bachelor days are almost over."

Arthur laughed. "I'm sure he'll be happy to see her, too."

"He misses her a lot."

"I bet." Arthur threw some crumbs onto the ground. "How was your game last night?"

"Good. I got a couple of hits, and we won."

"You're usually a little more animated about the games."

"When I do something great. I was just ordinary last night," he threw some crumbs.

Arthur smiled. "I see. Well, a win is a win. Congratulations."

"Thanks. My buddy Ned hit a nice home run."

"Are you sad because Ned hit the home run, and you didn't?"

"No. I just wish I had hit one too."

"Home runs aren't everything. Two base hits are nothing to scowl at. Do you know how many game's players will go without getting a hit at all? Do you know who Willie Mays is?"

"Of course I do. Dad said that he is one of the greatest of all time."

"That's right. Did you know he started his major league career 1 for 26?"

"One hit in 26 at-bats? Ouch!" Lincoln thought for a moment. "Didn't he hit a lot of home runs?"

"He did." Arthur nodded. "Okay, let's get back to the story."

Navin Field, Detroit, Michigan—May 13, 1935

Arthur was standing on first base. He had just driven a fastball from Yankee pitcher Lefty Gomez between the first and second base hole. The ball came back in from the right fielder, and Gomez stood behind the mound, shaking his head and talking to himself, clearly frustrated. The second baseman threw him the ball, and he resumed his position behind the rubber, staring at the catcher. Finally, the catcher called time and started his walk out to the mound. Arthur stood on first and watched. He heard laughter and then a voice to his right.

"He wanted to throw the curve, and Dickey made him throw the fastball."

Arthur looked to his right to see Lou Gehrig standing next to him.

"I guess he really wanted that curveball," Arthur responded as he smiled.

Gehrig extended his hand toward Arthur, and they shook.

"Lou," he stated, as if Arthur didn't know who he was.

"I know. Arthur," he responded.

"There's a lot of chatter about you, Arthur. How does it feel to finally be here?"

"Like I always thought it would. Amazing."

Gehrig laughed. "Whether you're twenty or forty, it always feels the same the first time you step onto your first major league field, I guess."

"I can't speak to the twenty-year-old part."

They both laughed together.

"I can," Gehrig answered. "Amazing is how I described it as well."

"How long do you think you'll play?" Arthur asked.

"Until I can't play anymore," he answered with a smile. "You?"

"I like that answer. I'm going to steal that one from you, too."

They laughed again. A little too loud this time as Gomez and Dickey stared over at them. Their conference on the mound ended, and

Dickey made his way back to the plate. Arthur took a lead at first as Gehrig straddled the bag and held his glove toward his pitcher. Gomez barely gave Arthur a look as he delivered to the plate. Gehringer took a strike and stepped out of the box and looked down to third. Arthur made his way back to the bag and waited for him to get set.

"He's not even giving you a second look, Arthur," Gehrig stated as he stood behind first.

"Are you trying to get me thrown out at second?" Arthur responded.

"Maybe," Gehrig replied with a smirk. "Billy is hard to run on. He's one of the best catchers I've ever seen."

"I know. An all-star the last two years."

Gehrig looked at him and smiled.

"You do your homework."

"I'm not just a pretty face," Arthur responded as Gomez got set and he took his lead.

Gehrig moved into position and held his glove toward his pitcher once more. Arthur glanced over at the third-base coach, who gave him the sign to steal. Gehringer was ready in the box and, without looking over at Arthur again, Gomez went into his motion. Arthur took off for second base. The fastball hit the catcher's mitt high and outside, and Dickey came up throwing. The ball sailed over the pitcher's head on a line and found the second baseman's glove perfectly in front of the bag. Just as the ball smacked the mitt, Arthur came sliding into second.

"Out!" screamed Dolly Stark, the second base umpire, who quickly reversed his call and screamed, "Safe!"

The ball had been kicked out of the second baseman's mitt as Arthur slid into the bag and was lying about six inches away. The second baseman stood and slammed his fist into his glove. Arthur called time and stood up to dust himself off. He looked over at Gehrig. Lou smiled and gave him a tip of the cap. Arthur tipped his cap back. The game resumed, and Gehringer doubled down into the left-field corner to bring Arthur in from second and give the Tigers a 1-0 lead at the end of the first. Tommy Bridges pitched a gem that day, throwing a nine-inning complete game, with five strikeouts, giving up four hits, and shutting out the Yankees 3-0. Arthur finished the day two for three with a walk, a stolen base, and a run scored. He threw out two baserunners and didn't allow a pitch to get past him in the win. After the game, Cochrane was questioned by some local reporters about the Tigers' chances of winning this season.

"Mickey. Do you think the team has a chance of repeating their success from last season?" Jack Williams of the Detroit Free Press asked.

He looked at Jack and answered, "I hope not."

"Why wouldn't…you want to…finish?" He stuttered.

Before he finished his statement, Cochrane rescued him.

"We don't want the runner-up prize. We want the championship," he stated as he smiled.

Williams laughed. "Poorly worded question on my part. Do you think the team has the firepower to win it all? After all, you are a huge piece of the puzzle that's missing."

"Jack, I have full confidence in this team, and in Arthur Graham, to lead us to the championship that this city deserves."

"Graham is going to be forty in two months. That doesn't concern you?"

"Why would that concern me? Arthur can play. End of story. You've seen him so far this season. What do you think about him?"

"I agree. He can hold his own against any catcher in the league from what I've seen so far. But do you think he can keep it up as the season wears on?"

"I have no reason to believe he can't." Cochrane answered.

The questions then shifted from Arthur to the team overall, and then eventually to Greenberg and his big bat. At the conclusion of the interview, the two shook hands, and Williams left to go write his story. Cochrane walked down into the dugout to grab a few of his things. He sat down on the bench and thought about William's question. "Do you think he can keep it up as the season wears on?"

He didn't know. That same question was in the back of his head when he went down, and Arthur started to play on a regular basis. Thirty-nine going on forty wasn't over the hill, but could he play consistently well for a hundred and fifty plus games? He looked up into the heavens and smiled.

"I guess we'll find out," he stated out loud.

In the second game of the series, the Tigers scored runs on every Yankee pitcher and walked away with a 10-4 win. Arthur caught his second game in a row and went three for four with a home run and two RBIs. In the third game of the set, New York dug in and walked away with a 4-0 win. Arthur went one for three with a walk and threw out one baserunner trying to steal. The Tigers took two out of the three games and improved to 10-12 on the season after starting 2-9. Williams stood outside the Yankee locker room, hoping to grab one of them for an interview before they got on the bus and headed back to New York. He was pleasantly surprised when the first one out of the room was Gehrig.

"Lou. Jack Williams, Detroit Free Press. Can I get an interview?"

"Sure," Gehrig stated as he stepped off to the side with the reporter.

"You guys got a 4-0 win today to end the series. What do you think was the difference between today and the first two games?"

"We scored more runs than they did," he stated with a smile.

"What happened to the offense in the first two games?"

"We went up against some tough pitching, and they brought their bats."

"Do you see the Tigers as your biggest obstacle to the pennant moving forward?"

"It's too early to tell, but it's a lot of the same players from last year's team. So, I would say they are definitely an obstacle. You can't count out Cleveland or Boston, though."

"Most of the same players, but they are minus a league MVP in Cochrane."

"Yeah, that was a tough break. Mickey's a great ballplayer, but they seem to have found another guy who can get it done."

"So you think Arthur Graham can fill the shoes of Cochrane?"

"I don't know all about that, but he's a good ballplayer."

"He's a 39, soon to be 40-year-old rookie."

Gehrig looked at Williams.

"Is there a question in there? You act like the guy has never played the game and suddenly decided he was going to pick up a bat this year. He's a seasoned player who finally got a chance that was long overdue. He's your guy on your team. Show him a little respect."

With that, Gehrig ended the interview and walked away. Williams stood stunned as he watched Gehrig get onto the bus. Williams folded his pad shut and headed for his car.

4

Arthur sat there staring at the birds with a big smile on his face.

"Mr. Gehrig had your back," Lincoln stated as he smiled.

"That's who he was. He was one of the very best to play the game, and he was just an all-around good guy." He laughed. "Jack didn't write that part in his article. He told me that a couple of years later, while we were having lunch."

"You went to lunch with that guy?"

"Sure. We had our differences here and there, but he was a good guy. He was a devoted member of this church for many years before he went to be with the Lord."

"You mean died."

"That's one way to put it, and it's true. But I prefer to state it in its truest form."

"I bet he got to interview a lot of famous ballplayers."

"He did. That's one reason I loved having lunch with him. I got to hear so many marvelous stories from those interviews."

"Still. Gehrig zinged him pretty good," he smirked.

"Yes, he did," Arthur smirked back.

"You guys were winning again, and you were playing good," he stated, changing the subject.

"I think the guys realized that even without Mickey behind the plate, we were a good team. Mickey was a great manager. He loved to match wits with other managers. Even though he couldn't catch, he was still the backbone of that team."

"My dad would say that he's a 'well-rounded guy.'"

"Your dad would be right. Mick is a perfect example of true sportsmanship. He was the very definition of a team player."

"So, did you keep winning?"

"We won six out of the next seven games to go to 16-13." Arthur smiled. "I remember we were in Boston playing the Sox, they had beaten us the night before, breaking our five-game winning streak, and as I passed by the front desk to get on the team bus to go to the game, the front desk told me I had a call."

"The front desk? Why didn't they call your room?" Lincoln asked.

"It was a little different back in those days. Hotels were getting phones in rooms, but some hotels only had them at the front desk, or in the hotel lobby."

Lincoln laughed, "Weird."

"Technology today is much more advanced. They say that within the next 20 years, people will carry a phone wherever they go."

"Wouldn't that be something?"

"It would. I don't know if it'll happen, but you never know. Anyway, I took the call at the desk, and it was Esther."

"Was something wrong?" He asked, worried.

"No. She just wanted to hear my voice. We were nine games into a twelve-game road trip, and she just missed me." He smiled. "I missed her too. And Dillard, of course. We only had a couple of minutes, so we told each other I love you and then she handed the phone to Dillard, who was turning 10 in a couple of months. He said, 'Daddy. Can you do me a favor and hit a home run over that big wall in left field?' I told him I would do my best, and he said, 'Just do it, please.' I told him I loved him and then got on the bus."

"I want to hit a home run over the Green Monster someday."

"Did you know it wasn't actually painted green until 1947?"

"What did they call it before that, then?"

"I guess they just called it a wall."

"Hmmmmmm... I bet it's robbed a lot of home runs in its day."

"I bet it has. It's quite a sight when you stand at home plate and stare at it."

"That's so cool," Lincoln stated with a big smile on his face. "What is?"

"You played at Fenway Park. Stared at the green, er, the wall. So cool."

Arthur laughed. "I guess that is pretty cool."

"Did you do it, Mr. Graham? Did you hit the home run?"

Arthur smiled and continued his story.

5

Fenway Park, Boston—May 25, 1935

Arthur was playing catch with Hank Greenberg along the third-base line to warm up for the game. Next to Cochrane, Greenberg had been one of Arthur's biggest supporters. They would remain friends for many years after baseball. When they had finished warming up, Greenberg jogged over to Arthur and handed him the ball.

"Who called you at the hotel?" Greenberg asked.

"My wife and son. They wanted to let me know they miss me."

"That's nice." Greenberg smiled. "It can be tough being out on the road for long stretches when you're a family man. I'm not there yet, but I can imagine."

"It is tough. I miss them."

"Just three more games after today, and we'll be home. Hang in there, pal."

"I will, thanks." Arthur laughed. "Dillard asked me to hit a home run over that big wall. When I told him I would try, he got really serious and said, 'Just do it.'"

Greenberg looked him in the eye. "Arthur, you've gotta do it."

Arthur smiled. "I'll try, but I couldn't promise the kid I would."

"You'll do it. If that kid wants his old man to hit a home run over that big wall in left, he will."

"I'm no Babe Ruth."

"There's only one Babe Ruth, but you're probably going to have four tries at it today, so like the kid said, 'Just do it.'"

Arthur really didn't know what else to say except, "Okay."

Greenberg slapped him on the back.

"That's a boy, Artie. In honor of the kid, I'll hit one too."

Arthur smiled. "I'll tell him you said that."

"Whoa. Don't tell the kid unless I actually hit one. You can't go around promising to hit home runs for people. The odds are never in your favor. Were no Babe Ruth, for crying out loud."

Greenberg smiled.

Arthur gave him a playful shove, and they headed into the dugout to get ready for the game.

Jo Jo White was in the box leading off the game in the top of the first. On the hill today for the Red Sox was the lefty, Fritz Ostermueller. He was an above-average pitcher who could bring the heat. He often relied on his fastball in most situations, which didn't bode well for him in the later innings. Hitters usually figured him out by then, which made it hard for him to pitch a complete game. Arthur watched the first pitch cross the plate from the batter's box. A fastball that was high and touched the inside corner for a strike. He dropped to a knee and bowed his head.

"Lord. I know it's silly to pray for a home run today, but I've gotta ask. It's for my kid. He's a good kid, and I love him. I

181

know that baseball is a game, and your will isn't centered on games, but I would really appreciate it if I could put a smile on Dillard's face. Anyway, as always, I ask that your will be done on this earth as it is in heaven. Amen."

He opened his eyes to see White walking back from the plate. He stood, and as he passed by him, White stopped him.

"His fastball isn't great today. I just missed it."

"Thanks," Arthur responded.

He made his way into the box and dug in. Arthur crowded the plate today with the theory that if he could just get the barrel on the ball with a full swing, he could pull it down the line and would have a better chance of at least hitting the wall. If he hit it, he could tell Dillard that he gave it his best shot. His fear was that he would come nowhere close to it today and his son would think that he didn't even try. Two practice swings later, his bat was on his shoulder, and he was watching Ostermueller go into the windup. His mind was a million miles away when the first pitch came in high and hard. It was a fastball that would have hit him square in the jaw if he had kept daydreaming. He snapped out of it just in time to drop his bat, lean back, and hit the deck. The ball popped the catcher's mitt.

"Ball," the umpire shouted.

Half of the Tiger team was on their feet in the dugout yelling at Ostermueller, while the other half yelled at the home plate umpire. Time was called while Arthur picked himself up off the ground and the umpire cleaned the plate with his brush. The Tiger players were still up out of their seats as Arthur stepped back into the box to get ready for the next pitch. He noticed that the indents from his feet were almost over the line in the box and understood why Ostermueller backed him off of the plate. No pitcher liked it when a hitter crowded the plate. This time when he stepped back in, he backed up almost ten inches and dug in. Ostermueller got the ball back from the catcher and shot him a smirk.

"Forget the home run, Lord. Please, just help me survive," he asked as he swallowed.

"Time," the umpire called and then looked at Arthur. "Did you say something?"

"No, sir," Arthur responded, a little embarrassed.

"Play ball," he shouted.

The next pitch was another fastball, but this landed right down the middle of the plate as Arthur leaned back from it.

"Strike one," the umpire shouted.

Arthur looked over into the Boston dugout to see players laughing and mimicking his actions. He took a deep breath and stepped back in. He was angry now. Arthur wanted to show both the Red Sox players and his own teammates that he wasn't scared. He dug in deep and stared Ostermueller down. The condescending look on his face only fueled his anger. He gripped the bat tightly and waited. The next pitch came in, and Arthur swung with all his might. It was a curveball that ended low and way outside, and his bat didn't even come close to touching it. He stumbled as he swung and had to catch his balance before he fell to the ground.

"Strike two," the umpire shouted.

The Boston dugout was alive with laughter. Arthur cleared his throat and looked into his own dugout. Cochrane was on the top step with both hands pushing down, mouthing "easy." He looked past him to see some of his own teammates hiding their faces or smiling, trying to fight back the laughter. He walked over to the box and stood just outside it for a moment. Arthur whispered to himself, "The worst is behind you. Now just play ball." He stepped into the box and steadied himself. Ostermueller stood on the mound staring at his catcher. He got the sign he was looking for and went into his windup. Arthur watched as the curveball landed low and outside again.

"Ball two," the umpire shouted.

There was clapping coming from the Red Sox dugout. He ignored it and stepped back in. The count was two balls and two strikes. He steadied himself once again and waited for the pitch. The fastball came in high and toward the inside corner. Arthur swung at the last minute and was able to get a piece, sending it out of play and foul down the third base line. The next four pitches were a combination of different pitches, and Arthur was able to foul all of them off to stay alive. Ostermueller was getting visibly frustrated with him, and the ninth pitch of the at-bat was a curveball that stayed inside and low, backing Arthur out of the way.

"Ball three," the umpire shouted.

The count was now 3-2, and the Boston dugout was silent. Arthur took an extra minute to collect his thoughts before he stepped back into the box. He knew Ostermueller did not want to walk him. He also knew that earlier in the at-bat, Ostermueller had thrown him a fastball right after backing him out of the box. Arthur stepped back in and dug in. He watched as the pitcher got his sign, and the catcher set up. He waited patiently for the tenth pitch of the at-bat as Ostermueller took a little longer than usual. The agitated pitcher went into his windup and delivered. It was a fastball that started and stayed belt high as it headed toward the inside edge of the plate. Arthur pulled his hands in and stepped forward as he swung. The ball leaped off the barrel of the bat as he followed through and made solid contact. He watched as the ball headed for the wall in left. Arthur didn't move from the box and seemed oblivious to the shouts of his teammates to "Run!" The ball just kept traveling toward that wall, rising as it went. Finally, it cleared the top of the wall and landed on the street. Arthur smiled as he flipped his bat and pumped his fist. As he ran toward first, he looked over at the mound to see Ostermueller staring at him, arms crossed, mouthing something that he couldn't make out. He rounded first and headed to second. He felt as if he were walking on air. Arthur slapped Del

Baker's hand as he rounded third and headed for home. Ostermueller never broke his stance or his stare. When Arthur finally touched the plate and headed for his dugout, the disgruntled pitcher walked toward him yelling. "You don't show a guy up like that." The umpire yelled at him to get back on the mound. Arthur was still reeling from the home run and didn't really comprehend what was going on. When he made it into the dugout, he walked toward the end, giving high fives to every player and coach along the way. He made it to the end and sat down to put on his equipment. Tommy Bridges sat next to him.

"That was a great shot, Artie," he stated as he slapped him on the back.

"Thanks, Tommy," he answered back.

"You know you're getting beaned when you go back up. Right?" Arthur stopped putting on his gear and looked over at him. "What?"

"Yeah. You can't show a guy up like that and not expect to get hit the next time you go to the plate."

"I wasn't trying to show him up. I was just happy I had hit the home run. It was for my kid."

"That's nice, but you're getting beaned. Hopefully, he throws a curve and not a fastball. My advice. When it happens, just smile and take your base. At that point, it should be over."

"And if I don't?"

"He'll probably hit Hank or Charlie. We don't want to take a chance of their getting hurt. So just smile and take your base." He patted Arthur on the knee and walked over to talk to one of the other pitchers. Arthur sat there, staring at the floor. He chuckled to himself and resumed putting on his equipment. If that's the way it had be, he was still glad he hit the home run. The inning ended, and he headed out onto the field. When he came to bat in the third inning, there was a man on second with two outs, and the Tigers were still ahead 1-0. He stepped into the box and braced himself. The first pitch was a fastball on the

185

outside corner for a strike. He stepped out and breathed a sigh of relief. Maybe Bridges was wrong. He stepped back into the box and dug in. The second pitch started inside and stayed inside. The curveball plunked him squarely on the left thigh. He grimaced for a moment, but then tossed his bat aside and jogged down to first. When he got to first, he looked over at Ostermueller and nodded. He didn't nod back or say a word. He turned back toward his catcher to face the next batter. In the sixth, Greenberg made good on his promise to Arthur and hit a two-run homer to give the Tigers a 3-0 lead. The Red Sox scored a run in the seventh and ninth, but the Tigers walked away with the win 3-2 that day on another great pitching performance by Tommy Bridges.

6

"Did it hurt?" Lincoln asked.
"It stung for about 10 minutes, but it went away."
"Did you cry?"
Arthur laughed. "No, I didn't cry."
"Did you want to?"
"I kind of did." Arthur smiled. "Have you been hit by a pitch before?"
"Yep. It hurts. I didn't cry, even though I wanted to."
"If you did, that's okay."
"Are you kidding me? If you cry, the fellas with never let you live it down."
Arthur laughed. "I suppose you're right."
"Was Dillard happy that you hit him the home run?"
"He was thrilled, and even happier when I told him that Hank hit one for him too."
Lincoln just sat on the bench, smiling.
"Did you ever talk to the guy who hit you and ask him why?"

"No. I knew why. Tommy was right. You don't show pitchers up like that. I was just thankful it was a curveball in the thigh and not a fastball in the ear," he laughed.

"A guy would probably cry if he got hit in the coconut."

Arthur laughed, "'The coconut.'"

"That's what my dad calls it."

"I like it."

"I'd like to go to Fenway Park someday to see a game."

"Maybe you will. It's very impressive. Maybe you'll play there someday."

"That would be awesome. Can you imagine if I did and hit a home run in the same spot you did?"

"I would love that for you, Lincoln. Then you would know exactly what I felt."

"So, you guys were back on your winning ways again?"

"Until the next game in New York, when we lost to the Yankees. We lost two in a row before we finally won the third game of the series. But then we got to go home for eight in a row."

"I bet your family was happy."

"They were, and so was I. I missed them something fierce."

"So at the end of your road trip, what was your record?"

"We were 18-16. We were on the right track. I know it doesn't seem like it, but we were really putting things together as a team. I was enjoying the game a lot."

"I bet. You were hitting homers and playing good defense."

"Throughout my twenty years of playing, I always played best when I enjoyed the game. When I got angry or frustrated, my game always suffered. I just needed to trust in my God-given talents and enjoy playing the game I was so fortunate to be a part of."

"It's hard when you're playing badly or in a slump."

"That's true, but I think we get into slumps when we overthink things so much, instead of just doing what we've been doing to be successful. In 1935, I was just playing the way I knew how to

187

play. Trusting in my experience and in my teammates to pick me up when I wasn't playing so well."

"Here comes my dad. I got to go early because he has a dentist appointment."

"I'll see you at the game tomorrow."

"Okay, Mr. Graham. See you tomorrow."

With that, he jumped off the bench and sprinted to meet his dad. Arthur laughed. What he could do with all that energy.

Chapter 14
Saturday—July 19, 1980

Arthur and Esther found a seat on the bleachers and watched as Lincoln and Chris played catch off to the side of the team dugout. Lincoln stopped momentarily to wave at them. They waved back, and he resumed playing catch.

"He has a good arm," Esther commented as she watched him.

"He really does," Arthur responded. "I think he would make a fine catcher."

A familiar voice to Arthur's right interjected.

"I think you're right."

They turned to see Chet Michaels sitting next to Arthur with a big smile on his face. Arthur returned the smile, and they shook hands. Esther reached across Arthur, and Chet took her hand and shook it gently.

"Chet, how are you?" She asked.

"I can't complain. You still look as young and beautiful as ever, Esther." He looked at Arthur. "You look like you've aged 100 years."

They all laughed.

"It must be like looking in a mirror," Arthur fired back.

More laughter.

"What brings you both here today? One of your grandkids?"

"No," Arthur answered. "Chris has been doing some renovations at the church, and young Lincoln there has been spending some time with me while his dad works. I have been telling him about baseball in the old days."

Chet smiled. "The good old days. We had some fun."

"We sure did. How long has it been since we've seen each other?"

Chet scratched his chin as he thought about it.

"Five years."

"Eight," Esther corrected him. "You moved to Arizona, and we lost touch."

"That long? I guess I hadn't realized how much time had passed," Chet responded.

"How's Shirley doing?" Esther asked.

"She passed almost two years ago," he answered.

"I'm so sorry, Chet. Shirley was a wonderful woman."

"She was one of a kind. Thankyou."

"I'm sorry, Chet," Arthur stated. "Why didn't you call?"

"It had been a while since we had seen each other. I was out of sorts for a long time after that. We had moved away and made a handful of close friends who were great, but I closed myself off after Shirley passed, and they eventually stopped calling. My daughter Melissa and her husband made the trip out and convinced me to come back about six months ago. They have a guest house, so I moved in there. I heard you retired."

"I did. It's been a few years now. Dillard took over."

"That's great. How's the church doing?"

"Fantastic. He's got a knack for preaching."

"I wonder where he learned that?" Chet smiled.

"Chet, why don't you come over to the house for dinner tonight? We can catch up."

"I can't tonight, but I'm free tomorrow night."

"Then it's settled. Tomorrow night at five for dinner," Esther pronounced.

"Tomorrow at five," Chet responded.

"Is lasagna okay?" Esther asked.

"You remembered," Chet stated.

She knew it was his favorite. Arthur slapped his old friend on the knee.

"Tomorrow at five for lasagna. It's settled. I see Jamie out there. Is he as good as his great-grandpa?"

Chet looked away and asked, "So, how about those Tigers this year?"

They all laughed. The players took the field, and the game started.

The game ended with Lincoln's team losing 12-4. Esther told Arthur that she was going to the car and that she would wait for him there. He walked over to a dejected Lincoln sitting on the bench, with Chris trying to console him.

"You'll get em next time, buddy," Chris encouraged him.

"We stink," Lincoln yelled with his arms folded and his lip out.

"Lincoln," Chris said firmly. "I don't want to hear you say that again. These guys out here tried their best. Sit here while I help the coach clean up, and then we'll head home."

Chris walked over to Arthur, and they shook hands.

"Kids taking it pretty hard, huh?" Arthur asked.

"Yeah. I'm not really digging this attitude. He's never really acted like this before. I don't know what to do. My first instinct is to yell, but I don't think that will help."

"Let me talk to him."

"Thanks, Arthur."

He turned to go help the coach, and Arthur took a seat next to Lincoln on the bench.

"So, 12-4. Not the team's best effort," he started out.

"We stink," Lincoln stated again, this time a little lower.

"You know you're a part of that 'we?'"

Lincoln looked up at him, tears in his eyes.

"I did good."

"Oh, so when you say 'we', you really mean they?"

"They didn't play the best today."

"Which of your teammates let the ball go through their legs today at third, allowing two runs to score?"

"Me," he stated as he looked away.

"Who struck out with men on second and third in the third inning when it was only 4-2?"

"Are you trying to make me feel bad, Mr. Graham?"

"No, son. I'm just trying to put things in perspective for you. Maybe the team didn't play great today, and maybe you had a better game than most, but you were far from perfect."

Lincoln's attitude softened.

"I hate to lose. It hurts."

"Nobody likes to lose, Lincoln. But it's part of the game. Who won the World Series last year?"

"The Pirates. They beat the Orioles."

"How many games did the Pirates lose last season?"

"I don't know."

"64. They were 98-64."

"They were probably really mad that they lost 64." Arthur looked down at him and stared. Lincoln broke the silence with laughter. "Okay, not too mad."

"When you play a team sport, your focus has to be on the team. They can feed off of good energy, or bad. So, when they see you sulking and yelling out things like, 'We stink,' that can affect the way they play. Lincoln, you're one of the best players on the team. Since I've gotten to know you and we've spent some together, I see someone who could be a leader."

"I want to be a leader," he interrupted.

"A leader picks the team up. He doesn't bring them down. In our story, when the great Mickey Cochrane injured his knee, did he bring the team down by sulking and being negative?"

"No."

"No, he didn't. He was a leader. He supported us and encouraged us in every way he could. When a guy was going through a slump, he didn't throw in the towel and criticize him. He did everything he could to help him. It's easy to be a good winner, but we must also be gracious when we lose. You don't have to like it, but you should respect it."

Lincoln looked around to see his team walking with their parents toward the parking lot. Their heads were down, and no one was talking.

"Maybe I could talk to them at the next practice and encourage them."

"Start out by apologizing."

"Okay." He dropped his head and continued, "but I still feel lousy inside from the loss."

"That's okay. It'll pass."

"Thanks, Mr. Graham. I'm going to go help my dad and coach pick up the rest of the equipment."

"Okay, Lincoln. I'll see you on Monday?"

"I'm coming to the church with my dad later today. Are you going to be there?"

"Yes. I just figured you wanted to go play with one of your friends today."

"I don't feel much like playing today."

"Okay then. I'll see you later."

"Thanks for coming to my game. Tell Esther I said thanks, will ya?"

"I will. See you later, Lincoln."

Arthur stood up, and Lincoln sprinted toward his dad. Chris looked up and waved to Arthur. He waved back and then turned to head to the car.

2

Arthur sat on the bench, feeding the birds. Lincoln walked up and sat down.

"Feeling any better, young Mr. Lincoln?"

"Yes, sir." He smiled. "Me and my dad had a long talk on the car ride home. He basically told me the same thing you did, and then he gave me an example of when he was a poor sport when he played. He actually shoved one of his teammates after a loss. I don't want to get to that point."

"It sounds like he learned from his mistake."

"You'd think, but he did it again about two weeks later. The kid fell

193

and sprained his wrist. The coach kicked him off the team, and my grandpa had to pay his medical bills. Grandpa also made him go over to the kid's house once a week and do his chores."

"Hard lesson learned."

Lincoln laughed, "Yep."

"Did your dad ever tell you that story before?"

"No, he said he was waiting for the right time."

"I guess he found it."

"Did you ever do anything like that?"

"Yes, but I skipped those parts."

"Why?"

"Because it paints me in a dark light. Nobody wants to be thought of as a hothead. It was about five years into my Texas League years. I developed an attitude of superiority. I thought we should win every game, and if we didn't, then I would get angry. Even in the games that I caused our loss, I blamed others. It wasn't a pretty sight."

"How did you get over that feeling?"

"I had a great support system. I had Esther, my parents, and Mr. Dillard. Their love and support meant everything to me. They always came at me with love and gentleness, and there were many times that we prayed together and asked God to help me with my anger. It subsided over time, and God revealed to me that my ability to play baseball was a blessing, and I wasn't being thankful for that blessing by dishonoring Him with my actions. I wasn't being a very good example for Him with all that anger and resentment. So, over time, I learned to enjoy his blessing in my life."

"So, you didn't get mad anymore at all?"

Arthur laughed.

"I wish. I still get mad from time to time, but I take a deep breath and ask Him to intervene for me. To give me peace in the moment. To give me love and forgiveness in my heart above all else."

"That works?"

"Most of the time," Arthur smiled at him.

Lincoln laughed and then pivoted the conversation back to his story.

"Yesterday you beat the Red Sox and hit a home run over the monster, but then the Yankees beat you two out of three.?"

"They did, but as the season progressed, we put together some impressive winning streaks." Arthur tapped his chin and thought for a moment. "Let's move ahead to the midpoint of the season."

"Aren't we going to miss a lot of baseball games?" Lincoln interrupted.

"You didn't expect me to talk about every single game, did you? We'd be here for weeks. Trust me, this story still has a lot of baseball left."

"Okay. I just didn't want to miss anything important."

"You won't. Let's jump to Game 76. We were on a nine-game winning streak and finishing up a home series with the St. Louis Browns."

3

Navin Field, Detroit, Michigan—July 7, 1935

Arthur was playing his 65th game of the season. He was holding up remarkably well, and Cochrane was taking advantage of it. He was mowing down baserunners at close to a 65% rate, and his offensive numbers were really helping the team. His batting average was strong at .335, with 13 home runs and 44 RBIs. He was sitting on the third-base side, stretching, when Cochrane walked over to him.

"How are you feeling?" Cochrane asked.

"Great," he responded.

"I was thinking about going with the kid today behind the plate. You've played the last nine games in a row."

"I can handle it, Mick, besides we're on a nine-game winning streak. It would be bad luck to pull me now." Arthur smiled.

"I would really hate to overplay you and wear you out."

"Is this because I turned 40 a week and a half ago?"

"It certainly is a factor."

"On my 40th birthday in Chicago, how did I do?"

"You went 4 for 4 with a homer and 3 RBIs in a 9-5 win." He scratched his chin. "I just don't want to lose you down the stretch."

"You won't. I feel great, and besides, my kids here today."

He pointed up into the stands. Sitting in the third row were Esther and Dillard. He smiled and waved to them, and they waved back.

"Fine, but if you feel any pain anywhere, you promise to tell me so I can get you out. Deal?"

"Deal. Thanks Mick."

Mickey walked back into the dugout and scribbled something on the lineup card. Just before the game, he walked out to home plate and handed the umpire the card, and shook hands with the St. Louis manager, who did the same. The game started, and Arthur took his position behind the plate. The 24-year-old Elden Auker was on the mound today. He was 7-3 on the season and had developed a solid rapport with Arthur. With one on and two out in the top of the first, Moose Solters stepped to the plate. Solters was a powerful kid whom they had just acquired from Boston last month. He hit the fastball well, so Arthur's goal was to flood this at-bat with curveballs or breaking balls that would hopefully throw his timing off. He gave Auker the sign for a curveball to start the at-bat, and Auker shook it off. Arthur then gave him the sign for the breaking ball, and Auker shook that one off as well. Arthur finally flashed the sign for a fastball low and inside, and he received the nod from his uncooperative pitcher. Solters dug into the box and waited for the pitch. Auker went into the windup and delivered. The fastball failed to go low and inside and headed right for the center of the plate. Solters took one giant step forward and put everything he had into the swing. He connected. The ball leaped off the bat and headed for the centerfield wall. Arthur stood and watched from behind the plate as the centerfielder took two steps back and then stopped. He turned to watch the ball land ten rows up into the seats and then turned to see Solter rounding the bases. St. Louis took an early 2-0 lead. The next batter struck out, and the Tigers headed into the dugout to bat in the bottom of the first. Auker walked over and sat next to Arthur.

"I guess I should have thrown the curveball," he joked.

"It's early. We'll get em back for you."

"He hit it pretty far."

"Yes, he did."

They looked at each other and laughed. Arthur was up third in the inning, so he removed his gear and waited for his at-bat. White and Gehringer both got on with base hits to start the inning. White stood on third and Gehringer on first. Arthur stepped to the plate and dug in. The Browns pitcher, Fay Thomas, was a 23-year-old righty who was on his fourth team in as many years. The young man from Southern California was having a hard time finding his rhythm in the majors. His first two pitches were both inside and low. The count was 2-0, with Greenberg looming on deck. Arthur fouled off the next two pitches, both fastballs up and away, to run the count to 2-2. The fifth pitch of the at-bat missed badly down and in, and the count was now 3-2. Arthur stepped out of the box and looked down the third base line, not at his coach, but at Esther and Dillard. His son was leaning in, watching his dad carefully. He smiled at Esther, and she smiled back. Arthur stepped back in and waited for the pitch. He wanted to hit this ball over the fence so badly for his family. He wanted them to be proud of him. The curveball came in so far outside that Arthur needed an ore to hit it.

"Ball four," the umpire screamed.

Arthur tossed his bat toward the Tiger bench and jogged down to first to take his base. He knew a walk would help the team, especially with Hammerin Hank batting next, but he wanted to be the one that Dillard cheered as he delivered a clutch hit. He stood on first and watched as time was called and the catcher walked out and talked to his pitcher. While they talked about strategy, his mind wandered to the dream he had last night.

He was waiting in the on-deck circle to hit. The Tigers were playing the Yankees, and Babe Ruth was on the mound. The Babe was striking out batters left and right. It was the bottom of the ninth inning, and the Yankees were beating the Tigers 5-0, and Ruth was throwing a no-hitter. He heard the umpire yell, "Strike three," and Greenberg walked by him, head down, whispering something to himself. Arthur looked over at his dugout, and Cochrane was standing on the top step, staring at him.
"It's up to you, Arthur."
"What is?" He asked.
"Break up this no-hitter. Don't let the team down."
He made his way to the plate and stared out at Ruth. The Babe laughed at him.
"This is who you send out?" He sneered and shook his head in disbelief. "'Am I a dog that you come to me with sticks?'"
"What?" Arthur whispered to himself as he stepped out of the box. He composed himself and stepped back in, but as he went to raise his bat, the only thing he was holding was a Bible. He looked out at the mound, and Ruth was gone. Arthur was staring at a church congregation looking back at him. He looked down and noticed his Bible open to Proverbs chapter three, and underlined were verses five and six. "Trust in the Lord with all your heart, and lean not on your own understanding; In all your ways acknowledge Him, And he shall direct your paths." He looked back out at the congregation. Sitting in the front row were Cochrane, Gehringer, Greenberg, Bridges, and the whole Tiger team.

"Arthur," came the shout from the first base coach.
"Yeah," he answered as he shook his head.
"Get ready," came the reply.
He looked over at third to see White with a lead off the base. He then looked over at second to see Gehringer with his lead off of the base. Arthur looked in to see Greenberg standing at the plate, awaiting the pitch. Thomas went into his stretch, and Arthur took his

lead off first. Thomas delivered a curveball that hung too long, and Greenberg crushed it. All three runners took off. The ball sailed through the air as the center fielder gave chase. It hit maybe three inches below the top of the fence and caromed back into right center. The center fielder gave chase, and by the time he threw the ball back in, all three runners had crossed the plate and Greenberg was standing on third with a triple. The crowd cheered, and the Tigers grabbed the lead 3-2. The next batter, Goose Goslin, lined a single into leftfield and Greenberg scored, giving the Tigers a 4-2 lead, and chasing Thomas from the game. Arthur watched as the young pitcher sat in the opposing dugout, head down, screaming something into his mitt. He wanted to go over and talk to the young man, tell him that tomorrow is a new day, but of course, that wasn't possible at this moment. The new pitcher, Patrick "Sugar" Cain, came in and retired the next three batters in order. The Tigers took the field in the top of the second with a 4-2 lead. Auker struck out the side, and the Tigers came to bat in the bottom of the second. Cochrane made it known to the team that Cain was infamous for walking batters and asked that they be selective in their approach. The first batter of the inning was Auker. He promptly walked to the plate, and after five pitches, walked to first. White was the next batter. On a 3-2 count, he sent a line drive up the middle for a base hit. Gehringer stepped to the plate with two on and nobody out. He watched four straight pitches miss the strike zone and walked to first. Cochrane looked over at Arthur, who was standing in the on-deck circle.

"Choose your pitch, Arthur," he encouraged him.

Arthur nodded and headed to the plate. He could read between the lines. 'Choose your pitch' was code for, let him walk you. Arthur stepped into the box and took a couple of practice swings. He stared down at his bat to make sure that it wasn't a Bible and readied himself for the pitch. Cain went into his windup and fired a fastball high and outside.

"Ball one," the umpire screamed.

Arthur looked over into the St. Louis dugout. The manager was looking at the floor, shaking his head. Arthur got ready again and waited for the pitch. This time it was a curveball that broke down over the center of the plate.

"Strike," the umpire shouted.

The count was 1-1. The next two pitches missed badly to drive the count to 3-1. Arthur was once again disappointed. Dillard wouldn't see that his dad could be the hero. He stepped in and waited for what was inevitably going to be ball four. As Cain delivered the pitch, something came over him. Pride. As the curveball broke, Arthur stepped forward and swung. The ball landed a good foot outside, and Arthur didn't even come close to hitting it. He swung so hard that he lost his balance and fell to the ground. The catcher had to get out of the way to avoid being knocked over. Arthur sat up and looked over at Cochrane. The look on Mickey's face told him everything he needed to know. He watched as Cochrane looked over at the young catcher and pointed at him. Arthur picked himself up off the ground and took a couple of practice swings before stepping back into the box. He wanted to look over at his family, but he was too embarrassed.

"I'll take my walk, Lord," he whispered to himself.

He got ready as Cain went into his windup. The pitch came in belt high and right down the center of the plate. A fastball that wasn't really fast and had no movement. Arthur once again stepped forward and swung. The barrel of the bat connected with the ball and sent it down the left-field line. It didn't deviate one inch to the left or right and kept rising. The dugout was up, looking down the line, and the fans held their breath. It landed in the left field seats, and Arthur had just hit his first big league grand slam. The fans cheered loudly, and the dugout roared with both laughter and cheering. As Arthur approached third, he looked into the stands to see his wife and son on their feet, with everybody else cheering and smiling. He made it home, and the three on base were there to congratulate him. As he made it to the dugout, Cochrane slapped his hand, and he made his way all the way to the end, getting congratulated. He took a seat at the end of the bench. Cochrane came down and sat next to him.

"You know you're out of the game. Right?"

"Why…I…just." He couldn't get the words out. He was stuttering so badly.

"You could have walked easily. Instead, you put your own pride before the team's success and almost injured yourself. I can't have that."

"But Mick. I."

"This isn't up for discussion. Accept the decision and move on." Before Arthur could say another word, Cochrane was already gone and standing at the front of the dugout on the top step. He thought about Mickey's words. He wasn't wrong. Pride was in his heart, and if he had struck out or got injured, it would have hurt the team. He took the lesson and didn't say another word about it.

Later that night, he explained the decision by Mickey to Esther and Dillard after the game, because it was a good lesson for all of them. When Dillard was tucked in, they sat on the porch and enjoyed the nice cool breeze together.

"How are you feeling tonight, Arthur?" Esther asked.

"I feel great. Why do people keep asking me that? 40 isn't ancient." He responded.

"That was a nasty fall at the plate earlier today. I thought you might have injured something," she smiled as she paused, "but that was a much-needed breeze on a hot July day."

He laughed as he turned toward her. "I knew that pretty little head was thinking of something to zing me with."

"Stop being so sensitive. I was just concerned."

"I know." He smiled. "But I really got a hold of that next pitch."

"You sure did. That was four runs the fun way."

He put his arm around her.

"Thanks," he stated.

"For what?"

"Always being my rock."

"We're each other's rock, my love," she responded as she kissed his cheek.

"I had a crazy dream last night, and I thought about it today while I was standing on first waiting for Hank to hit."

He told her about the Babe Ruth dream, as it would come to be called later, and stated that he didn't really know what it meant.

"That's a wild dream. If it has any significant meaning, then He will reveal it to you in time."

"I guess. Maybe when I'm not so tired, I'll be able to figure it out."

"Maybe."

They sat there for a few more minutes together in silence. Enjoying the night.

"I'm not mad at Mick for taking me out," he stated out of the blue.

"Plus, it sounds like you both got what you wanted today."

"How do you mean?" he asked.

"Well. He got to teach you a lesson in pride, sure. But both of you benefited before that. He didn't really want to play you, and you wanted to show your son that you're a hero. The second inning gave both of you a chance to accomplish that. You hit the grand slam in front of Dillard, and he gets to take you out before you can get injured."

Arthur thought for a long moment about this.

"I guess it worked out for both of us." He smiled. "Now I get two days off before we have to be in Washington on the 10th."

"I'll take it," she smiled and hugged him.

4

"Man, I love that woman," Arthur stated as he smiled.

"A grand slam. You hit a grand slam. Mr. Graham, that's so awesome. I dream that one day I'll hit a grand slam in front of a sold-out stadium." Lincoln had stars in his eyes again.

"It was pretty cool. The best part was that I hit it in front of my son."

"Awesome, but why did you get two days off?"

"The All-Star game was on the next day, so we all got a couple of days off. Except for the fellas that had to play in it."

"You didn't make the All-Star team?"

"I did not. The ownership, team, and fans were angry about it, but I saw it as a chance to relax with my family and get a little rest. As much as I didn't want to admit it, my bones were aching."

"Who made it?"

"Mickey was the manager. Gehringer, Bridges, and Rowe made it."

"Hank didn't?"

"No, and there was outrage throughout the whole league on that one."

"Why didn't he make it?"

"That might be a story for another day. But just know that it made him so mad, he played the second half of the season with a big chip on his shoulder."

"I don't know what that means."

"Sorry," Arthur laughed. "He played with fire in his gut. He wanted to show everybody that Hank Greenberg was one of, if not thee, best players in baseball right now."

"Did he?"

"Without a doubt, he did. Anyway, Mickey managed the AL to a 4-1 win, and we were riding a 10-game winning streak going into the second half of the season."

"I can't wait." He stated as he watched his dad walking toward them. "See you on Monday, Mr. Graham."

"See you Monday, Lincoln."

He jumped off the bench and sprinted to meet his dad. Arthur watched as they walked toward the parking lot. Lincoln was obviously sharing his animated version of the grand slam. His arms were all over the place, and his dad was laughing as he watched. He turned back around and fed the birds the last of the bag.

Chapter 15
Monday—July 21, 1980

Arthur watched in amusement as Lincoln illustrated Lou Whitaker at the plate in last night's Tiger game against Seattle in the Kingdom. The Tigers won the game 5-2, but it was Lou's hustle double in the sixth inning of the game that Lincoln focused on. He ran around in a big circle and then did a headfirst slide into the imaginary bag. The birds scattered as he slid and yelled, "Safe!" Arthur laughed so hard his face hurt. As Lincoln popped up and ran back over to the bench to sit down, Arthur was wiping tears from his eyes.

"That was the best reenactment that I have ever seen. Bravo young Lincoln," he stated as he clapped.

Lincoln smiled. "It was a great game."

Arthur was finally catching his breath when he asked, "Did you stay up and watch the entire game?"

"Yep. That's why I love summer vacation. I get to see all the games I want without having to go to bed early because of school."

"You might have a career as a broadcaster."

"I figured I'd play for about twenty years and then step into the booth."

Arthur laughed some more. This kid was in a groove today.

"Did your dad watch the game with you?"

"Yeah, but he fell asleep around the fifth inning. He was in and out."

"Well, I'm sure you let him know what he missed."

"Yep. My mom called last night too."

"How is her dad doing?"

"Great. She says that they're coming home this weekend."

"That's great news. Are you excited?"

"Yeah. I miss her."

"What about your brother and sister?"

He shrugged his shoulders, which made Arthur laugh some more.

"She says that my grandpa is doing great with his physical therapy. I told her all about your story."

"That must have been a long conversation?"

"It was getting there, but my dad told me I could fill her in on the rest when she got back. She really loved the story so far. I told her maybe she could make it into a book."

Arthur smiled. "Who knows? Your dad talked about the same thing." Arthur scratched his chin. "Did he put you up to this?"

"No." He studied Arthur's face and then added, "I'm honest."

Arthur chuckled, "I believe you."

"She's a good writer. Dad says she took a lot of writing classes in college, and she used to be a journal...journal..."

Arthur helped him out. "Journalist."

"That's it. A journalist. She cut back when I was born, and then eventually quit when my brother and sister were born. She says she'll do it again when we all go to school."

"I'm sure she misses it a lot, which goes to show how important you guys are to her."

"Yeah." Lincoln smiled. "I forgot to ask you, how was your Sunday?"

"Mine was good. We went to church, had some lunch, and then had the family over for dinner. What did you do, aside from watching the Tiger game?"

"Dad had the day off, so we went to church, then played catch in the yard, and then made a giant sub. We ate it while we watched the game. It was awesome."

"That sounds like my kind of evening."

"It was a lot of fun. It's been nice having my dad to myself for the last couple of weeks. Don't get me wrong, I love my brother and sister, but they demand a lot of time."

"I'll bet. If you ask him, I bet he'll say the same thing. He's probably enjoyed the one-on-one time between the two of you."

"He said that yesterday."

Arthur smiled. "Has it made you appreciate how hard he works for your family?"

Lincoln looked up at him. "Yes, sir. He and my mom do a lot to take care of us. I don't think my brother and sister will realize it until they get older. They're still in the, me, me, me stage."

Arthur laughed, "Maybe you can help a little more so they can give your parents a break once in a while."

"I'll try, but I'm a kid too. I don't want to waste these years doing too much adult stuff."

"I understand," he laughed as he patted Lincoln on the back. "Are you ready to get back to it?"

"Yep, let's get to the second half."

"Well, in the first game back from the break, we had our ten-game winning streak snapped by Washington 12-11. There were a lot of hits and errors in that game. We won the next two, but then we rolled into Philadelphia and got crushed by the Athletics, 18-5."

"Phillies."

"What?"

"The A's are in Oakland. The Phillies are in Philadelphia."

"In 1935 there were 16 teams. Eight in the American League, and eight in the National League. There was no team in Oakland, and in Philadelphia the team was the Athletics."

"Okay. Sorry, Mr. Graham."

"It's okay. That's how you learn. Anyway, the A's beat us like a drum 18-5, and after the game Mickey really let us have it. We felt awful about the way we played, and to a man, we vowed not to let that happen again. Over the next 30 games, we played as hard as any team could play. We went 22-8 and ran our record to a division-leading 70-39-1. The only team that could keep up with us was the Cubbies in the National league who were 67-44. We had built a six-game lead over our division rivals, the Yankees."

"I bet you were hitting good."

"The entire team was playing great baseball. My average was over .310, and I was contributing a decent number of RBIs. Gehringer was playing great baseball, as usual. I tell you this, Charlie

Gehringer is one of the greatest players in the game's history. He defined second base. A homegrown product that was in the MVP conversation every year."

"Did he ever win it?"

"In 1937. He hit .371 that year. Won the batting title too. Man, he was a joy to watch. A player who genuinely loved playing the game and brought that attitude every time he took the field."

"Were you two good friends?"

"Were? We still are. Charlie and Josephine attended my church for a long time. It was a bit of a drive for them, so after I retired, they found a great little church closer to home, but we still talk on the phone a couple of times a month and have breakfast together a couple of times a year."

"I'd like to meet a legend like that someday."

"Maybe I'll see if your dad wants to come the next time we have breakfast. That's the guy you're going to want to talk stats with. He's a baseball encyclopedia."

"That would be great, Mr. Graham. Thanks."

"Sure kiddo. Anyway, Hank was hitting homers and killing it in the RBI category during that stretch. I think it was after Mickey's speech and during that 30-game stretch that our team really gelled into the machine that we knew we could be." Arthur smiled. "Let's jump ahead to August 26, 1935. We were playing Philadelphia at home. Remember, we lost to them 18-5?"

"I remember. Mickey gave you a real tongue-lashing."

Arthur smiled. "That's right. I had one of my best games as a player."

2

Navin Field, Detroit, Michigan—August 26, 1935

Ty Tyson informed his audience, "It's an absolutely gorgeous day here in Detroit for a doubleheader. The Tigers are getting ready to go up against the Athletics from Philadelphia, who are having a very dismal season at 50-63." He paused to wave to some fans, who had caught his attention in the press box. "Meanwhile, your Detroit Tigers have won six out of the last seven, including a 6-3 win over the Athletics here yesterday."

On the field, the two teams were getting ready to start the game, and Arthur had just finished warming up today's starting pitcher, Alvin Crowder. This was the 36-year-old's second season with the club, and 10th overall. He was another one of those pitchers who didn't really have great stuff, but when he was on, he was on. In the top of the first, he wasn't on his game. Jimmie Foxx drilled a fastball over the centerfield wall with a man on, and Philadelphia took a 2-0 lead. In the bottom of the first, Bullfrog Dietrich got the first two Tiger batters out. Arthur stepped to the plate, determined to extend the inning. Dietrich was in his third major league season, and so far, it had been a struggle. He was becoming what managers called a "serviceable pitcher who could eat up some innings." Arthur dug in and waited for the pitch. The first three balls came nowhere near the strike zone. With a 3-0 count, he had already told himself that he was not swinging at the next two pitches. The fourth pitch of the at-bat was a fastball that possibly touched 90 and was directly in the center of the plate. Arthur grimaced as he watched it go by. It literally hurt not to swing at it, but he was determined to show Mickey that he was a team player, and that a walk could mean a run. The next pitch was identical, and Arthur grimaced again as the umpire yelled, "Strike two!" It was now a 3-2 count. Arthur took a deep breath and stepped back into the box, praying for a pitch that was so bad he wouldn't have to think about swinging at it. The prayer was answered. The pitch was a curveball that didn't come close to breaking and plunked Arthur in the middle of the back. He grimaced for a third time, but this time the pain was physical. He walked around in circles for a moment, shaking off the effects. "You okay, Arthur?" The umpire asked.

"I'm good, Joe. Thanks."

"Take your base," he shouted and pointed to first.

Arthur jogged down to first while the guys in the dugout yelled and pointed at Dietrich. Arthur took his lead as Greenberg stepped to the plate. He looked at the third-base coach and got the sign to steal. He dug in as Dietrich got set. At the first sign of his windup, Arthur took off. He delivered a curveball low and outside, and as soon as the ball hit the catcher's mitt, he came up throwing. The throw was high, and Arthur slid into the bag before the tag was applied.

"Safe!" yelled the second base umpire.

Arthur dusted himself off and took his lead toward third. Greenberg watched two more pitches sail wide of the plate, and with a 3-0 count, the third-base coach gave him the sign to steal third. Arthur dug in once again, and as Dietrich delivered the ball to the plate, he took off for third. With his head down, focused on his mission, he heard that distinct Greenberg crack of the bat. He turned his head toward the plate just in time to feel the breeze of the ball across the back of his neck as it flew by the shortstop and into left center. He continued running hard, and Baker gave him the sign to keep going. Arthur rounded third and picked up speed as he headed for the plate. The catcher took his position to receive the throw, and Arthur flew into the air with a beautiful headfirst slide. His hand touched it first as his body flew past. He looked up at the umpire.

"Well?" Arthur asked.

"I already said safe," the umpire stated as he laughed.

Arthur sat up and looked at the catcher. He didn't have the ball. The shortstop was jogging in toward the pitcher to hand him the ball. The catcher smiled at him.

"Nice slide, Artie."

Arthur picked himself up and started walking toward the dugout. The fans were roaring, and his teammates were covering their faces as they laughed. Mickey smiled at him as he entered the dugout.

"Heck of a nice slide, kid," he stated as he laughed.

Arthur didn't say a word. He moved all the way to the end of the bench, enduring the jostling of his teammates. As he sat putting on his equipment, he had to laugh at himself. He looked down the bench once more, and they were still smiling at him. Arthur laughed out loud, and they joined in. He would learn later from Greenberg that he had received that same 90 mile an hour fastball right down the middle of the plate on the 3-0 count. He asked Hank, "Didn't you look to take the walk?" to which Greenberg replied, "You'd have to be crazy to let a pitch like that go on any count."

In the third inning, Arthur hit a sharp line drive up the middle for a single. In the fifth inning, he dug in on a 3-2 count and hit a bullet down the first-base line, right by a diving Foxx, for a double into the rightfield corner. In the sixth inning, he hit a seed down the third-base line into the left-field corner. The left fielder misplayed the ball as he ran into the corner, and the ball caromed around the wall before he ran it down and threw it into third. A sliding Arthur made it to the bag first and was standing on third with a triple. When Arthur stepped to the plate in the eighth inning with a man on first and two out, the crowd stood and cheered.

"The forty-year-old rookie with the magic bat is coming to the plate," Ty Tyson screamed into the microphone. "The fans are on their feet in anticipation of Arthur Graham completing the cycle." After taking a drink of water, he continued, "Not just the cycle, a natural cycle."

Arthur continued toward the batter's box and stopped before entering. He couldn't believe his eyes or ears. The crowd was on its feet, going nuts. The pageantry of the moment had completely escaped him until this moment. In his head, he quickly ran through all his at-bats. None of his teammates said a word in the dugout for fear of the baseball gods taking this chance from him. He looked at the umpire.

"Your Highness," he stated as he pointed to the batter's box. The catcher chuckled and dropped into his squat. Arthur stepped into the box and dug in. He looked out at the mound to see Bullfrog looking back at him. In the bottom of the eighth, he was still pitching. The Tigers were up 11-7, but he was still pitching. Arthur readied himself for the pitch as Bullfrog went into the windup. The crowd was now silent. The curveball missed low and outside.

"Ball," the umpire shouted as the crowd remained silent. Arthur didn't leave the box. He stood firm and waited for the next pitch. Another curveball low and outside.

"Ball two," he shouted. The crowd was now getting a little restless, and a few boos rang throughout the stadium. Arthur again stood firm and got ready. The third pitch was a fastball that backed Arthur out of the box and came close to finding a home in his ribcage.

"Ball three" came the call. The count was 3-0, and the boos came raining down from the Tiger faithful. Bullfrog walked off the mound and looked for composure. Arthur stepped out of the box and cleared his head. As he stepped back in and Bullfrog took the mound, the crowd was once again silent. As the pitcher got the sign and went into the windup, the crowd sprang to life and cheers filled the stadium once more. Arthur gripped the bat tightly and watched as the fastball came his way. It never veered off course and stayed right toward the center of the plate. He took a mighty step forward and put everything he had into it. The ball rocketed off the barrel of the bat and took flight into center. The runner on first sidestepped his way to second as he watched the ball and motioned for it to keep going. The crowd erupted and watched with Arthur as it made its way toward the center field seats. Bullfrog watched from the mound, hand on hip, hoping that his centerfielder, Doc Kramer, would make a spectacular catch. Kramer kept going back and as he approached the wall, he dug his cleat into the bottom of the wall and jumped.

"Kramer uses the base of the wall like a springboard," Tyson shouted as he stood and leaned forward in the booth. The crowd's noise was deafening. The ball traveled toward Kramer's open glove, and as it arrived, it brushed the top and landed in the second row.

"Home run! Graham got every bit of that one," Tyson shouted into the mic. "He's done it. Arthur Graham has done it."

The crowd stood and cheered the whole time Arthur was rounding the bases. As he touched home plate, he looked into the heavens and whispered to himself, "Thank you, Lord." He turned his attention to his teammates, who were clapping their hands and cheering for him as he walked toward the dugout. He stopped to look up into the stands and see everyone still on their feet, somehow cheering louder. He tipped his hat to them. They screamed his name and clapped harder. He walked down into the dugout and got mobbed by his teammates. Hank Greenberg came up and gave him a big hug.

"I knew you weren't crazy," he stated, laughing.

The Tigers 13-7 victory gave them four wins in a row and a nice lead on the Yankees in the division race. In the second game of the doubleheader, Tommy Bridges pitched a four hit complete game gem, but the Tigers fell to the Athletics 3-2. Arthur went 1 for 3 with an RBI.

3

"Wow, the cycle." Lincoln stated, "How did you not know you had a chance at it?"

"I guess I was just focusing on calling a good game behind the plate and doing my part at the plate when I got up." He smiled and paused before continuing. "Guys were walking around the dugout smiling and feeling good, so I was just enjoying that. Maybe in the back of my mind I knew, but it really dawned on me when I walked to the plate and the crowd wouldn't stop cheering."

"None of the guys said anything about it?"

"No way. Baseball players are among the most superstitious people in the world. If a pitcher is throwing a no-hitter, no one dares say a word about it for fear of jinxing him."

"Do you believe that, Mr. Graham?"

"I don't think anybody really does, but no one wants to be the guy that talks about it and then gets blamed for ruining it." He laughed.

"I guess. How did it feel to hit that home run?"

"Awesome. It wasn't even getting the cycle that pumped me up. It was the fans. To have all those people cheering for you at once, and to come through, it's hard to describe."

Lincoln had a big smile on his face. "Yeah. I can see how it would pump any guy up. You really were taking advantage of your first major league season."

"I was. It had taken me so long to get there. I guess I felt I had a lot of catching up to do."

They both laughed.

"Which moment was better? The grand slam or the cycle?"

After thinking for a moment, he answered, "Both had a different but wonderful feeling. The grand slam was one of those moments you dream of as a kid, but the cycle is something much rarer, and I believe the crowd's enthusiasm was much stronger for the cycle. I guess I can't answer that, young Lincoln. Both were equally thrilling for me."

"I figured."

Arthur smiled. "You'll have to let me know someday."

Lincoln smiled at the thought of playing in the big leagues and accomplishing those feats.

"I hope I do, Mr. Graham." Changing the topics quickly, as a 12-year-old boy can, he asked, "Why did they call the guy Bullfrog?"

"I don't really know for sure. I think someone told me once it was because of the thick glasses he wore, but honestly, I don't really know. His name was William or Bill."

"What about Doc Kramer? Was Doc his first name?"

"No. That one is actually an odd one. He had a good friend who was a doctor, and he would often accompany him on calls."

"That's strange."

"I agree. Although I guess you could really call him Doc because of his surgical play in centerfield. He played it for 20 seasons, and he played it well."

"20 years is a long time."

"Tell me about it. 20 years in the minors seems even longer."

They both laughed.

"Did he ever win a World Series?"

"He won it in 1945. In 1942, he came over to the Tigers and played the last seven years of his career with us. He was a good ballplayer, and a great person. It stumps me he isn't in the Hall of Fame."

"Did he hit a lot of home runs?"

"No. He hit something like 35 in his career, but he had over 2,700 hits and over 1,300 runs scored."

"That's a lot."

"I know. I don't understand their election process at all. There are many players in there with far fewer accolades, but Doc didn't make the cut. Anyway, we lost the second game that day, but we were still playing great baseball. We ended up taking five out of six games in that series with Philadelphia. Altogether, we went 22-7 on that homestand."

"You played 29 games in a row at home?"

"From July 30th to August 28th. Remember, there were only eight teams in each league, and we didn't cross over during the season. You could just as easily play 29 to 30 games on the road."

"Wow, that's crazy."

"That was baseball. Over the years, more teams have been added, and the playoffs have evolved a bit, but in 1935 we played 152 games against seven teams in a season."

"You really got to know your competition."

"We sure did." He smiled. "Okay, let's see. We were coming down the stretch, and we held a decent lead over the Yankees, but they still had some fight left in them. We went into New York for a five-game series against them, and in the opener, we won 8-5. The next day we tried to put em away."

Yankee Stadium, Bronx, New York—September 13, 1935

"The Tigers come in nine games up on New York with only 15 games to go in the season. It would take a meltdown of epic proportions for the Tigers to lose the pennant at this point." Tyson cleared his throat and continued. "In the National League, it's still a two-team race with St. Louis holding a slight edge over the Cubbies of Chicago."

On the mound for New York was the crafty 27-year-old, Lefty Gomez, 1-4 against the Tigers this season with a 3.8 ERA, and 11-13 on the year. Pitching for the Tigers was Schoolboy Rowe, 3-3 against New York on the season. Rowe had three complete game shutouts in his six outings against them, but had a 4.3 ERA in his three losses. Rowe was 8-2 in his last 10 games and boasted a record of 17-11 on the season. Arthur was sitting on 27 home runs for the year and desperately was looking to get to 30 with 17 games left in the season. Mickey had been resting him more lately for fear of him getting hurt, so Arthur had to make each game count. The Tigers were up 5-2 in the fifth inning. Both of New York's runs came from two solo shots by Gehrig in the second and fourth innings, when Arthur stepped to the plate with two outs and no one on.

"Arthur Graham steps to the plate with two out and no one on. He had a single in the first and then grounded out in the third. Graham has 27 home runs on the season and is truly one of the unsung heroes on this Tiger team. Gomez goes into the windup and delivers a fastball high and outside for ball one." He paused for dramatic effect. "Graham has hit the fastball pretty well this season, which surprises me that Gomez didn't go with the curveball." Someone next to Tyson shuffled some papers and handed them to him. "Thanks, Mel," he whispered into the mic as he looked at the papers. "It looks like Graham has had moderate success against the curveball as well. Gomez stares in at his catcher and gets the sign as Graham waits for the pitch."

"Hit it out," a fan yelled before the delivery.

"That was a Tiger fan all the way from Plymouth, Michigan," Tyson laughed as he said it and then shrugged at Mel for looking at him funny. "Here's the windup and the pitch. Graham makes solid contact with that one," he screamed into the mic, "it's way back in leftfield...and...gone! Graham hit it out of the ballpark and with number 28, the Tigers led it 6-2."

The Tiger fans in the stadium sent out a noticeable cheer, which prompted the proud New Yorkers to drown it out with a chorus of boos. Tyson high fived Mel, and with a big smile on his face announced, "Detroit is barreling toward a showdown with the Cardinals of St. Louis, or the Cubbies from Chicago. What a season!" he shouted as he high fived Mel again. The Tigers continued to hit, and at the end of the 7th inning, Gomez was out of the game and the Tigers were up 11-3. Rowe struck out the final Yankee hitter to end the ninth, and the Tigers walked away with a 13-5 win. They were now 10 games up on the second-place Yankees with only 16 games left in the season.

5

"You hit 28 homers? Wow! I hope you get to 30," Lincoln smiled.

"Do you want me to tell you if I did?" Arthur asked.

"No, I'm learning Mr. Graham. I like the journey."

Arthur laughed. "Well, at least I taught you that." After throwing some breadcrumbs onto the ground, he glanced up at Arthur, but didn't say a word. "Are you okay, Lincoln?" Arthur asked.

"I think I just realized something." He put the bag on the bench. "If you're the top team in the division, does that mean you play the second-place team for the right to go to the World Series?"

"No," Arthur answered with a big smile on his face. He watched as the wheels turned in Lincoln's head.

"You go right to the World Series, don't you?" He blurted out in excitement, barely able to contain himself. "I'm right, aren't I? The announcer said that you guys were barreling toward a showdown with the Cardinals or Cubs. That can only mean that you are in the World Series. Right, Mr. Graham?"

"Well, let me answer, son." Arthur laughed. "Yes. That's exactly what it means."

"I knew it. I knew it. Did you play in the World Series, Mr. Graham?"

Lincoln stopped talking and gazed at Arthur. With no expression on his face, Arthur looked at him.

"Didn't you just say something about the journey?" Arthur asked him.

Lincoln gave a big sigh, "All right. I'll wait. But come on, a 10-game lead with 16 games to go would be a historic collapse."

"Baseball can be a tricky game, Lincoln." He smiled.

"Did you guys blow it? You did, didn't you? You blew it." Lincoln responded as he dropped his head into the palms of his hands. He was devastated.

Arthur placed his hand on the young man's shoulder.

"Enjoy the journey. Let the story play out."

Lincoln looked up at him. "Okay. I'm just really excited."

"Really. I hadn't noticed." Arthur smiled at him. They both laughed.

"Here comes your dad. I'll see you tomorrow morning."

Lincoln hugged him and ran off to meet Chris.

Chapter 16
Tuesday—July 22, 1980

Chris opened the door to Lincoln's room to tell him it was time to get up. To his amazement, Lincoln was lying in his bed, looking up at the ceiling with a big smile on his face. Chris walked over and sat down at the corner of the bed.

"You're really throwing me for a loop with how early you're waking up. When did you get up? And why the big smile?" Chris asked.

"About half an hour ago." Lincoln answered. "I've just been thinking about my time with Mr. Graham. I was mad when I had to go to work with you on this project. I wanted to go to my friend's house to play and hang out, but then they went on vacation, and I was forced to go with you for a week. But now I'm glad. I got to meet Mr. Graham and hear the greatest baseball story ever." There was genuine gratitude in his voice.

Chris smiled, "Like your mom always says, 'The Lord works in mysterious ways.'"

Lincoln laughed. "Yeah, mom says that at least once a week."

"Yeah," Chris smiled, "she does." He sighed. "It seems like she's been gone forever. I miss her and the two little ones."

"You forgot their names," Lincoln laughed.

"I did not. It's Lucy and…James…no…wait…Jeff."

Lincoln laughed and responded, "It's Jack, dad."

"Oh yeah. Jack." He smiled. "I'm glad you're enjoying time with Arthur. I feel blessed that I get to benefit from it too. It's a great story. He has met and played with so many great players."

"I know. I mean, I didn't really know, but I like getting to know the history of the game, and it's the coolest thing in the world that he played for the Detroit Tigers."

"Arthur has led a very interesting life." He looked at Lincoln and gave him a pat on the leg. "I really appreciate your sharing it with me."

"I knew you would like hearing about it too." Lincoln smiled.

"We've talked a lot these past couple of weeks. It's nice."

"Yeah," Chris stated with a lump in his throat. "You know I love all of you very much. I just have to work…"

"Dad, I know. You work hard to take care of us. It's okay."

"Thanks, son. But God takes good care of us and has given me the ability to choose the jobs I take so that I can prioritize family over wealth. We are truly blessed in that way."

"I'm glad you took the church job."

"Me too. This is one of those jobs I'm talking about. We made good money, and I could spend more time with you. I took this job instead of a bigger, more time-consuming job. It would have meant a lot more money, but it would have been a 7:00 a.m. to 9:00 p.m. type of job every day until the project was finished."

"I'm glad you didn't take that job."

Chris sighed and looked his son in the eye.

"I was going to. I saw those big dollar signs and got lost in the numbers."

"What stopped you?"

"When I got the call from Dillard, and he asked me to do this job, it was at the same time as the bigger job, and paid a lot less, but still enough for our needs."

"And you took the church job? What changed your mind? Mom?"

"Another example of His mysterious ways. I told Jessica about my conundrum."

"Your what?" Lincoln asked with a very inquisitive look.

"Sorry. Conundrum means, difficult problem, or just a problem."

"Oh. I like that word. Conundrum."

Chris laughed. "You'll have to use that one to impress Arthur."

"Yeah." Lincoln smiled.

"Anyway, I told your mother, and instead of telling me which one to do, she told me to pray about it. She said she would respect whatever decision I made. It was around 3:00 p.m. and I didn't think it could wait until bedtime."

"You can pray whenever you want, dad. You don't have to wait until bedtime. Remember, you told me that."

"I know. I guess it's just one of those things we lose sight of sometimes. We can talk to God anytime we want, but we restrict it to early morning, or dinnertime, or bedtime. Anyway, I went into the bedroom and closed the door. Mom took you guys outside to play to give me some quiet time."

"Probably a good idea," he smiled.

"It was," he stated as he smiled back. "I got on my knees and bowed my head and asked God to please guide me in my decision. To show me what was best for our family. Then I got up and came outside to play with you guys."

"That's it?"

"That's all it takes. To acknowledge the Father and ask for His wisdom and blessing."

"And he showed you?"

"He did. Right around 6:00 p.m. your grandma called and told your mom that your grandpa was having surgery the same day these jobs were supposed to start, and that she didn't know if she could handle it by herself. I could see the concern in your mom's eyes and told her to go be with her parents that week. She told me she could take all of you if I wanted to do the bigger job."

"So, why didn't you let her?"

"In my mind, that was God giving me the answer I was looking for. It would be the bigger job, but your mom looked at me and asked me to sleep on it. I told her I would give her my answer in the morning. When we went to bed that night, I had a hard time sleeping. I tossed and turned and finally got up around 4:00 a.m. to grab a glass of water. It was a full moon that night, and it was bright. I went to take a drink of water and noticed your bat and glove lying in the yard."

"I don't remember ever leaving my stuff in the yard," he stated nervously.

221

Chris smiled. "It got me thinking about baseball, and about how much you loved playing. I knew your mom would be there for at least a week, but probably longer. You would miss a lot of practice and some games if you had to go."

"So, you took the smaller job for me?"

Chris smiled. "I knew it would be an opportunity for us to spend some quality time together, and it appeared we both needed that. So, the prayer was answered, and the decision was made. The church job."

"Thanks, dad." He moved to the side of the bed next to his dad and gave him a big hug.

"You're welcome, Link."

"Was mom surprised the next day when you told her about your decision?"

"No, she wasn't surprised at all. She told me that she's the one who accidentally left your mitt and bat in the yard."

"What?"

"Yeah. She said she had been playing with your brother and sister, trying to get them interested in the game, but after a while she just gave up and they played something else. She just forgot to go back later and pick it up."

Lincoln smiled. "I knew I hadn't left my stuff in the yard."

Chris laughed. "Let's go eat some breakfast before we head out."

2

"Good morning, Mr. Graham," Lincoln stated as he sat down next to Arthur.

"Good morning, Lincoln. You look a little tired this morning. Did you sleep okay?"

"Yeah. I just woke up early. Had some thinking to do."

Arthur smiled. "Nothing too serious, I hope?"

"Naw. Sometimes you just gotta think."

Arthur laughed as he answered, "I agree."

"Do you ever just sit back and think?"

"Lincoln, I'm 85 years old. Some days, that's all I do."

They both laughed.

"I was excited about today. You're coming down the stretch, and I want to know what happens."

"Maybe we should talk about something else today. All we've talked about is baseball lately."

"Mr. Graham," Lincoln interrupted.

Arthur laughed, "Okay, okay. I'm just kidding."

"Did the Yankees catch you?"

"First things first. I was trying to hit 30 homers in a season, remember?"

"That's right. Did you?"

"Well, I was sitting on 29 home runs and 99 RBIs for the season going into the last game of the year in Chicago."

3
Comiskey Park—Chicago, September 29, 1935

"The Tigers lost the first game of the doubleheader 3-2. They'll see if they can rebound and take game two and end the regular season on a winning note." Tyson sipped his water as he watched the players take the field for game two. "The Sox have taken the field to get this game started." He looked at his watch and then up at the sky. "We're steadily losing daylight, and I'd be surprised if we're able to get nine innings in."

Cochrane announced the starting lineup, and Arthur wasn't in it. He played the first of this four-game series, but Mickey was resting his 40-year-old catcher for the series to come. Arthur walked over to him.

"Mick, I feel great. I can play," he pled.

"I'm not taking any chances, Artie. To be honest, I hope darkness shuts this game down before anyone gets hurt."

"Mick, I waited a very long time to play at this level. I just want to play as much as I can."

He turned toward Arthur. "I get it, but I have to do what's best for the team right now. If I can get you in late in the game, I will."

"Thanks, Mick."

A dejected Arthur took a seat at the end of the bench and watched. If Chicago was angry about the way their season went, they were taking it out on the Tigers today. When the third inning finally ended, the Sox were up 14-0. The Tigers offense was nonexistent today, and at the end of five innings the score hadn't changed. The umpire walked over to Cochrane before the Tigers came to bat in the sixth.

"Hey, Mick. I think this is going to be the final at-bat in the game."

"You can call it now if you want to," he stated as he smiled.

"I don't think I can justify calling it just yet, but by the time your team finishes batting, we'll be there."

"Okay. Thanks, Jim."

Jo Jo White led off the inning with a line drive single up the middle. Gehringer was due up next, but Cochrane sent out Henry Schuble, a utility player that he used to give rest to his starters. Cochrane wasn't taking any chances of losing his star second baseman right before the big series. Schuble fouled off pitch after pitch. Finally, on a 3-2 count and the twelfth pitch of the at-bat, he went down swinging on a curveball in the dirt. The ball got away from the catcher, and White took second without a throw. Owen was due up next, but Cochrane substituted Flea Clifton into hit. Clifton was another utility fielder used to give his starters a rest. He also put up a fight at the plate and went down on strikes eleven pitches in. Cochrane stared at Arthur sitting at the end of the bench. Before he even knew what he was saying, he yelled down at him.

"Arthur, grab a bat. You're hitting for Reiber." Arthur's head popped up, and he ran down to grab a bat before Mickey could change his mind. Before he exited the dugout to go to the plate, Cochrane stopped him. "He's tired after the last two batters. He wants to get ahead of you in the count. Be ready to swing."

Arthur nodded and then exited the dugout. He stepped into the batter's box and stared out at the pitcher. He was sitting on a fastball. White had a modest lead off the bag at second when he went into his windup. He delivered a fastball right down the center of the plate. Arthur jumped all over it. He connected and sent the ball into the air toward right center. The Chicago centerfielder just looked up and watched it as it went over his head and landed in the bleachers behind him.

"That's number 30 on the season," Tyson screamed into the microphone. "And RBIs 100 and 101."

Cochrane smiled and looked up into the sky as Arthur ran the bases. He shook his head and looked over at Greenberg, who was already looking at him and smiling. They both watched as Arthur rounded third. He touched home plate and hustled into the dugout. You would have thought that it won them the game as his teammates mobbed him. The Tigers lost 14-2 that day, but it was one of the sweetest losses that Arthur was ever a part of. They ended the season with a record of 93-58-1, edging the Yankees by three games to take the pennant.

4

"You went to the World Series?" Lincoln screamed.

The construction crew stopped working for a moment and looked at them. Arthur laughed and gave Lincoln a pat on the shoulder.

"I sure did."

"I never in a million years thought this story would end up in a World Series," he shouted as he clasped his hands behind his head and started rocking back and forth. "Oh my gosh," he shouted.

"I told you it was a good story."

"It's a great story," he shouted. "Mr. Graham, you got to play in a World Series championship. Did you win? No. Wait. I want to hear the rest without spoiling it. Did you win?"

He was all over the place with his emotions. Arthur smiled and waited for him to calm down before he finally spoke.

"You'll find out over the next couple of days. I know you're excited, but if you wait for the ending, you won't regret it."

"You won, didn't you? I'm sorry. Can we start now, please?"

Arthur looked at his watch.

"I think we have time to get through the first game today."

Lincoln leaped from the bench and pumped his fist.

"Yes. Wait. Who did you play?"

"The Cubs won 100 games that year and edged out the Cardinals by four games."

"The Tigers and the Cubs. Wow."

"They were a tough bunch."

"Tougher than the Tigers?"

"I didn't say that," Arthur laughed, "but they played with heart. Charlie Grimm was their manager, and he knew strategy. The Cubs weren't the biggest or strongest team. They would not beat you with the long ball, but they could hit, and they played good defense. Grimm was the manager when they went to the series in 1932, but they lost to the Yankees. They were hungry, but so were we."

"Yeah. You guys lost the year before and were playing with a chip on your shoulder," Lincoln stated as he nodded his head.

Arthur smiled. "Yes, we were. I wasn't a part of that group, but there was plenty of chatter in the clubhouse from guys still stinging from the 1934 loss to the Cardinals."

"Mr. Graham, do you think they wanted to play the Cardinals again?"

"Boy, did they. They were mad when the Cubs took the National League Pennant. They wanted revenge in the worst way. Mickey knew he could use that energy to get the best out of the boys in the upcoming series, which is what made him a brilliant manager."

226

World Series Game 1—Wednesday, October 2, 1935—Navin Field, Detroit, MI

"The Cubbies of Chicago come into Navin Field for game one of the World Series as the hottest team in baseball. Chicago went an astounding 23-3 in the last month of the season. The Tigers, however, are happy to see September go, as they finished below .500 at 12-14." Tyson stated as he gathered more stats on the two teams. "On the mound today for Chicago is Lon Warneke. The 26-year-old right-hander is coming off his third 20-win season and looking to silence those big Detroit bats. Pitching for the Tigers is Schoolboy Rowe. He finished the season with 19 wins. Rowe has a big arm and is hoping to use it to help the Tigers open this series with a win." Tyson cleared his throat and continued. "The city is buzzing with excitement in anticipation of its first World Series championship. The Tigers are no stranger to making it to the dance, but they haven't been able to win it. They lost in 1907 and 1908 to the Cubs, and in 1909 to the Pirates. Last year they had high hopes but lost in seven games to the Cardinals. This city is hungry for a championship."

Arthur stood on the top step of the dugout staring out at the field, as both teams were going through their warmups. His heart was pounding, and his adrenaline was high. He took a deep breath and exhaled slowly. He smiled as he looked up into the sky.

"Thank you, Father." He whispered to himself. "In my wildest dreams, I never would have predicted this moment in my life." He had a lump in his throat as he whispered, "Please let me glorify You in deed and word." He closed his eyes and thought about the journey. It wasn't just about baseball. He thought about his parents, Mr. Dillard, Esther, and all the great friends he had made along the way. He thought about the war and his friends he had lost, and the injuries that threatened to derail him time and time again. Last, he thought about the ministry. He thought about his theology degree and how much he loved preaching the gospel. God was his rock and his foundation. Everything he had directly resulted from God's love for him.

"Are you having a moment?" Mickey asked as he stood next to him.

"Yeah," Arthur responded as he laughed and turned toward him. "I can't believe I'm here."

"Well, believe it. You earned every bit of it. I have never in all my days seen such perseverance. You, Arthur Graham, are a lesson to every boy with a dream to make it to the big leagues." Mickey smiled as he slapped Arthur on the shoulder. "I'll let you finish your moment, but wrap it up. We've got a game to win."

"Yes, sir," he stated as he looked out at a packed stadium. "I'm ready."

"Let's show em how we play ball in Detroit," he stated with a smile on his face.

Arthur sat down on the bench and finished putting on his equipment. The Tigers took the field to a roaring crowd. Arthur caught some warmup pitches from Rowe, and the home plate umpire, George Moriarity, yelled, "Play ball."

Augie Galan, the Cubs speedy 23-year-old left fielder, led off. Rowe and Arthur agreed on a fastball to start the at-bat. The pitch was perfectly placed low and inside for a called strike one. The second pitch of the at-bat was another fastball, high and outside. Galan nearly came out of his shoes as he swung and missed.

"Strike two," Moriarity yelled.

Arthur called for the fastball a third time, but Rowe shook it off. He wanted to throw the curve high and inside. Arthur set up and Rowe delivered. Instead of hitting his mark, the ball broke back toward the center of the plate. Galan connected and sent a line drive into right center. As White got to the ball, he backhanded it and looked up. Galan was already on his way to second base. He threw the ball to Gehringer, but Galan had already slid in safe for a leadoff double. Rowe pounded the palm of his glove in anger and then took the throw from his second baseman. He stepped back onto the mound and prepared to face the Cubs All-Star second baseman, Billy Herman.

"Herman is having an MVP-caliber season," Tyson stated as he sipped his water. "He hit .341, lead the league in hits with 227, and in doubles with 57." He watched and commentated as Rowe got ahead of Herman in the count, one ball and two strikes. "Schoolboy goes into the windup and delivers. Herman swings and catches the ball on the end of the bat. Rowe fields it as it dribbles down the third-base line. He turns and throws to Greenberg. The throw is in the dirt and gets by Greenberg." His voice went up a whole octave as he yelled. "Greenberg chases the ball down as Galan is rounding third and headed home." He stood and looked on from the press box. "Greenberg finally corrals the ball and turns to throw home, but it's too late. Galan crosses the plate and gives the Cubs a 1-0 lead in the top of the first. Herman is still standing on first on Rowe's error, and the Cubbies have a man on with still no one out."

The crowd was silent, and Cochrane was furious as he paced in the dugout. The next batter laid down a bunt and pushed Herman over to second. The cleanup hitter, catcher Gabby Hartnett, lined a single through the infield and Herman scored from second. When the top of the first concluded, the Cubs held a 2-0 lead. The bottom of the first was very uneventful for the Tigers. White struck out looking, Gehringer popped out to the shortstop, and Arthur flew out to left field. After the first inning, the pitchers took over. Neither allowed a run to cross the plate until the Cubs right fielder, Frank Demaree, led off the top half of the ninth with a homer to left. Game one of the World Series ended with over 47,000 walking away disappointed their Tigers couldn't put a single run on the scoreboard. The Cubs finished the game with three runs on seven hits and no errors. The Tigers finished with no runs on four hits and committed three errors. "The Cubs start October like they finished September…dominating. A 3-0 win now gives them the home-field advantage in this best of seven series. The Tigers just couldn't get the bats going today as they finished with just four hits. One from White, two from Fox, and one from the pitcher, Rowe. The rest of the team laid a big goose egg."

Arthur's day at the plate was one he wanted to forget. He went 0 for 4 with two strikeouts and two fly-outs. His defense was better. Arthur didn't allow a passed ball, and he threw out the only baserunner trying to steal. The team played uninspired baseball in the first game, and Cochrane saw it as his job to get them back on course. When they got into the locker room, he had them all gather around and take a seat. He stood on one of the benches.

"Did we get it out of the way, boys?" He asked.

They looked confused as they stared at their manager, but no one said a word.

"What's the matter? You look confused. The question was, did we get it out of the way?"

Arthur spoke up. "We did, skip."

"Good," he shouted. "Good. Then I don't have to stand up here and drone on about how you guys looked today. Like it was the first game of the year, and you didn't know what you were doing. Like you were a bush-league team making bush-league plays. Like you forgot how to hit and how to field like a pennant-winning team. I want you boys to come back here tomorrow looking like the team that won 23 games in August. That team," he pointed his finger at them one by one before continuing, "is the team that better show up tomorrow. Because if it doesn't, then kiss another championship goodbye. You are the best the American League has to offer, and the city of Detroit expects you to play like it. That's all I'm gonna say." He stepped down from the bench and made his way to the office, where he slammed the door and didn't come out until the last man was gone.

6

"He was pretty mad, huh?" Lincoln asked.

"Yes, very mad. But it had to do with our effort that day. He knew, actually, everyone knew we were a much better team than that. We didn't give it the effort we should have, and that's why he was so angry."

"Plus, you lost the World Series the year before."

"That didn't help. I'm sure there were lingering feelings there." Arthur laughed. "He was doing what Mickey did. Inspiring us to look at ourselves and respond like champions."

"I really hope you guys get it together, Mr. Graham." Lincoln sighed. "Because as cool as it is that you went to the World Series, it would be so much cooler if you won one."

"I see your dad coming. We'll get into game two tomorrow."

"Did the Cubs have any really good players on that team? You know. Like a Greenberg or a Gehringer?"

"They did. Their catcher, Gabby Hartnett, was not only a Hall of Famer, but he also won the National League MVP that year. Billy Herman was a Hall of Famer and ten-time All-Star. Their first baseman, Phil Cavarretta, won the National League MVP in 1945. Chuck Klein was a Hall of Famer, a National League MVP, and a Triple Crown winner in his career. That's just to name a few."

"Wow. They were good."

"Of course they were. They won 100 games that year. They had great individual talent, but more importantly, they played well as a team. It was going to be a tough series."

Lincoln stood and gave Arthur a hug.

"Tough first game. See you in the morning."

Arthur laughed.

"See you in the morning." He laughed again and shook his head. "What a great kid."

Chapter 17
Wednesday—July 23, 1980

Arthur sipped on his coffee as he read a passage from 1 Chronicles 16:1. "Seek the Lord and his strength; seek his presence continually." He smiled. "You are my rock and my redeemer, Father. Please use this day for your glory. Amen." Esther walked into the kitchen as he said, 'Amen.'

"Good morning, my love," she stated as she walked over and kissed the top of his head.

"Good morning, my dear." He responded. "You see how much God loves you," he continued.

"How much does he love me?" She asked, half knowing the answer.

"He removed the hair perfectly from that spot just for your lips," he responded as he laughed.

She kissed his head again. "Then I shall thank Him for loving me so."

They both laughed.

"What gets you up at this hour?" He asked as he looked at his watch. "It's 7:00 a.m."

She smiled. "It's only half an hour earlier than I usually get up."

"True. But it is something. Right?"

"Yes, I'm having breakfast with our granddaughter, Alyssa, and great-grandson Adam."

"What time?"

"8:30 a.m. at Connors Family Diner."

"I love that place. Big breakfast for a low price. How old is Adam again?"

"He's one."

"Give him a kiss for me. Tell Alley that grandpa loves her."

"I will. Would you like to join us?"

"Not today, my love. We're in the thick of the story, and if I show up late, Lincoln might have a meltdown. He's an excitable kid, you know?"

She smiled. "I know."

"Did you want to go to his game again this Saturday?"

"I would love to." She smiled and put her arms around his neck. "He's fun to watch."

He squeezed her arms and laughed.

"The kid's got gumption. I think he has the heart to make it if he wants to."

"If he's got your perseverance, then the sky's the limit." She kissed his head one more time and then let go so she could get ready. "Just a reminder that we are having another family dinner on Sunday."

"Here?"

"Dillard and Claires."

"That'll be nice. I look forward to it."

She smiled and headed to the bathroom to shower. He finished his morning Bible study and placed his coffee cup in the sink. He said goodbye before he left and then headed off to see Lincoln.

2

They were done with breakfast and were getting ready to walk out the door when the phone rang. Chris answered it. It was Jessica.

"Is everything alright with your dad?" he asked.

She laughed. "You assume its bad news because it's early? I just wanted to hear your voice."

"Oh, that's sweet. Well then, good morning. It's great to hear your voice too." He paused. "Wait. Do you have to stay longer?"

"I didn't realize you were such a pessimist in the morning."

"Sorry. I'm just wired that way, I guess, and I miss you."

"I miss you too. Actually, I have good news. My parents are doing great, and it looks like we'll be home on Sunday."

"That's fantastic news." He looked over at Lincoln, who was pointing at the clock. "One second, buddy. We'll get there soon enough."

"Is our son up and pressuring you to leave already? This must be important."

"He's just eager to hear Mr. Graham's story. They're kind of in the meat and potatoes part of the story."

"Dad," Lincoln stated in a self-serving voice. "Can we go?"

"Don't talk to me in that tone, young man. I'm on the phone with your mother and…"

"Can I talk to him?" Jessica asked.

He handed the phone to Lincoln.

"Hi mom."

"Hey sweetie. How are you doing?"

"Good. I'm sorry about being anxious, but Mr. Graham gets antsy if I'm late. He's an excitable guy, you know?"

She laughed. "It sounds like the story is good enough to keep your attention."

"It's the greatest story ever. He played in a World Series, mom. A World Series."

"Wow. That is exciting. I can't wait to hear this story when I get home."

"That's why I want to get going. I'm just excited to hear the rest."

"I understand. Okay. Let me say goodbye to your dad."

"I love you, Mom."

"I love you too, sweetie."

He handed the phone back to Chris and then sat down on the couch.

"I'll call you when we get home later," Chris stated as he looked at Lincoln.

"That sounds good. I love you."

"I love you too. Tell the kids I love them and miss them."

He hung up the phone, and they were off to the church. On the way, he talked to Lincoln about his disrespectful tone and impressed upon him the need to correct his behavior. Lincoln apologized and stated that he would be better in the future.

3

Arthur smiled as he stood in front of the bench and watched Lincoln get out of the truck and sprint from the parking lot to the bench.

"Good morning, Mr. Graham," an out of breath Lincoln stated.

"Good morning, Lincoln. Impressive sprint."

"Thanks."

Chris waved from the parking lot as he walked toward the building. Arthur waved back.

"How was your morning?" Arthur asked.

"I got in trouble for being disrespectful," he responded.

"Oh." Arthur sat down on the bench. "What happened?"

"We were leaving the house to come here, and my mom called. That's why I'm late."

"We don't have a set time. When you get here, you get here," Arthur stated.

"I know, but I wanted to get here sooner so we could start."

"I take it you rushed the conversation?"

"Yeah. My dad got mad and talked to me about it on the way here."

"I see. Lincoln, you've got to remember, your mom and dad have been apart for a couple of weeks. They miss each other."

"I know. I miss her too, but I really wanted to get back to the story."

"I get that, but she misses you too and was probably excited to speak to you."

"She was. She understood."

"Moms can be pretty understanding."

"She said they're coming home on Sunday."

"That's nice. So, your grandpa is doing well?"

"Yep."

"Good." He smiled. "We should have this story wrapped up by Friday."

"Me and dad talked about it last night. He's excited too."

"Probably because you tell it better than I do."

"I doubt that," he stated as he smirked.

"I don't, and that smirk tells me you know I'm right."

Lincoln laughed. "When I tell a story I'm excited about, I can't help it."

"I know. That's what makes it so fun."

"Thanks, Mr. Graham. It was hard retelling the story of the first game of the World Series, though, because you guys didn't score any runs."

Arthur laughed. "I think you'll like the second game better. Let's get started."

4

World Series Game 2—Thursday, October 3, 1935—Navin Field, Detroit, MI

"The Tigers are looking for some offense today as the Cubs kept them off the scoreboard yesterday in a 3-0 opening series win." Tyson let that sink in for his listeners. "Rumor has it that Cochrane let his team know how disgraceful they played and is expecting that offense to make a statement in today's game." Tyson listed the starting lineups, and questioned the Cubs manager, Charlie Grimm, about starting pitcher Charlie Root today, instead of 20-game winner, Bill Lee. "Lee is 9-1 in his last 10 starts. Grimm said he has confidence in the veteran Root, who went 5-1 in September."

As warmups concluded, Cochrane pulled his team into the dugout. "I will not give you a big, long speech about what you need to do today. You already know. I do, however, want you to take a moment to look at all the people who came to watch you play today. People who work hard and decide to spend some of that hard-earned money on a ticket to see you win. Now, look across the way at the other team, laughing and smiling. They can afford to do that because they came in here yesterday and smacked us in the mouth. They are so confident right now that they plan to do it again today. Last, look at each other. We've given our blood and sweat for each other this season to make it to this series. So, this is what you're going to do today. You're going to go out onto that field and show these hard-working people that their money is well spent. You're going to wipe those smug looks right off that teams," he pointed at the Cubs, "faces, and you're going to play Tiger baseball so that this team and this city become champions."

The dugout exploded with clapping and cheering. Each man pumping the other up. The team's adrenaline was through the roof. They were ready to get back to Tiger baseball. Cochrane let the boys whoop it up for a bit and then silenced them.

"Before we take the field. Arthur, will you lead us in a prayer?"

Arthur and the team stopped talking altogether and stared at Cochrane. Mickey had never brought religion into the dugout or clubhouse before. Not that it wasn't encouraged or permitted, it just never happened. Arthur stood up, and the team huddled in close around him. Everyone removed their hats, and Arthur started.

"Lord, please help us play to our full potential today. Give us your blessings on this field and allow these fans to leave happy. Thank you. Amen."

Tyson stared down into the Tiger dugout, trying to figure out what was happening. "I don't know what the team is doing down there, but it looks like they're huddled around Arthur Graham. I'll have to ask Mick after the game to get some clarity." Tyson shuffled some papers before continuing, "The Tigers are getting ready to take the field for this important game two."

When Arthur had finished, the team looked up, and Mickey shouted, "Go get em boys."

The adrenaline started pumping again, and the starting nine leaped from the dugout to take the field. Cochrane stopped Arthur as he was leaving the dugout.

"What's up, Mick?" he asked.

"I'm sorry to put you on the spot like that."

"It's okay, Mick. I felt at home doing it. Thank you for letting me."

Cochrane smiled. "Let's show Chicago what we're made of."

Arthur smiled and nodded before running out to take his position behind the plate. The Tigers sent their 20-game winner to the mound today to try to even up the series. Tommy Bridges ended the regular season with a 6-3 loss to the White Sox and was determined not to lose back-to-back games to a Chicago team. The top of the first started rocky. Bridges walked Galan on five pitches. Arthur called for a pitchout on the first pitch to the next batter, Herman. Galan had stolen 22 bases during the year, and Arthur wanted to see if he was going to make it 23. He also wanted to see if Herman was trying to bunt Galan over to second base. If he tried this, it would affect the pitch sequence. Bridges threw the fastball wide. Herman showed no signs of bunting, and Galan stayed out.

"Ball one," the umpire yelled.

Bridges and Arthur settled on the curveball for the next pitch, and Herman got on top of the ball, sending it right up the middle. Bridges snagged it, turned and gunned it to the shortstop Rogell, who flipped it to Greenberg for a double play. Just like that, it was two outs and nobody on base. The next batter struck out swinging, and the side was retired. The Tigers centerfielder, Jo Jo White, led off the bottom of the first. On a 2-2 count, he lined a fastball up the middle for a base hit. Arthur was hitting second today and walked to the plate with the goal of advancing White into scoring position. He settled in and waited for the pitch. Root delivered a fastball high and outside. Arthur attempted a bunt, but the ball glanced off the top of the bat and ended up foul behind the plate. The next pitch was a curveball that landed low and outside. Arthur showed bunt but didn't offer.

"Ball," yelled the umpire, Ernie Quigley. "1-1," he stated.

As Arthur stepped back into the box, he had a strong feeling that the next pitch was going to be a curveball. Root went into his windup, and Arthur edged a little closer to the plate. White took off for second base. The ball broke low and to the outside. As it crossed the corner of the plate, Arthur swung and connected. The ball shot off the bat and headed down the first-base line. The first baseman dove for the ball but just missed as it landed a foot behind the bag and sent chalk flying into the air. Ty Tyson captured the moment.

"Graham sends a line shot down the first base line just past a diving Cavarretta. White is already rounding second as the ball heads for the right-field corner. Demaree scoops it up as White rounds third and Graham is digging for second. Demaree tosses the ball into Herman as White touches the plate and Graham is safely in at second base with a double. The Tigers take a 1-0 lead."

Tyson's excitement echoed throughout radios all over the Detroit area as fans leaped and yelled for their team. Esther and Dillard were huddled around a radio in the living room and started jumping and yelling when it was announced that Arthur was into second with an RBI double. Gehringer strolled to the plate with Arthur on second and no one out. On a 2-2 count, and on the seventh pitch of the at-bat, Gehringer lined a single up the middle. The third-base coach gave Arthur the signal to round the bag and go home, and that's exactly what he did. The center fielder charged the ball and came up throwing. Arthur slid just as the catcher received the ball, and his foot crossed the plate before the tag.

"Safe," Quigley yelled as he emphatically threw his arms out.

The crowd roared as the call was made, giving the Tigers a 2-0 lead. Arthur entered the dugout to a host of happy teammates. There was yelling, slapping, and a lot of laughing. The atmosphere was electric. With Gehringer on first and nobody out, Greenberg stepped to the plate.

"Root is already in big trouble, and we're only in the bottom of the first," Tyson stated as he drank some water. "Hammerin Hank is up, and his season stats are MVP-worthy. He batted .328, with a league-leading 36 home runs and 170 RBIs." The fans were on their feet in anticipation of a big inning. Tyson let the radio audience know Root was way outside on his first pitch to Greenberg, making the count 1-0. The second pitch was a fastball that was high and inside, but caught the corner of the plate for strike one. "The count is 1-1 on Hank with a runner on first and no outs. The Tigers already have two runs this inning and are hoping for more. Root sets and deals. Greenberg connects!" Tyson stood and shouted, "The ball is heading for leftfield, and it's heading there fast. That ball is long gone," Tyson screamed into the mic. "A monster shot for Greenberg gives the Tigers a 4-0 lead in the first, and still, no one out. Whatever Mickey said to the team before the game, worked."

In the bottom of the fourth with the score still 4-0, the Tigers offense came alive once more. Root left the game in the first inning, having given up four runs and not recording a single out. Roy Henshaw entered the game and had not allowed a Tiger to cross the plate in his three innings of work. In the fourth, he retired the first two Tiger hitters. He then hit Owen with a pitch and allowed Bridges to get a single. He walked Jo Jo White to load the bases, which brought Arthur to the plate. Arthur watched as the first two pitches missed the strike zone. With a 2-0 count, he knew the next pitch would be a strike, and most likely a fastball. He stepped out of the box and looked at his third-base coach. They were on the same page. Arthur stepped back in and waited for the pitch. Tyson was on the edge of his seat, waiting to make the call.

"Henshaw goes into the windup, and the runners are off," he screamed into the microphone again. "Graham lays a bunt down the third-base line. Hack sprints in from third. He scoops the ball barehanded and throws it to first," his voice clear with excitement. "Safe! Graham is safe!" Arthur's foot hit the front of the bag as the ball smacked into the first baseman's mitt. "The Tigers lead it 5-0 on a very gutsy call by Cochrane."

Gehringer then stepped to the plate and singled in White and Bridges to give the Tigers a 7-0 lead. Henshaw was knocked from the game, giving way to the third Cub pitcher of the game, Fabian Kowalik. Greenberg grounded out to third to end the inning, but the Tigers offense had made a statement through four innings of play. The Cubs finally broke through in the run column in the top of the fifth, and again in the top of the seventh. Heading into the bottom of the seventh, the Tigers led 7-3. Kowalik was pitching well, but Arthur led off the inning with a walk. Gehringer struck out, and then Kowalik hit Greenberg with a pitch, putting runners on first and second with one out. Goslin was the next batter, and he flew out to left field. With two outs and two on base, Pete Fox came to the plate. This at-bat would change the complexion of the entire series.

"Stepping to the plate is right fielder Pete Fox. He had two of the Tiger's four hits in game number one." Tyson's voice conveyed the intensity of the moment, and through the first three pitches, he had Tiger fans on edge. "The count is 1-2 on Fox with Graham on second and Greenberg on first. Kowalik goes into the windup and delivers. Fox sends a line drive over first and into the rightfield corner. Graham is going to score easily to give the Tigers an 8-3 lead. Demaree throws the ball to the cutoff man as Greenberg touches third." Tyson's voice erupted. "Greenberg ignores the sign to stop at third and is rounding third to head home. Herman turns and guns the ball into Hartnett, who is waiting for Greenberg…who lowers his shoulder and barrels into Hartnett."

"Out," Quigley screamed.

"Greenberg is out at the plate. Both Greenberg and Hartnett are on the ground not getting up. The dust is still settling, and both players are still down." Tyson's voice tapered off as he explained the disastrous scene for Tiger fans.

Bridges finished a complete game as the Tigers won 8-3 and took game two of the series. Both Greenberg and Hartnett finished the game, but Arthur sensed something was definitely wrong with Hank. Greenberg had an X-ray of his wrist before the team boarded the bus for Chicago. It was broken. He was done for the series.

Lincoln sat wide-eyed, not saying a word. Arthur let the severity of the circumstances sink in before he finally spoke.

"Yeah. That was our reaction when Mickey told us the news."

"No, he can't be done. He worked hard. He deserved to play," Lincoln stated with a quivering voice, as if the moment had just occurred.

Arthur placed his hand on the young man's shoulder.

"It's okay, Lincoln. Our team was still determined to give it everything we had."

"But…but…he deserved to play," he only got out. "It's not fair."

"Life is not fair all the time. It can be cruel. He deserved to play after the work he put in that season, but it wasn't meant to be."

"Why does God allow that to happen, Mr. Graham? Why now? He was a good person. Right?"

"One of the best. He mirrored God's command to 'Love thy neighbor as thyself.' He often helped people down on their luck."

"So, why?"

"Only God knows why He allowed it to happen. We can ask all day long. Sometimes we know why, and sometimes we don't. Sometimes we find out later in life, and still, sometimes we never do."

"Was he angry?"

"At first, but then he took Mickey's attitude. He realized that just because he couldn't play, it didn't mean that he couldn't contribute. He was a great help the rest of the series with his scouting knowledge of the pitchers."

"So, he made lemons into lemonade?"

Arthur laughed. "That's a great way to put it, kiddo."

Lincoln smiled. "You had a great game, Mr. Graham, and you guys tied the series."

"Yes, and yes."

"Was it weird when he asked you to pray before the game?"

"It was strange. He had never done that before, but I loved it. It gave me the opportunity to thank Him, and to kind of let the others know that if they wanted to talk about God, I was there."

"So when was the next game?"

"It was the next day in Chicago."

"The next day?" he asked in amazement.

"We didn't mess around. It was October, and nobody wanted to play deeper into a month that was already getting colder."

"Good thing it was close."

"Yep. We could still get there in plenty of time for a good night's sleep and wake up ready to go the next day."

"Who replaced Hank?"

"Mickey moved our third baseman, Marv Owen, over to play first, and put in, Flea Clifton, to play third."

Lincon laughed. "Flea. Was he good?"

"He was a good infielder, but not so good at hitting."

"That's not good. Greenberg was a big power bat."

"Yep. But we weren't the first team to battle through losing a big player. To win a championship, the rest of the team must step up. It was going to hurt, but we still had enough talent to win. We lost the reigning American League MVP right at the beginning of our season, and here we were in the World Series."

"That's because a 40-year-old rookie stepped up and delivered," Lincoln stated as he winked at Arthur.

Arthur laughed out loud and then winked back.

"Game three would prove tough. It was forty-eight degrees at game time."

World Series Game 3—Friday, October 4, 1935—Wrigley Field, Chicago, IL

Ty Tyson was back on the air for game three in Chicago, with some disappointing news for Detroit fans. "The Tigers suffered a tremendous blow yesterday. After the game, they found out that Hank Greenberg broke his wrist in that collision at the plate with Cubs catcher, Gabby Hartnett, and will be out for the rest of the series." After a brief pause and some shuffling of papers, he continued, "Tiger Manage Mickey Cochrane has moved Owen over to first and inserted Flea Clifton at third. The 26-year-old Clifton," Tyson paused again and could be heard covering the mic and whispering, "that can't be right," before continuing, "has 116 major league at bats under his belt. In those 116 attempts at the plate, he is batting .256, with no home runs and 10 RBIs." He looked over at his stats guy and shook his head. "The Tigers could be in trouble."
In the clubhouse, the Tigers sat in silence. The news of Greenberg's injury devastated the team, and as they stared at their injured slugger, they couldn't help but feel defeated. When Mickey broke the news to his guys after the diagnosis, he could see the doubt in their eyes. Hank could see it too. He asked to speak to the team before Game Three. Greenberg stood in front of his team and addressed them. "We won the pennant and made it this far as a team. I'm looking at a group of guys that won the pennant without their MVP catcher from last season because Arthur Graham stepped up and grabbed the reins. This team has dealt with a lot over the season, and if I had to define you boys in one word, it would be resilience." There was passion in his voice, and his words resonated with every man in that room. "I have complete confidence that Flea can do the same thing." The players stood one by one, staring at Greenberg, feeding off of every word he said. "Come on, boys. Go out there today and punch these guys in the mouth," he shouted as he scanned the room. The team erupted in applause. They were slapping each

other and cheering on their injured star. Greenberg smiled and then sat down as Cochrane stepped into his place. "I think nothing else needs to be said. Let's go," he shouted.

"On the mound for the Cubs today is their other 20-game winner, Bill Lee, 20-6 on the season. The Tigers will throw Elden Auker on the hill, 18-7 this season. A great matchup that will see one team take a 2-1 series lead." Tyson stated.

In the top of the first inning, Arthur reached on an error but was ultimately stranded at second base. In the bottom half of the inning, Auker gave up a single to the first batter but struck out the next batter and then induced a ground ball double play from Hartnett that ended the inning. After one it was still 0-0. The Cubs struck first in the bottom of the second inning when on a 0-2 count, Frank Demaree drove an Auker fastball into the rightfield seats. Later in the inning, Clifton committed an error that would produce Chicago's second run. At the end of two innings, the score was 2-0 Cubs. In the top of the third inning, the first two Tiger batters made an out before Arthur took a walk. Gehringer singled to put a man on first and second, but the rally came up short when Goose Goslin sent a line drive to left field that saw Galan make a beautiful diving catch to end the inning. In the bottom of the fifth inning, Auker walked Jurges to start the inning. The next batter sacrificed him over, and then Galan hit a single up the middle to score him, giving the Cubs a 3-0 lead. Galan took second on a throwing error and then took third on a single by Herman. With runners at the corners and only one out, the Cubs were threatening to break the game open. The next batter, centerfielder Freddie Lindstrom, hit a line drive to Gehringer at second, who started an inning-ending double play. At the end of five innings, the Cubs lead 3-0. In the top of the sixth, Goslin singled. Tiger right fielder Pete Fox then tripled into the gap to score Goslin all the way from first, giving the Tigers their first run of the day. A promising inning ended with Fox getting picked off third by Lee, and Billy Rogell striking out.

"Well, Tiger fans, as your team comes to bat in the top of the eighth inning, they are trailing 3-1. The bat of Tiger slugger Hank Greenberg is noticeably absent." Tyson watched as the first hitter of the inning, Jo Jo White, walked. "Graham is coming to the plate with White on first and no one out. The Tigers are looking for a spark, and Graham could be that spark with a base hit in this at bat." Arthur walked to the plate and stopped short of the batter's box. He took a deep breath and closed his eyes. He listened to the screaming Cubs fans yelling their insults and cheering for their team. He smiled as he opened his eyes and took two practice swings. He stepped into the box with a smile on his face. Cubs catcher Hartnett looked up at him.

"What are you smiling about? Your team's done without Greenberg."

He looked down at Hartnett and simply stated, "God is so good."

He shook his head. "To the Cubs."

Arthur continued to smile as he waited for Lee's pitch. Lee delivered a fastball that hit the corner low and inside.

"Strike!" home plate umpire Bill McGowan shouted.

Hartnett threw the ball back to his pitcher and watched as Arthur continued to smile. He shook his head again and gave Lee the signal. Lee delivered another fastball. This time it touched the corner high and outside.

"Strike two," came the call.

Hartnett threw the ball back and looked up at Arthur. "Are you going to swing or stand there grinning like an idiot? I'm okay if you watch the next pitch too."

Arthur didn't say a word. He readied himself for the next pitch. White took a good lead off second and waited. The third fastball came in low and on the outside corner. Arthur took a step forward and extended his arms. The swing was late, but the barrel of the bat solidly met the ball and sent it into the air. The crowd was silent as they watched the ball fly toward the right-field corner. Arthur watched as he ran toward first, willing the ball to stay fair. Demaree ran toward the corner and then leaped into the air to make the catch.

The ball cleared his mitt by a foot before ringing off the foul pole and ricocheting into the second row of seats. Arthur leaped into the air and raised his fist as he approached first base. The Tiger dugout exploded, and the crowd remained silent. The smile never left Arthur's face. In the booth, Tyson was screaming like a madman and walking back and forth.

"Home run…home run…home run…Arthur Graham has done it. The game is tied, and the Tigers have new life."

As he crossed the plate, he looked up into the sky and pointed to his God. He then looked at Hartnett, who was standing behind the plate with his hands on his hips, shaking his head. When he got to the dugout, he was showered with the adoration of his teammates. The game was now tied at 3-3. Feeding off the energy of that home run, the Tigers pushed two more runs across the plate in the inning, and after eight innings in Chicago they led 5-3. Schoolboy Rowe entered the game in the ninth inning, looking to secure the Tiger win and a 2-1 series lead. The ninth started out with a fly ball out to centerfield, but the Cubs refused to go away quietly. Three straight singles produced a run and put runners on first and third with just one out. Augie Galan, a thorn in the Tigers side, then hit a deep fly ball to centerfield. White was able to make the catch, but Klein tagged from third and the score was now tied 5-5. The next batter grounded out and sent the game to extra innings. The score remained tied until a Tiger unsung hero came forward in the top of the eleventh inning.

"Flea Clifton will start us off in the top of the Tiger eleventh. Clifton has no hits in four at-bats today." Tyson sipped his water when he almost choked as he stated, "French hit him with the pitch." With Clifton on first, Cochrane did the expected move and had Rogell bunt him over to second. The next batter, Marv Owen, hit a lazy ground ball to second, which moved Clifton to third, but gave the Tigers two outs in the inning. "Jo Jo White steps to the plate hoping to give his team a one-run lead. French checks on Clifton and then deals to the plate," Tyson's voice raised again as he called the play.

"White hits a line drive up the middle and into centerfield. Clifton is in to score, and the Tigers take a 6-5 lead in the top of the eleventh." Rowe struck out the side in the bottom of the inning, and the Tigers escaped with a 6-5 win and a 2-1 series lead. The celebration in the clubhouse was brief as each man showered and got dressed so that they could get back to the hotel, eat, and then get some rest for tomorrow's game.

7

Arthur looked at his watch and then looked at the church. Chris was walking toward them as Lincoln sat in front of him with a smile on his face.

"That's it for today, kiddo."

"You hit a home run in the World Series."

"I did. It felt incredible. The only thing better would have been if we had been at home. The Chicago crowd didn't appreciate it as much," he laughed.

Lincoln laughed. "Yeah, I bet they didn't. My dad and I have a lot to talk about tonight at dinner."

"When you tell him about the home run, Lincoln it up a bit."

Lincoln started laughing hysterically. Chris walked up and smiled. "What did I miss?" he asked.

"I'll tell you on the way home, dad. You're going to love today's story."

"I like the sound of that," he responded as he shook Arthur's hand. "Good to see you, Arthur."

"Good to be seen," he replied.

"You ready, son?" Chris asked.

"Yep. Are you coming, Mr. Graham?"

"I have a few more crumbs to get rid of before I leave. Good luck in the game tonight."

They bid him farewell and started toward the parking lot. Arthur could hear Lincoln's voice fluctuating as he left. The story was already being retold.

When Arthur got to the bench today, Lincoln was waiting for him.
He was feeding the birds as he hummed, *Jesus Loves Me.*
"Well, good morning, Lincoln," he stated as he sat down. "How long
have you been here?"
"Good morning, Mr. Graham. Not long. My dad had to get here
early today to meet a guy for some special equipment he needed."
"I see. How was the game last night?"
Lincoln smiled. "I was on fire. I got four hits in four at-bats. They
were all singles, but I had never done that before."
"Impressive. Whenever you bat a thousand in a game, that's a good
game. Did you win?"
"Yep. Do you remember the kid who can never hit the ball?"
"Yes, I do."
"I helped him during the game, and he almost got a base hit," he
stated proudly.
"That's some good coaching. Where did he hit the ball?"
"To third base. That kid has a great arm. Any other third baseman in
the league and he would have gotten a base hit."
"Something to build on. So, what did you tell him to do differently?"
"I told him to concentrate on the swing and not the stance. Too many
people were trying to position him every time he came up. I just told
him to stand how he wanted to, and to focus on keeping his eye on
the ball. That he would find his stance later."
"And that worked?"
"He grounded out three times. Once to third and two to the pitcher.
Before this game, he would strike out every time."
"Did it make him smile to hit the ball?"
Lincoln smiled, "Yeah. He had a big smile on his face."
"Good. Baseball is supposed to be fun. Smiling is always
encouraged." Arthur smiled. "Did you update your dad on our

story?"

"Oh yeah. We talked about it on the way home, and then at dinner. He said that your journey to the majors is inspiring."

"That was kind of him to say."

"He seriously wants mom to write about it. He thinks people will love it."

"From 1935 to around 1938 there were many people trying to interview me and tell my story, but I was focused on other things."

"Did you ever sit down and write about it?"

"No, but I've penned many sermons over the years."

"Well, I think it's the greatest baseball story ever told."

Arthur smiled. "That's very kind of you to say."

"Heck, I would much rather do a book report on you than on the solar system or some other boring topic." He turned to Arthur and put his hand on his shoulder. "It's a real page-turner, Mr. Graham. I heard my mom say that once when she was reading a good book."

Arthur laughed out loud. When he was finished, he looked at Lincoln. "You have a way of making me laugh, Lincoln. I think you should be a writer. From what I can see, you know how to tell a story."

"That's what my dad says. He says my mom and I share that trait."

"I believe he is right. Are you ready to talk baseball?"

Lincoln started rubbing his hands together as he looked at Arthur. "Game four."

Arthur laughed. "Alright, let's get to it."

2

World Series Game 4—Saturday, October 5, 1935—Wrigley Field, Chicago, IL

"With game four of the World Series coming to you from Wrigley Field in Chicago, I'm Ty Tyson. The Tigers took game three yesterday in a 10-inning nail-biter, 6-5. They lead the best of seven series, 2-1. Taking the mound for Chicago today is Tex Carleton. He was 11-8 on the season. The Tigers will send General Crowder to the hill. He was 16-10 on the season, but winless in September."

The two teams were warming up on the field. Arthur jogged in to grab a drink and took a seat next to Greenberg on the bench. Hank appeared to be looking out at the field, but Arthur could tell he was looking through it. Arthur cleared his throat, and Greenberg looked at him.

"How are you feeling today, Arthur?"

"I'm good, Hank. How are you?"

"Oh…I'm fine." He answered as he smiled and looked away.

Something inside Arthur told him that Greenberg needed a win today. He was feeling depressed because he couldn't be on the field with his team. He felt he was letting the team down, and he felt helpless for doing that.

"I'm actually not fine, Hank."

Greenberg turned toward him.

"Why? What's wrong?"

"It's not physical. It's mental. I just…I'm having a hard time with reading these pitchers. And when a runner gets on, I fear they're going to steal a base and then score. I don't want to let the team down."

"Arthur. You've gotta rely on the confidence and skills that got you here. You're a smart player."

"Thanks, Hank. I'm just all in my head, that's all."

"You hit 30 home runs this year and over 100 RBIs. Defensively, you were one of the top three catchers in the league."

"Thanks. I needed a confidence boost. We miss you on the field, but having you here in the dugout is a giant help to the team."

"Hank Greenberg. Professional motivator."

They both laughed. Hank looked forward, crossed his arms and smiled.

"The Cubs take the field. Dolly Stark is behind the plate today, calling the game. The Tigers send up Jo Jo White to lead things off,"

Tyson barked into the microphone. The first inning was uneventful as both teams failed to score a run. Arthur grounded out to second in his at bat, resulting in a 1-2-3 first inning. At the top of the second inning, the Tigers had something cooking. "If you're just joining us, Goose Goslin singled to start the inning, Pete Fox doubled to put runners at second and third, and Carleton walked Rogell to load the bases for Marv Owen." The excitement was building in Tyson's voice. Owen popped out to the second baseman, failing to advance the runners. "Flea Clifton steps to the plate now with the bases loaded and one out. Clifton was thrust into the starting lineup after star first baseman Hank Greenberg broke his wrist in the second game of the series." The count was 2-2, with Clifton having fouled off three balls to stay alive. "Clifton is putting up a fight against Carleton. He looks in at his catcher and gets the sign. Carleton goes into the windup and delivers." He stood, and his voice went up an octave as he called the play. "Clifton smashes a line drive that's speared by the second baseman Billy Herman, who tosses the ball to Jurges standing on second base completing an inning-ending double play. You've got to be kidding," he yelled into the microphone as he plopped back down into his seat. "The Tigers had the bases loaded and no one out and couldn't get a run across the plate. That might come back to haunt them."

The crowd was cheering as the Cubs charged in from the field celebrating. In a situation that would most certainly yield a run, maybe two, they denied the Tigers. Adrenaline and spirits were high in that Chicago dugout, and Cochrane had to settle his team down while suppressing his own feelings of defeat. The first batter in the bottom of the second inning was three-time All-Star catcher Gabby Hartnett. He walked to the plate with a swagger in his step and smirked at Arthur as he took his position in the batter's box. Arthur tried not to let it affect him, but there it was again. Pride

"What are you smirking about?" He asked.

"That was pathetic." Hartnett responded.

"It's still 0-0. You have nothing to smile about."

"Yet," he responded curtly.

"We'll see after this game who is smiling," Arthur shot back.

He looked down at Arthur. "Are you going to give your pitcher a sign or keep making empty threats to me?"

Arthur looked up to see Crowder shrug his shoulder and stare at him. He finally gave him a sign, and he nodded.

"Thank you," Hartnett remarked.

Crowder threw a fastball that caught the outside corner, but Hartnett got around on it and hit it a mile down the line. It was just foul. Hartnett smiled as he stepped out of the box to take a few practice swings.

"It's gotta be straight to count," Arthur snapped.

"If he throws that fastball again, it'll be 1-0," he shot back.

Arthur could feel his blood boil. He called for the fastball again, but Crowder shook it off. He threw a curveball that landed low and outside. Arthur called for another fastball, but Crowder once again shook it off. Crowder threw a curveball that landed low and outside once more, but Hartnett swung through it for a strike. Crowder threw his third curveball in a row that landed for a ball and put the count at 2-2. Arthur called time and went to the mound to talk to his pitcher.

"What gives? Why do you keep shaking off the fastball?" he asked him.

"He's locked in. The curve is the way to go with Hartnett right now." He answered.

Pride swelled in Arthur again.

"I want to see a fastball. He can't hit your fastball."

"You could have fooled me after that first pitch. I still don't think it's landed."

"Fastball," Arthur reiterated.

"I tell you what, Artie. This next pitch is going to be another curve. If I don't get him out, then I'll throw the fastball."

Arthur turned and ran back to his position behind the plate.

"You boys have a good chat?" Hartnett asked.

"Don't worry about it," Arthur answered.

"Just stay away from the fastball," he stated again.

Arthur was angry that Crowder was going back to the curve on the upcoming pitch. He wanted the fastball to get Hartnett out, and more importantly, shut him up. Crowder threw another curve high and outside, and Hartnett fouled it off.

"2-2," Stark bellowed.

Arthur gave Crowder the fastball sign. He sighed but reluctantly agreed. Hartnett steadied himself in the box and waited for the pitch. Crowder put a little extra on it as he released it toward the plate. The ball came in hot, high, and on the outside corner. Hartnett swung and connected. The crowd roared as everyone watched the ball sail through the air toward the left-field seats. Tiger left fielder Goose Goslin turned and watched as the ball landed near the back row of seats. Arthur took off his mask and massaged his forehead as he watched Hartnett circle the bases. When he made it back to home plate, Hartnett simply smiled and stated, "Call me what you want. But I'm not a liar." He jogged to the dugout to celebrate with his team when Arthur took a step that way. Dolly Stark stepped in between Arthur and the Cubs dugout.

"Let it go, son, and just play the game," Stark stated as he handed Arthur a new ball.

When the bottom of the second inning was over, Arthur jogged back to the dugout, head down. Cochrane didn't say a word to him as he passed by. He sat down at the end of the bench. Crowder stood in front of him.

"I told you he was locked in. Maybe next time you'll listen. This one is on you," he stated and then walked away.

Arthur just looked at the floor and sighed. Greenberg sat next to him and put his arm around him. Arthur looked up, and he was smiling.

"Tough lesson to learn in the fourth game of the World Series," he stated as he laughed.

"He was talking trash, and I let my pride get the best of me," he responded.

"You preach in the off-season. Right?" Greenberg asked.

"Yeah."

"Isn't pride a bad thing? Isn't that what's contributing to a lot of problems in the world?"

Arthur laughed, "Indeed it is, Hank."

"Great. We've identified the problem, so don't do it again."

Arthur smiled. "Hank Greenberg. Man of wisdom."

They both laughed. Arthur walked down and sat next to Crowder.

"Sorry General. I won't let that happen again."

"Don't sweat it, Artie. Theres plenty of game left for you to make it up to me." He smiled.

With two outs and nobody on to start the third, Arthur stepped to the plate and took a four-pitch walk. Gehringer was up next. The third-base coach gave Arthur the sign to steal second. He took a liberal lead, and Carleton threw over, forcing him to dive back into the bag. He got his hand in before the tag was applied. Arthur stood and took another extended lead. This time, Carleton delivered to the plate. Arthur took off with his head down. He heard the crack of the bat but never looked up. He hit second base and kept going. Arthur looked up to see Baker winding his arm to send him home. Arthur kept running as fast as he could and crossed the plate without a throw. Gehringer had lined a double into the right-center field gap, and the Tigers tied the game at 1-1. The score stayed tied until the top of the sixth inning. The first two batters hit fly ball outs to the right fielder. The third batter of the inning, Flea Clifton, followed suit by hitting a fly ball to right field. After catching the first two with ease, Demaree misjudged Clifton's, and it bounced off the front of his mitt. Clifton was able to reach second base on the error, and the Tigers had a man on second with two outs. The pitcher was the next batter of the inning and sent a line drive to the shortstop. Tyson made the call. "On an 0-1 count, Crowder hits a sharp line drive to short…oh my goodness." He screamed into the mic, "Jurges misplays the ball, and it's off his mitt into centerfield. The center fielder Lindstrom throws the ball back into the infield, but Clifton crosses the plate to give the Tigers a 2-1 lead. Back-to-back errors silence this crowd."

The next batter struck out, but the damage had been done. In the top of the ninth, Arthur led off with a single. Gehringer bunted him over to second base, but he was stranded there when the next two batters struck out. In the bottom of the ninth with the Tigers leading 2-1, the Cubs speedy left fielder, Augie Galan, singled to start the inning. Grimm was an aggressive manager, so Arthur knew he could be on the move. Arthur called for the fastball to be low and outside. Crowder agreed. Demaree awaited the pitch.

"Galan takes his lead off first. Crowder goes into the windup," Tyson's voice exploded in excitement, "Galan takes off! The pitch is low and outside as Graham comes up throwing. Galan slides in as Gehringer drops the glove in front of the bag on a perfect throw by Graham. Out! He nailed him at second," Tyson yelled.

The crowd silenced and stunned watched as Galan jogged to the dugout with his head down. The Tigers were two outs away from taking a 3-1 series lead. Demaree singled to left and then Cavarretta singled to right. The Cubs had men on first and second with one out. The crowd came alive once more as Cochrane paced the dugout nervously. The next batter was third baseman Stan Hack. He hit .311 on the season in 504 plate appearances. Crowder and Arthur were on the same page with Hack. Curveballs at the bottom of the zone. On a 2-1 count, Crowder threw a curveball that broke over the center of the plate and just below the strike zone. Hack connected and sent a sizzling ground ball right to Rogell at short. He fielded it cleanly, tossed the ball to Gehringer for the out at second, who gunned it over to Owen at first for a game-ending 6-4-3 double play. Tyson was yelling on the radio, and the fans in Detroit were cheering for their Tigers, who took a commanding 3-1 series lead.

Lincoln was jumping up and down as Arthur described the game-ending double play that propelled the Tigers to a 3-1 series lead. "How were you feeling at that moment?" Lincoln yelled, not realizing he was yelling.

Arthur laughed.

"Incredible. We played a great game and got rewarded with a great win."

"I wasn't even in it and I'm so excited," Lincoln continued to yell.

"It's a very exciting story. Even to this day when I tell the story, I can feel my blood pumping and the excitement of winning that game. General pitched a complete game 2-1 win. It was an amazing game to be a part of."

"Up 3-1 in the World Series. Wow!"

Arthur smiled. "I couldn't believe it either."

"What a rush."

They paused for a few moments to feed the birds, which scattered when Lincoln started jumping up and down. When the adrenaline had subsided, they talked about the game a little more.

"The Cubs had a good game too. The sixth inning did them in that day. They had two errors all day, and in resulted in a loss."

"I wonder if those guys thought about that game for a long time after that," Lincoln asked.

"I would say yes. As humans, we're often way more critical and harder on ourselves than anyone else could be. Years later, I talked to some of those players who still held that inning in their hearts. Good men and good ballplayers. But they couldn't let it go."

"It's hard because they felt like they had let the team down."

"That's exactly right. Life is like that sometimes. That's why it helps to have a loving savior to take all of life's problems too. Even in our failures, He loves and cares for us. There's great comfort in that."

"Amen," Lincoln stated as he threw more crumbs to the birds.

Arthur smiled. What a great kid, he thought. "Shall we move on?"

"Wait. The Cubs guy who hit the home run…"

"Hartnett."

"Right, Hartnett. He got under your skin, didn't he?"

"Boy, did he ever." Arthur scratched his head and smiled. "I was an active man of God who loved the Lord deeply, got a degree in theology, and even preached on some Sundays up to this point in my life. But my pride really got the best of me there. It just goes to show you we're all human and struggle to live godly."

"At least you had Hank there to talk you right."

Arthur laughed, "Yep. He was right. Pride starts wars, fosters greed, and even drives a godly man to lose his cool."

"Did you ever talk to Hartnett after the series?"

"Oh yeah. We laughed about the encounter and talked a few times throughout the years."

"It seems like all of you played against each other, but you were all kind of friends."

"We all knew what it took to make the big leagues. There was always a type of respect between us. Sure, there were a few who nobody wanted to talk to, but mostly ninety-five percent of the guys in the league got along."

"Even through the smack talk?"

"Smack talk was just part of the game. You tried to get into a guy's head to get an edge. Some guys and teams took it way too far, but those are the guys you didn't associate with much."

"That's not cool."

"I agree. But enough about smack talk. Let's get to game five."

World Series Game 5—Sunday, October 6, 1935—Wrigley Field, Chicago, IL

"Game five of the 1935 World Series between the Detroit Tigers and the Chicago Cubs will be underway shortly, and the Cubbies are fighting to stay alive today." Tyson cleared his throat before continuing. "Yesterday's game was a defensive battle in which the Tigers came out on top 2-1. On the mound today for Chicago is game one winner, Lon Warneke. He held the Tigers scoreless at Navin Field, en route to a Chicago 3-0 victory. On the bump for the Tigers will be the man he beat in that first game, Schoolboy Rowe. He gave up only two earned runs in that game but took the loss. He is 1-1 in this series."

The first two innings of the game remained scoreless. In the bottom of the third inning, Billy Herman led off with a triple. The next hitter was right fielder Chuck Klein, who was getting his first start in this series. During the regular season, he batted .293 and led the team with 21 home runs. Klein watched the first pitch fastball hit the zone for a strike. The second pitch was a curveball that broke to the outside and stayed low for a ball. With the count at one and one, Tyson called the action.

"Herman is standing on third, representing the first run of the game. The count on Klein is 1-1. Rowe gets the sign from Graham. He checks on Herman at third. The windup and the pitch…and there she goes!" Tyson bellowed. "A long drive to left center. White goes back to the track and looks up as the ball lands halfway up the stands. Home run and the Cubbies lead 2-0 in the bottom of the third."

Rowe closed out the third by retiring the next three batters in a row, but the damage had already been done and his team trailed by two. Through six innings of work, Warneke silenced the Tiger bats. Bill Lee came on to pitch a scoreless seventh inning, and through the top of the seventh the Cubs led 2-0. In the bottom of the seventh inning, Rowe gave up a leadoff single to Jurges. Lee bunted him over to second base, which brought Galan up to the plate with a man on second and one out. On the first pitch from Rowe, Galan smashed a hard liner to Clifton at third base. He fielded the ball cleanly, but the throw was over the head of the first baseman. Jurges rounded third and headed for home. Right fielder Pete Fox scooped up the errant throw and came up throwing. He threw a perfect strike to Arthur, who caught the ball in front of the plate and did a sweeping tag. Jurges slid to the back half of the plate and extended his foot to avoid the tag. Stark was in the thick of the action looking down on home plate.

"Out," he screamed as Arthur came up with the glove.

Jurges sprang up and started arguing his case. The manager came out of the dugout and argued with Stark some more. Eventually order was restored, and the inning resumed with Galan now on second and two outs. Herman came to the plate. On the first pitch from Rowe, Herman delivered a line drive into right center for a two-out double. Galan crossed the plate, and the fans cheered as the Cubs led the game 3-0. The top of the ninth rolled around and the Tigers were looking at getting blanked for the second time in this series. Gehringer led off the ninth with a single. The crowd continued to cheer as Goslin came to the plate, hoping for a double-play ball. On the first pitch, Goslin singled to right field. The Tigers now had runners on first and second with nobody out. Fox was the next batter.

"Gehringer is on second and Goslin is on first. The Tigers are trying to mount a comeback and to end this series and take home their first World Series championship in team history." Tyson sat on the edge of his seat in anticipation. Fox swung and missed at the first pitch, and Lee missed with a fastball on the second. "1-1, the count. Fox gets ready as Lee delivers. It's a base hit!" he screamed as the ball went over the shortstop's head. "Gehringer rounds third as Galan tosses the ball into second. He crosses the plate, and the Tigers cut the lead to 3-1. Goslin is on second and Fox on first with no one out."

The crowd was silent as the Cubs manager made his way to the mound. Rogell waited on deck as the powwow on the mound lasted a few moments before Grimm headed back to the dugout. The crowd started cheering the Cubbies on to get the final three outs and move the series back to Detroit. On an 0-1 count, Lee got Rogell to reach out for one and hit a weak fly ball to shallow rightfield. With one out and two on, Cochrane pinch-hit Gee Walker for Owen. Walker hit .301 on the season and had decent power. On the second 0-1 count of the inning, Lee was able to get Walker to hit a weak ground ball to second. Herman scooped it up and threw Walker out at first. The crowd cheered as there were now two outs in the inning. The Tigers still had a chance. They had runners on second and third with two outs and Flea Clifton coming to the plate. The crowd stood and cheered wildly for their team to get that last out. Clifton didn't have a hit in the series, and some second-guessed Cochrane for not letting Owen bat and putting Walker in for Clifton. Tyson was one of those people.

"I don't understand this at all. Clifton is not known for his bat when the Tigers desperately need a bat to come through. I don't know what Mickey is thinking." Tyson bellowed as he shook his head in disagreement. Lee worked the count to 1-2. "Lee has Clifton where he wants him. The count is 1-2. Lee goes into the windup and delivers." Tyson rose out of his seat and screamed, "Clifton smashes the ball down the third base line…oh…a diving catch by Hack. He robbed Clifton of extra bases and the Tigers of possibly tying this game." He sat back down and settled into his seat. "Cubs third baseman Stan Hack might have just saved this series for Chicago. What a play. Clifton gave it everything he had and got completely robbed."

The fans cheered loudly as their team celebrated on the infield. They lived to see another day and were happy to be back on the bus headed for Detroit. In the dugout, the Tigers players tried to console Clifton as his hitless slump continued.

"That was a tough break for such a nice guy," Arthur stated.

"It sounds like Hack made a great play."

"It was a great play. I still don't know how he stretched out that far. He used every bit of his six-foot frame," Arthur laughed.

"Was he good?"

"He played 16 years, all for the Cubbies, and was a career .301 hitter. He played great defense too."

"I'd say that's pretty good." Lincoln sighed. "So, back to Detroit, but you're up 3-2."

"Yep. The city was excited at the possibility of winning a championship at home."

"At least you don't have to face that Warneke guy again. He really had your number, Mr. Graham."

Arthur laughed. "He sure did. But we had to face Larry French in game six. He won 17 games on the season and had a better ERA at 2.96."

"Who was pitching for you guys?"

"Tommy Bridges."

"He's one of your best pitchers."

"True, but he had a 3.51 ERA during the season, which shows you how impressive French's was."

"I can't wait to get to Game Six. Do you think we have time?"

Before he finished his sentence, he heard his dad's voice.

"You ready to go, buddy?"

Lincoln sighed, "Already?"

"Already. It's been a long day." He looked at Arthur and winked. "How's the story going?"

"We were just about to get to the sixth game."

"That'll be a great game to talk about tomorrow," Arthur chimed in.

"The sixth game, huh," Chris stated as he scratched his chin. "I agree, buddy. That'll be a great way to spend tomorrow."

"Okay," Lincoln reluctantly agreed.

"Tonight, we dine on pizza." Chris smiled.

"Yes," Lincoln pumped his fist. "I'll see you tomorrow, Mr. Graham."

"See you tomorrow, Lincoln," he smiled. "Enjoy that pizza."

"That's a given," he responded.

Arthur and Chris laughed.

"Hey buddy, meet me at the car. I have to talk to Mr. Graham."

Lincoln made his way to the car as Chris sat next to Arthur.

"Is there anything wrong?" Arthur asked.

"No. I just really wanted to thank you again for spending time with Lincoln while I worked on this project."

"It's been a pleasure," Arthur responded. "You have a wonderful boy there. I think I've enjoyed it as much as he has."

"I don't know about that. His love of baseball before was big, but now it's off the charts. He has loved hearing about your career. When he talks about it, he really gets into it. I feel like I'm there sometimes watching you."

They both laughed, and Arthur smiled.

"I'm going to miss our talks."

"Lincoln would love it if you still came to his games. Jessica and I talked, and we want to have you and Esther over for dinner one night to thank you both."

"Is your wife a good cook?"

"An excellent cook."

"Then we would be delighted. Thank you."

"When she gets home, we'll figure out a good day and time. I know Lincoln would really like that."

"That sounds lovely, Chris."

"Well, I better get to that truck so he can fill me in on today's games."

"He tells the story better than I do."

Chris laughed. "He might have a future in that."

"Maybe, but I think it'll be in baseball. He radiates passion for it."

"You might be right." Chris stood and shook Arthur's hand. "See you tomorrow."

"God willing," he smiled.

Chapter 19
Friday—July 25, 1980

Arthur sat at the kitchen table reading his Bible and finishing his toast. He was wearing his jersey from the 1935 season today. He loved the enthusiasm of Lincoln and wanted to finish his story with a bang. Arthur stood and walked over to the sink, rinsed his dishes and placed them in the sink. He looked out the window and smiled at a cardinal that was sitting on the fence. It was glowing in the morning sunrise.

"I love a man in uniform," stated the soft, loving voice from behind him.

He smiled. "It's loose these days. No muscles to hold it up."

She walked over and wrapped her arms around his waist and laid her head on his back. "You look as dashing as the day I met you."

"As do you, my love," he stated as he cupped her hands with his.

"The story ends today?"

"The story ends today," he repeated. "I have so enjoyed telling it to him."

"He must really love hearing it. It's not often that a twelve-year-old boy sits still for a two-week story."

"He doesn't sit still." He laughed. "Even when I'm telling it, he gets his cardio in."

She laughed.

"I believe you have pointed out in the past that he is a very animated young man."

"He is, but that's the thing I love about him. He's so full of passion and energy. Lincoln says what he thinks, but he's not rude or disrespectful. He knows his Bible, too. He's a good kid, Esther."

She squeezed his waist. "So you've said."

"Did I tell you? His mom is supposed to be home on Sunday."

"No. So her dad is doing well?"

"The kid says everything is great."

"Good. I'm sure he misses her…and his siblings."

They both laughed.

"Brothers and sisters don't realize how special their relationship is until they get older."

"That's the truth."

He looked at his watch. "Well, I'd better get going. You know that…"

"I know. He gets excitable if you're late."

He turned and gave her a hug and a kiss. Arthur grabbed his bag of breadcrumbs off the counter and headed for the car.

2

Arthur sat on the bench feeding the birds when Lincoln leaped over the bench and landed on the seat next to him.

"Good morning, Mr. Graham," he stated with a big smile on his face.

Arthur leaned back in his seat and placed his hand on his chest. "Are you trying to give me a heart attack, kid?"

Lincoln laughed, "No."

"You could have fooled me." Arthur dropped his hand. "That's quite an entrance."

Lincoln grabbed a handful from the bag and threw it on the ground. "I'm just excited to hear the rest of the story. My dad and I talked about it for most of the night as we watched the Tigers game."

"That was a real stinker. Losing 5-3 to Oakland."

"It wasn't great, but we talked about how cool it was knowing someone who played in the World Series."

"Your dad didn't tell you the ending, did he?"

Lincoln looked up at him. "No…hey wait! Is that your jersey from when you played?"

"It is. It's been in a box for 45 years. Esther had to wash it delicately and let it air dry, but it's still in good shape."

Lincoln touched the sleeve and smiled. His eyes were wide, and for the first time since Arthur had been talking to him, he was speechless.

Finally, "Awesome" was the only word he could get out as he stared at the jersey.

"It feels good to put on the old English D once more." Arthur ran his fingers across the D and smiled. "It feels like only yesterday."

"My dad brought his camera today. Can we get a picture later?"

"Of course," he stated as he cleared his throat.

"Mr. Graham, are you okay?"

"Yeah. I get a little sentimental sometimes when I think about those days. Wearing this jersey takes me back."

"To all the great games?"

"The games are a small part of it. It's the people I remember most. The men I played with, and against. My parents, Mr. Dillard, and all their incredible support. A lot went into getting me to the majors. I needed every bit of that support from the key people in my life."

"Don't forget Esther."

"I could never forget Esther. She is still going above and beyond in her support. God has blessed us with over 65 years together."

"I hope my mom and dad get 65 years together. Sometimes she says, 'That man's going to be the death of me.' I hope not."

Arthur laughed. "I think all our wives had made that statement at one time or another. It's a playful way of saying, 'He's driving me crazy right now.'" He shook his fists for effect.

"Yeah." Lincoln smiled. "So, game six."

"Game six." Arthur repeated.

World Series Game 6—Monday, October 7, 1935—Navin Field, Detroit, MI

Ty Tyson settled into the booth with his partner and stats guy, Dirk Totten. "This stadium is busting at the seams today, Dirk. They want to see their Tigers take home their first World Series championship." "So do I," Totten responded. He was a former Tiger player who had a short playing career over a decade ago. Until this point, he had been a stats guy, cynical by nature and more focused on stats than optimism. Tyson had decided that today they would try a back and forth. If the response was good, then next season Totten would be his partner on air. "The city of Detroit deserves a champion during these hard times."

"I couldn't agree more, Dirk. The Tigers have played inspired baseball this year to get to this point. They lost last year's American League MVP, Mickey Cochrane, to an injury ten games into the season, and what could most likely be this year's MVP, Hank Greenberg, to an injury in the second game of this series. These players have really bonded together with each other and this city."

"It's a beautiful thing, Ty, but can they finish it is the question on my mind, and I'm sure the city of Detroit?"

Mickey addressed his team in the clubhouse.

"This is it, boys. I hear the media and people in Chicago talking about Game Seven. I gotta tell you, I don't see it. I'm looking at the best team in baseball, and I don't see a Game Seven in their future." Some were nodding their heads, and others were punching the insides of their gloves. "Let's send these boys back to Chicago tonight," he shouted as he looked at every man in that room. Hands clapped and players started pumping each other up. He smiled as he watched his warriors pumping themselves up to do battle. He gave it a few moments and then looked over at Arthur. "Take us home, Arthur." The room fell silent as Arthur began.

"Lord, we have fought the good fight, we have kept the faith, please let us finish this race as champions today. Give us your strength, we pray. In your son's name. Amen."

The players jumped up and headed for the field. Each one slapped Arthur on the back as they passed. He grabbed his mitt and walked toward the entrance to the field. He stopped and looked around the clubhouse one last time. In his heart, he knew that this would be the last time he would exit this room as a player. A lump entered his throat, and he took a moment to really appreciate the gift that God had given him. "God is good," he whispered under his breath as he walked through the tunnel and out onto the field.

In the top of the first, Bridges set the Cubs down in order and only used eight pitches to do it. As the team came off the field, the adrenaline from Mick's speech in the clubhouse still had them energized and feeling good. In the bottom of the first, Cochrane tried to shake things up a bit and had Flea Clifton lead off. Clifton grounded out to third, making him 0-12 in the series since coming on for the injured Greenberg. Arthur was hitting in the number two spot today and took a 1-1 fastball into left field for a base hit. The next batter, Gehringer, singled as well, putting runners on first and second with one out. Goslin hit a shallow fly into right field for the second out of the inning, failing to advance the runners. Pete Fox. The most consistent Tiger hitter in the series stepped to the plate with two on and two out. All of Detroit listened as Tyson spoke. "Pete Fox has a real chance to put the Tigers on the board first. The runners take their leads and await the pitch." The first pitch was a curveball that Fox swung over to make the count 0-1. Tyson grabbed his mic and leaned forward as he called the next pitch. "Fox waits for the pitch as French checks the runners. He goes into the windup and delivers." Tyson leaped from his seat as he shouted, "Fox hits a line drive down the left field line over the head of Hack at third. Galan goes into the corner to field the ball. The throw is to third base as Gehringer slides in safely. Fox takes second, and Graham crossed the plate to give your Tigers a 1-0 lead."

270

The crowd of over 48,000 roared as Detroit scored in the bottom of the first. Throughout the city was cheering and jubilation for their beloved Tigers. The second inning saw both pitchers have their way, and going into the top of the third the Tigers clung to a 1-0 lead. Billy Jurges led off the inning with a single into center field. The pitcher French struck out, which made the crowd feel more at ease. Galan stepped to the plate and promptly singled to right, and Jurges took third. With runners on first and third and one out, Billy Herman took a 1-1 pitch into rightfield. Jurges scored, and Galan was thrown out at third. Chuck Klein flew out to end the inning, but the Cubs tied the game, 1-1. In the bottom of the fourth inning, the first two Tiger hitters each singled on the first pitch of the at-bat. On the third pitch of the inning, Marv Owen bunted down the third baseline. Hack threw the runner out at second, and the Tigers had them on the corners with only one out and the pitcher, Tommy Bridges, coming to the plate.

"Bridges hit .239 on the season across 119 plate appearances. Not awful, but not the player the Tigers would rather have up right now," Tyson remarked.

"Well, Tommy can certainly help his own cause here, Ty. He is a better option than the next batter, Clifton." Totten responded.

"You might be right, Dirk." He looked at his partner and smiled. They watched as Bridges battled to a 3-2 count. "The first three batters of this inning saw three pitches total. Tommy has seen six and is sitting on a 3-2 count. French gets set and checks the runners. He goes into his windup and delivers. Bridges hits the ball down third. Hack fields it and guns it to second to get Rogell, Herman flips it to first to complete the double play...no, safe. The first-base umpire Bill McGowin calls Bridges safe. Walker scores and the Tigers take a 2-1 lead."

"Wow, Bridges knew he had to hustle down the line, and he did." Totten yelled.

The next batter, Clifton, grounded out, and the Tigers took a 2-1 lead into the top of the fifth inning. In the top of the fifth inning, Jurges led off with a fly ball out. French, feeding off the success of the Tiger pitcher, singled into rightfield. Galan struck out looking, and the Tiger crowd breathed a sigh of relief. There was one on and two out with Herman coming to the plate.

"Billy Herman coming to the plate," Tyson let his audience know. "Not really known for his power, but a hitting machine with 221 hits on the season, Bridges must focus on not letting Klein come to the plate next. Klein led the Cubs with 21 homers on the season and could change the complexion of this game quickly."

"Bridges must be careful with Herman. He had 57 doubles on the season to lead the league," Totten chimed in.

They watched as Bridges was cautious with Herman, taking the count to 3-1. Arthur called time and walked out to the mound to have a word with his pitcher.

"What are you thinking here, Tommy?"

"I don't want to walk Herman and have Klein come up with two on. I don't want to give him anything good to hit either."

"You want to hit the high inside fastball? Maybe he goes for it and pops it up. If he walks, we'll worry about Klein then."

"Okay Artie. Let's try it."

Arthur jogged back to the plate and took his position. Herman stepped into the box and waited for the pitch.

"The count is 3-1 on Herman. Bridges checks on French at first and gets set. He goes into the windup and delivers. Herman connects," he screamed into the mic. "That ball is demolished to left, and all Goslin can do is look up and wave goodbye. Home run! The Cubs take a 3-2 lead on one swing of the bat."

Klein walked to the plate and shot a single into center on the first pitch. Bridges dropped his head and stared at the ground as the ball came back into the infield. Gehringer walked it to his pitcher and said a couple of words to him as he gave him the ball. Hartnett was the next batter. And he strolled to the box with a big smile on his face. Arthur noticed a lot of chatter and celebrating in the Cubs dugout and looked down at first to see Klein nod to his third base coach. Hartnett awaited the pitch as Arthur gave the sign for Bridges to pitch out. He agreed and threw a fastball outside. Klein took off from first. Hartnett swung and missed, and Arthur popped out, caught it, and then fired the ball down to Gehringer.

"Out!" yelled second base umpire Stark.

The inning was over, but not before the Cubs took a 3-2 lead and silenced the crowd. The score stayed that way until the bottom of the sixth. Fox and Walker started the inning with fly ball outs. Rogell then hit a ball deep into the left-field corner. The crowd went wild. The ball hit the chalk and headed for the corner when a fan reached out and touched it. Rogell was held to a ground-rule double. With a man on second and two out, Marv Owen hit the first pitch from French into left field. Rogell scored from second, and the game was tied at three. The fans and the city of Detroit yelled and rejoiced once more. The pitchers once again took over for the seventh and the eighth, and the game went into the top of the ninth inning tied 3-3.

"The Cubs come to bat in the top of the ninth, sending Stan Hack to the plate to start it off. The speedy Hack hit .311 on the year and had 36 extra-base hits," Tyson recapped. Everyone watched and waited as Hack took the count to 3-2. "Bridges sets and then delivers. Hack gets a hold of the pitch and drives the ball to deep centerfield." Tyson is shouting into the microphone. "The ball is over Walker's head and hits the base of the wall. Hack hits the bag at second as Walker picks it up and gets it to the cutoff man, Gehringer. He guns the ball over to third, but Hack is standing on third base with a leadoff triple." Tyson fell back into his seat, and the crowd was completely silent.

"Stan Hack has silenced this crowd with a leadoff triple to start the ninth inning," Totten echoed over the airwaves.

The Cubs dugout was going crazy. The Cubbies fans who had made the trip from Chicago could be heard in the stands for only the second time today. The Tigers and the crowd were stunned.

Cochrane walked out to the mound to talk to Bridges and his infield.

"The only way we lose is if we panic," Cochrane started out. "You okay, Tommy?"

"Great," Bridges responded with confidence.

"Good. The next two batters are Jurges and French. A .241. and .141. hitter. Go right at them. If you get ahead of them, see if they'll help you out by swinging at a bad pitch. Got it?"

"Got it," he responded.

"The rest of you guys play in. If they hit a ground ball your way, don't even check the runner. Just throw home. Artie, watch for the bunt. I don't think it'll happen, but be prepared for anything. Everybody good?"

They all nodded that they understood, and Cochrane walked back to the dugout while everyone else took their positions. Bridges started Jurges off with a curveball low and on the inside corner. He didn't show bunt and let the pitch go by.

"Strike," Quigley screamed.

The next pitch was another curve. This one was high and headed for the outside corner. Jurges swung and caught the ball at the end of the bat and shot it toward the Cubs dugout. The coaches and players dove for cover.

"Foul ball, strike two," Quigley yelled.

With an 0-2 count, Bridges reached back and fired a fastball high and inside. Jurges couldn't catch up to it.

"Three," Quigley yelled as he came up with the right hand to signify the out.

The crowd showed some life again. They were making noise to support their team and willing for that run on third not to cross the plate. French stepped to the plate. Bridges tested the bunting waters and threw him a fastball high and inside. He swung and missed for strike one. The second pitch was a curveball that landed high and outside. French watched it go by, and the umpire called strike two. On the third pitch of the at bat he threw a fastball in the middle of the plate but low. French swung and connected. It was a one hop line drive to a surprised Bridges. He looked over at third, and Hack dove back into the bag to keep from getting picked off. Bridges turned and gunned the ball to Owen at first to get the out. The crowd went wild. The leadoff triple that silenced them was now standing on third base with two outs. The pesky Galan was the next hitter. Galan worked the count to 1-2.

"Bridges stares in at Graham and gets the signal. He goes into the windup and delivers. Galan swings and gets under the ball. The left fielder Goslin has plenty of room. He gets under it and makes the catch. Oh, my goodness, Tiger fans!" Tyson yelled. "A leadoff triple to start the ninth is stranded at third, and the Tigers have a chance to win it in the bottom of the ninth."

The crowd was cheering at the top of their lungs. The stadium noise was deafening as the Tigers prepared to come to bat, and the Tiger dugout was buzzing after getting out of that inning. Bridges, Clifton, and Arthur were the hitters due up. Cochrane sent White up to the plate to pinch hit for Bridges. White attempted to put a bunt down, but Hartnett popped up quickly from his catcher's position and threw him out by a step. Clifton took French to a full count before striking out on a curveball outside. Arthur kneeled in the on-deck circle. His head bowed and his eyes closed.

"Lord. No matter what happens today, I am yours. Thank you for everything. Amen."

He opened his eyes and walked to the plate. The crowd was on its feet screaming his name.

Ty Tyson smiled as he surveyed the field from the broadcast booth. "It's a great day to be alive if you're a baseball fan. These two teams have given us exactly what we expected. A hard-fought series that will see a new champion crowned at its conclusion. The Tigers lead the series three games to two, but the Cubbies are doing their best to force a game seven tomorrow. We're in the bottom of the ninth with the score tied at three. French retired the first two Detroit batters and now Graham steps to the plate."

"You can't ever count these Cubbies out," Dirk Totten, Tyson's partner, responded as he scratched some notes down in his notebook without looking up.

"Graham, a remarkable story this year, is one for three on the day. The Cubs know well that they still must be careful with him, as he hit 30 home runs during the season. What do you know, Dirk? I know more get the words out of my mouth as the Chicago pitching coach Roy Johnson is out of the dugout and headed toward the mound." Tyson stated as he took a drink of water.

Totten looked up from his notebook. "Johnson wants to talk strategy with his pitcher. There's no sense in playing with fire at this stage of the game." He chuckled. "French doesn't want to go down in history as the pitcher who lost the World Series on a home run to a 40-year-old rookie."

Tyson laughed and then leaned into the mic. "Well, Dirk, it looks like the meeting on the mound is over, and French is ready to pitch. Graham closes his eyes and looks up into the heavens. He smiles and then steps into the box and digs in."

"Has anyone ever asked him about his ritual? Who's he smiling at?" Totten chuckled some more.

Tyson continued. "French gets the sign from Hartnett. He goes into the windup and delivers. Ball one."

"That wasn't even close," Totten remarked.

"No, it wasn't. High and very outside. French gets the ball back and wipes his brow. Graham has one foot out of the box and is staring out at French. He steps back onto the mound and peers in at Hartnett. Graham steps back into the box. He has his signal. French goes into the windup and delivers. Ball two."

"Another high and outside pitch, Ty. I think this might be the strategy."

"I think you're right. They seem content to walk Graham and take their chances with Gehringer. French takes a trip around the mound. Wait. Something has him staring into the Tigers dugout. French is now pointing in Cochrane's direction and yelling something. Cochrane is now pointing at French and yelling."

"Whatever Cochrane said didn't sit well with French because now he's walking toward the Tigers' manager." Totten noted.

"The home plate umpire is walking toward French and pointing toward the mound. He looks over at Cochrane and points for him to get back into the dugout."

"Tempers are hot," Totten smiled.

"I'll say. Tensions are running high on both sides right now as each tries to bring home a championship. Order is restored, and French takes the mound. Graham digs back in. Here is the windup and the pitch. Strike one. Whoa, baby, that was a heater down the center of the plate."

"Whatever Cochrane said didn't sit well with French, and it showed in that pitch," Totten stated.

"Graham takes an extra second to collect himself and steps back into the box. French stares in at Hartnett. He shakes off the first sign. Now the second. They don't seem to be on the same page right now. Finally, he gives his catcher a nod. French sets and goes into the windup and delivers the pitch. Strike two. Another fastball right down Broadway."

"Whatever the plan was for Graham going into this at bat, French has now changed it," Totten stated.

"Two balls and two strikes to Graham. French stares his opponent down, refusing to blink. He goes into his windup. Ball three. Another fastball that was just low to run the count full."

"French really wanted that pitch, Ty. He started toward the dugout before the umpire called it," Totten stated.

"It was definitely low, but I'm really surprised that Graham took it after those two fastballs down the middle."

"He has shown incredible patience at the plate this year," Totten remarked.

"You can say that again. Graham steps back into the box and digs in. French gets the sign from Hartnett." Tyson grabbed the microphone and leaned in. "A long pause here as French and Graham seemed to be locked on to each other. Here comes the payoff pitch. French goes into the windup and delivers. Graham connects," Tyson's voice boomed with excitement, "It's a deep fly ball to centerfield."

"Graham is really moving out of the box," Totten added.

The stadium was going nuts. Both benches were standing and leaning over the railing, watching the ball and the Cubs center fielder tracking it.

Tyson focused completely on the ball. "Demaree going back. He's almost at the wall. He leaps and...the ball is over his glove. It hits the top of the wall and caroms toward right field. Klein is just standing in right field watching the play." He looked down to see Graham motoring around the bases. "Graham is rounding second base as Klein runs to pick up the ball." Tyson is out of his chair screaming into the microphone. "Klein gets to the ball and throws it in to Herman. Graham rounds the bag at third and is heading home." His screams at this point were almost inaudible. "Herman turns and throws the ball to a waiting Hartnett at the plate...Oh baby! He catches the ball and turns as Graham is coming in. Graham lowers the shoulder and runs into Hartnett at full speed." The players and the umpire became hidden in a thick cloud of dust. Everyone's heart stopped as they waited to see the umpire's call. Tyson could now see Quigley materialize out of the dust. "Safe...safe...safe..." he shouted at the top of his lungs. "Arthur Graham has just hit an inside the park home run to win the World Series for the Tigers." Tyson collapsed into his chair, exhausted from the call. The Tigers came pouring out of the dugout to pick up Arthur. The stadium was shaking, the noise was so loud, and the city of Detroit was engulfed in celebration.

"This is one for the history books," Tyson stated as he sat back in his chair and looked at his partner.

Lincoln was jumping up and down. "Safe…safe…safe," he shouted. "That's one of the greatest things I've ever heard. Mr. Graham, you won a World Series. You hit the series-clinching home run, but not just any home run. An inside the parker that will never, ever be forgotten. How has my dad never told me this story?" He shouted at the top of his lungs without taking a breath.

Dillard and Chris were standing at the construction entrance staring down at the scene unfolding. Dillard laughed.
"He got to the end, I see."
"Yeah," Chris laughed, "I'd say so. Look at that smile. That excitement."
"Dad is one heck of a storyteller, and that's one heck of a story," he responded.
"I'll say. Your dad has really helped while Jess has been gone. Lincoln loves him."
"I think the feeling is mutual. Believe it or not, no one else in the family talks baseball with him. They all know the story, but he has never gotten a reaction like that from one of his grandkids or great-grandkids."
"Really? What about you? Not a big baseball fan?"
"No. I never really got into it like he did. He passed on the preaching gene, though."

Arthur laughed as Lincoln continued to dance around.
"Come sit, my boy."
Lincoln sat down next to him, sweaty and out of breath.
"I can't believe you're still not jumping around after that home run."
Arthur smiled. "Well, it's been 45 years now. I still get a charge when I think of that day, but now it's just a fond memory that I get to share."

"That's the greatest baseball story I've ever heard," he said with a very serious face. "Amazing."

"I'm glad you liked it."

"Liked it? I loved it." He looked at Arthur's jersey. "Is that the jersey you were wearing?"

"Yep." He turned slightly so Lincoln could see the tear at the top of the left shoulder. "That's from the collision at the plate."

"Whoa!" he stated as he touched it. "So did you touch the plate before he tagged you?"

"Nope. He got the ball, turned, and tagged me as I plowed into him. When we fell back, the ball got dislodged from his glove and fell to the ground."

"You would have been out?"

"Yep. And who knows how the series would have ended. What most people don't talk about from that game is how I ignored Del Baker's sign to stop at third. I ran right through it."

"Was he mad at you?"

"No. But if I had been thrown out, and we had lost the series, the history books probably would not have been too kind to me."

"Was anybody hurt in the collision?"

"No. As a matter a fact, Hartnett was such a great sport he came into our locker room later and congratulated us on a series well played. He gave me the ball from the collision. We both signed it, and I got it at home."

"What made the pitcher so mad? Was Mickey yelling at him?"

Arthur smiled. "It was a big misunderstanding on French's part. Mickey was shouting at me to get ready. He couldn't believe they would just walk me to get to Gehringer. Nobody could. French thought he was yelling at him and got angry and started yelling at Mick. So, Mickey gave it right back."

"Pride," Lincoln stated as he shook his head.

"Pride," Arthur repeated as he laughed at Lincoln. "It can take down kingdoms, and lose you a World Series."

Lincoln smiled. "I can't wait to see all the stuff you have."

Athur smiled. "It's a lot, but I look forward to showing all of it to you."

"So, what happened after that season? You know, with your career."

"I was one and done. Mickey wanted to sign me to a two-year deal, but I just didn't feel it anymore."

"Really? What happened?"

"After all the hoopla died down, and I reflected on everything, God revealed to me it was time. He had waited long enough."

"How did He let you know?"

"He talks to everyone differently. Through dreams, other people, circumstances, or His word. If you open your heart to receive His wisdom, then He will reveal to you what He wants. Over the years I beat myself up because I thought I wasn't honoring His will by going into the ministry sooner."

"But you won a World Series."

Arthur laughed. "While that is true, I came to understand that through the perseverance he instilled in me, coupled with the people he put in my life, I was doing exactly what He wanted me to do. Even when I doubted myself, He carried me through that doubt and blessed me greatly." He smiled. "God is so good."

"Was Mickey mad at you for not coming back?"

"No. I told Mick that the Lord had called me into the ministry. He was of course understanding and wished me the best of luck. Over the years I've seen a lot of the ballplayers from the Tigers and from other organizations come through my church. I had the opportunity to counsel and witness to a lot of those guys. I even became a sort of unofficial chaplain to the team down the road."

"Cool. I bet you've met a lot of famous players."

"I have."

"Did being a baseball star help you get the pastor job here?"

"No. I was the associate pastor here from November 1935 until December 1936. I became the head pastor in January 1937 when the previous pastor retired."

"Why did he retire?"

"He was ready, I guess. His associate pastor left in October 1935 to pastor a church in Tennessee."

"I guess God wanted you here."

Arthur laughed. "I guess he did."

Lincoln smiled at him and sat back in his seat. "I'm glad he did, Mr. Graham."

"Me too, Lincoln. Me too."

The End.

Baseball has been around for almost 200 years. It has a rich history that has grown into a worldwide phenomenon. The Detroit Tigers organization has a long history of excellence. Along with four World Series Championships (1935, 1945, 1968, & 1984) they have sent many players to Cooperstown to be enshrined in the baseball Hall of Fame. I remember the 1984 World Series win like it was yesterday. The excitement, the thrill, and the incredible rush when that final catch was made to seal the series. The 40-year-old Rookie combines a love of God and baseball. It is a testament to what you can accomplish when you place your faith and trust in His plan for your life, and even if you deviate from that plan, it is a testament to the grace and love that He has for you. God is good.

Jeremiah 29:11 - For I know the plans I have for you," declares the Lord, "plans to prosper you and not to harm you, plans to give you hope and a future. (NIV)

Thank you for reading The 40-year-old Rookie, a Major League Story of Perseverance and Faith.

I would like to take the time to thank a few people:

foremost, God in heaven above for giving me the words to write this novel. My darling wife Crystal, for her love. My daughter Jessica and my sister Donna for their feedback and support. To my parents, Don and Irma, for always showing me the love and support I needed growing up, and throughout my life. Finally, to all my wonderful family and friends, who are way too numerous to list, but have all had a loving impact on my life. I say thank you.

www.ingramcontent.com/pod-product-compliance
Lightning Source LLC
Chambersburg PA
CBHW071850220626
47052CB00002B/49